Did I Read This Already?
Place your initials or unique symbol in
square as a reminder to you that you have
read this title.

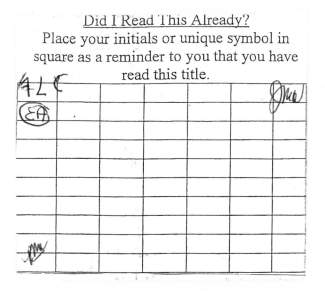

All Is Bright

Center Point
Large Print

Also by RaeAnne Thayne and available from
Center Point Large Print:

The Cliff House
Coming Home for Christmas
The Cottages on Silver Beach
Season of Wonder
The Path to Sunshine Cove
The Sea Glass Cottage
Sugar Pine Trail
Summer at Lake Haven
Summer at the Cape

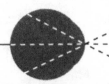

**This Large Print Book carries the
Seal of Approval of N.A.V.H.**

All Is Bright

A Hope's Crossing Novel

RaeAnne Thayne

CENTER POINT LARGE PRINT
THORNDIKE, MAINE

This Center Point Large Print edition
is published in the year 2022 by arrangement with
Harlequin Enterprises ULC.

The text of this Large Print edition is unabridged.
In other aspects, this book may vary
from the original edition.
Printed in the United States of America
on permanent paper sourced using
environmentally responsible foresting methods.
Set in 16-point Times New Roman type.

ISBN: 978-1-63808-522-5

The Library of Congress has cataloged this record
under Library of Congress Control Number: 2022942243

For all my readers who have been asking me to write Sage McKnight's story since I introduced her more than a decade ago.

Thank you to Jill Shalvis, Michelle Major and Molly O'Keefe for your invaluable help. Love you all! Also, special thanks to reader Ali Hird for suggesting a name for the Fire & Ice Festival.

1

Sage

Sage McKnight inhaled a breath that smelled of pine, snow and home as she walked up the new curving sidewalk of sculpted concrete that led toward the front door of a massive log and glass structure in Silver Strike Canyon.

She had been away far too long.

Her home base in the Bay Area, a small loft near the California offices of her father's architectural firm of Lange & Associates, was an easy flight to her hometown of Hope's Crossing, Colorado.

Under normal circumstances, she should have been able to come back often, but she had spent most of the past year overseeing a pair of major commercial projects overseas while keeping tabs on the progress at Wolf Ridge through the occasional visit and reports from her father.

This season was a gift, one she fully intended to savor. Somehow, almost miraculously, both commercial buildings had finished ahead of schedule and the rest of her commitments had eased enough to allow her to spend the entire month of December staying with her family.

On the flight in, she had been shocked to realize this would be the longest span of time she had spent in Hope's Crossing since her sophomore year of college, when she had temporarily put her schooling on hold to deal with more urgent matters.

She drew in another deep breath, as if the mountain air could scrub both her mind and her lungs clean from the residual particulates of urban living.

This wasn't wholly a vacation. She would be working on several other designs virtually as well as being available nearby while crews put the finishing touches to this gorgeous house in front of her, on a forested hillside a mile from the Silver Strike ski resort.

Sage considered Wolf Ridge her crowning achievement, the project she had poured her heart and soul into over the past nine months.

No vehicles except her rental were out front but she had spoken with Sam Delgado, the contractor handling the construction end of what had turned into a complete overhaul. He told her he wouldn't be on-site but had given her the access code so she could walk through and check the progress.

Anticipation swirled through her like the light snowflakes that brushed her cheeks. She had kept up with the progress of the job virtually and with pictures from Sam and her father, but that wasn't the same as actually having her boots on the ground.

Sage punched in the code and pushed open the door, nerves jumping inside her.

She always loved this sense of discovery when she walked onto a job site she hadn't visited in a few months, that thrill that still washed over her at seeing an abstract vision she designed months ago taking shape, becoming reality.

She had just pushed open the door when her father's SUV pulled up behind her rental car. A moment later her dad climbed out and walked toward her, smiling broadly.

With anyone else, she might have felt a little resentment that she wouldn't have the chance to see the progress of her passion project on her own. But her father was Jackson Freaking Lange, one of the world's preeminent architects. She still sometimes couldn't quite believe it, even after ten years of having him in her life.

She had spent her first nineteen years without a father of her own, though she had gained a loving stepfather when she was three and she still deeply loved Chris Parker, even after he divorced her mother.

Still, not knowing so much as the name of her birth father had left a small void in her heart, an empty spot she hadn't known how to fill when she was younger.

Since they found each other a decade earlier, Jack had become a steady source of support, professionally and emotionally.

"Welcome back," he said now, his deep voice so dearly familiar. He opened his arms and hugged her with a warmth that touched and comforted her.

"How did you know where to find me?" she had to ask.

He gave a little laugh. "Where else would you be? I knew what time your flight was coming in and guessed this would be your first stop. In your shoes, I would have done the same thing."

They were so alike, both of them passionate about the art and aesthetics of architecture. Of course, she could never begin to compare to all her father had achieved, but she was working to make her mark in her own way.

"I'm going to assume you didn't stop at the bookstore to see your mother first before rushing out here."

After Jack and Sage had found each other, during the most difficult season of her life, he and her mother had reconnected. They had been wildly happy together since then. In a way, she felt as if she had played a part in bringing them back together.

Sage shook her head now, feeling a little guilty. "I'll see her soon enough. Remember, I've got Taryn's birthday party in an hour. I wanted to squeeze in a stop here first."

"Naturally." He smiled. "Do you mind me tagging along? Don't feel obligated. If you would rather check things out first by yourself, I can wait in my car until you've had time to bask in the glow."

She had to laugh that he could read her with such accuracy. "No. You've been in on Wolf Ridge from the beginning. It will be fun to see it together."

The two of them walked into the grand foyer, with its soaring ceiling and commanding staircase.

She had seen this part before but was thrilled all over again at how bright and welcoming the space was now, compared to how it had been before the massive renovation, with afternoon light pouring in from several new windows to play across the wood plank floor.

"Oh wow!" she exclaimed. Everything looked even better than she had dreamed.

Built thirty years earlier when the Silver Strike resort was new, the massive estate had good bones and a gorgeous view of the surrounding mountains and the Silver Strike Reservoir, glittering in the distance. But for all its size, the interior spaces had been dark, cramped, with small rooms, narrow hallways and no cohesive design.

In many ways, it might have been easier for the owner to sell the property and start over after his life circumstances changed. She was glad he had decided to keep it, instead hiring Jackson Lange & Associates to rehabilitate the space.

Sage had gone for a mix of rustic and industrial throughout the eight-bedroom, ten-bathroom house, with a mix of glass, wood and metal.

Others might not have seen the potential of Wolf Ridge. She could only be grateful that her client, difficult as he might be, hadn't been one of those people.

"Have you heard from Tucker?" her dad asked, again guessing her thoughts with uncanny accuracy. "Is he happy with the progress?"

She made a face. "Who knows? Mason Tucker is a tough nut to crack. We have had more change orders on this job than any other residential property in my experience."

Jackson nodded. "The man has been through hell and I imagine his circumstances are still fairly fluid. I'm sure he only wants to make sure everything will still work for him exactly as he needs it."

She did understand that. She also knew the internal conflict a man like Mason Tucker must be experiencing, to know his life would never be the same as it once was. With that in mind, she had tried to approach all aspects of this renovation with compassion and consideration.

Mason had turned out to be a tough man to please, but she could only hope he would be reasonably happy with the finished project.

They walked through the house, each room a new discovery for Sage. Since she had been here, most of the finish carpentry had been done, the multilevel kitchen cabinets installed and new flooring laid throughout.

Part of her enjoyment at seeing the changes came from her father's admiration. "Everything works together perfectly," Jackson said. "I love the industrial look, with all the support beams showing and the turnbuckles and rivets. It's perfect for a house here in Hope's Crossing, especially in this canyon where mining was such an integral piece of the history."

"Many of these elements were already here, just hidden behind drywall," she said. "It made sense to highlight them."

"It's beautiful," her father said, the pride in his voice warming her all over again.

"I think it's some of my best work," she admitted, something she hadn't said aloud to anyone else, even her father.

"I suppose it helped that Tucker was willing to throw piles of money to the renovation."

"Definitely."

Her father's phone pinged suddenly, while they were still walking through the rooms on the main floor. He glanced at his smartwatch. "Oh shoot. I'm going to have to run. That's Nick. He's done early with basketball practice. Since your mom is busy at the bookstore getting ready for the party, I'm on pickup duty."

Her breath seemed to catch a little, as it always

did at the thought of her nine-year-old brother.

"Yes. Go. You don't want to leave him waiting out in the cold at the community center. Thanks for stopping by to take a look, Dad. It was fun to share at least this much with you."

He gave her another hug. "Are you kidding? I know how important this one is for you. It's fantastic, Sage. I'm so proud of you."

She tucked his words of praise into her mind to take out in those moments of doubt. Jackson Lange thought her work was fantastic. Yeah, he was her father but he wouldn't say the words if he didn't mean them.

"Thanks, Dad."

"I'll see you at Taryn's party."

With another hug, he hurried out of the house, leaving her standing near the empty gas fireplace of the great room.

On impulse, she pulled out her phone to document her steps as she finished the tour, wishing she had thought to bring her gimbal or at least a selfie stick.

"We're now walking into the home theater," she spoke to her outstretched camera, "one of the more challenging rooms of the renovation. Prior to this update, the room had a series of steps leading to the different levels of recliners. Obviously, that would no longer work for the homeowner, so we chose to remove the steps completely, instead building a gradual slope with room to maneuver around each level of seating. Beyond featuring state-of-the-art electronics that will be easily upgradeable, everything in here—from the blackout window shades to the sound system to the recliners themselves—can be controlled through a single smart home phone app."

She turned the camera to face her. "Doesn't this look like a wonderfully cozy place to watch a movie or catch your favorite sporting event?"

She smiled into the phone camera, then moved back into the wide hallway leading to the library/office, her own favorite spot in the house.

"You can see here we have sliding pocket doors that open and close with the push of a button. We chose to replace the traditional doors in many of the spaces with these pocket doors, which gives more room for the homeowner to navigate, and we also . . ."

Her words trailed off as she heard a sound behind her and turned to see a large, dark-haired man using a wheelchair, framed in the doorway.

He frowned, an expression she had become all too used to seeing there, during their few in-person interactions and their more frequent video conferences.

"What are you doing?" he demanded. "You're not filming this, are you?"

Sage dropped her phone with an inward wince and stopped recording. Technically, this was still her job site, which meant she had full permission to check on the progress of the work until they handed the finished home over to the owner, who happened to be this man, former professional baseball player Mason Tucker.

With effort, she forced herself not to show any of her dismay. Out of all the clients she had worked with during her career thus far, Mason Tucker was the only one who made her palms sweat and her stomach feel knotted with stress.

"Mr. Tucker. Um, hi." She forced a smile, feeling awkward as hell and wishing she had waited until the contractor would be here to take a tour.

"I haven't been here in weeks and wanted to document the progress that has been made since I visited last. I didn't see any vehicles outside and assumed everybody was gone for the day."

"I'm parked in the garage of the guesthouse."

"I didn't even know you were in town. Have you been here long?"

The last she knew, Mason had been living in Portland, where he had once played for the same baseball team as another town resident, Spencer Gregory, who was married to Sage's friend Charlotte. Sage knew Spence and Mason had remained friends, despite life circumstances that had led to both of them retiring.

For a moment, she wasn't sure Mason would reply, then he finally shrugged. "I wanted to be close as we started to wrap things up so I can keep an eye on things and be on hand if there are any questions or problems. My daughter and I moved into the guesthouse a month ago."

Why hadn't her dad or Sam Delgado told her Mason was already living in Hope's Crossing?

Beyond that, she suddenly thought, how in the world was he making the guesthouse work? That place wasn't at all wheelchair accessible, with three steps leading into the place, narrow hallways and no accessible bathroom like those she had designed for this main house.

Renovating the guesthouse was part of the master plan but not until all the work was finished on Wolf Ridge itself.

"That place is a mess. How are you getting around?"

"I'm managing," he said, his voice curt. "I can still get around on crutches, as long as I don't have to go far."

"You shouldn't have to go far, from one end of the guesthouse to the other. It's tiny." She imagined a man Mason's size would make the space shrink to almost nothing.

"It works fine for me and Grace. It's only a few more weeks anyway, right?"

"I suppose."

Sam Delgado had assured her when they spoke earlier that the renovations to Wolf Ridge would be finished shortly before Christmas.

Sage had to admit, she wouldn't be sorry to put the job behind her.

While she was thrilled with the way her designs had transformed the mountain estate, working with Mason Tucker himself was another story.

She tried to be compassionate. Whenever she grew frustrated with him, she would remind herself that Mason had endured the sort of tragedy that would have completely destroyed someone without his resilience. While she was only charged with renovating this house, Mason had to completely rebuild his life.

He had every right to be surly and unco-operative.

While she might know that intellectually, it was difficult to remember when she was dealing with yet another last-minute change order.

Still, he had superb taste and basically unlimited financial resources. In a few more weeks, when the job was finished, Wolf Ridge would meet his needs now and long into the future.

The home now featured a new indoor pool, spa and high-tech exercise room on the bottom level, two new elevators at either end of the house and heated floors throughout. Wolf Ridge also featured a kitchen that worked for people of any mobility level and wheelchair accessible bathrooms on each level, including the extensive owner's suite on the second floor.

Sage loved everything about this house, from

the skylights to the beams her dad had mentioned to the wider doorways and hallways. It was warm, luxurious, comfortable.

She wanted to show off her work to the world. The only trick would be convincing the intensely private Mason Tucker.

Faced with his glower now, Sage felt as if she faced a Herculean task.

She had to try, though, didn't she?

Her fledgling internet show had exploded in popularity over the past year, allowing her foundation and personal pet project to help far more deserving people than she had ever envisioned.

Sage could only imagine the vast number of views—and thus ad revenue—a video featuring Wolf Ridge would bring in. People would love a glimpse inside the house redesigned for the reclusive and private Mason Tucker.

The public still clamored to know everything it could about the former professional athlete who had endured so much physical and emotional pain.

If she could showcase Wolf Ridge on the Homes for All internet channel, she would also bring awareness to some of the issues and obstacles noninclusive design presented to those with mobility challenges.

She drew in a breath, not sure where to start. Yes, he would likely slap her down but she wouldn't know unless she asked, right?

"The progress while I've been overseas is amazing. I can't believe how different everything looks, with the finish work and the new flooring."

"Sam and his subs have put in some long hours."

"It shows. And Jean-Paul tells me he's going to have nearly all the furnishings ready to go in a few more weeks, except for a few custom pieces."

"That's what he tells me."

"I can't see any reason you and Grace can't move in before Christmas. How exciting!"

A shrug was his only response, which she supposed was about as eloquent as Mason Tucker could be.

She stuck her hands into the pockets of her wool coat.

He was going to say no. She knew it and braced herself for it.

"There's no easy way for me to ask you this so I'm going to come straight out with it." She drew in a breath. "For the past year, I've hosted a YouTube channel, Homes for All, which features projects with the kind of innovative universal design elements we have tried to incorporate here at Wolf Ridge."

He raised an eyebrow but said nothing.

"While it's called Homes for All, we feature commercial as well as residential projects. I hope to continue raising awareness of how limiting and even discriminatory some design practices can be for those who are, er, differently abled."

He again said nothing, only continued to look at her out of those hard blue eyes that concealed his emotions completely.

"I have poured so much energy into Wolf Ridge, and I'm absolutely thrilled with the way the house has turned out. It's everything I dreamed and more. I feel like more people should see it. Don't you? I would absolutely love to feature your home on my channel."

She held her breath, hands curled inside her pockets.

As she might have predicted, he didn't leave her waiting long for his answer.

"Hell no," he said with blunt finality, then turned away and started to roll back down the hall so abruptly she could only stare at him.

After a moment, she pursued him. This was too important to give up at the first obstacle. "Just like that? You don't even want to hear the details?"

He paused and maneuvered to face her. "Why waste both our time? I don't need to hear the details. Whatever you have to say doesn't matter. My answer will remain a hard no."

The man was impossible. Her grandfather Harry might have called him *pigheaded,* but Sage preferred the more diplomatic *obstinate.*

And yes, how could she blame him for that? Mason was trying to rebuild a life for himself

21

and his daughter in Hope's Crossing, away from the prying eyes of the tabloid press. She already knew he was an intensely private man. He had made her sign a nondisclosure agreement before even talking to her about what he wanted done at the house.

She might have been more surprised if he *had* agreed to let her feature his house on her channel.

Still, she had never been good at taking no for an answer. She could be every bit as pigheaded as Mason Tucker. She figured she had inherited that from Harry Lange himself.

"What I love most about your home is how seamlessly we have managed to integrate the new design into the existing structure without altering the basic style and grace of the home," she said. "I'm sure you can agree that the changes will benefit everyone who lives here, not only you."

"Sure," he said after a moment. "You definitely know what you're doing. The house is exactly what I wanted. That still doesn't mean I want the whole world peering in at the transfer bars in the shower or the damn lift I need to use so I can get in and out of my spa."

Sage was so caught up in the first part of what he said, the unexpected praise coming from her difficult client, that she almost missed the second part.

"That's exactly what I try to showcase on my channel. When done right, universal design can blend with the overall style of a home or commercial property, small and sometimes barely noticeable changes but enough to make a huge difference to those who need them."

"No," he said again. "Judging by how seldom you're here, you must have other projects. You can focus on those."

"I have. You can watch the videos online. We have about thirty of them up now. But Wolf Ridge is the most ambitious residential renovation I've ever undertaken. Most people would never have poured the kind of resources you have into making such extensive changes to an existing structure. They would have sold the house as is and built a custom home somewhere else. Because of the location and the basic sound structure of the house, you chose to renovate instead. The results are beautiful, and I want the whole world to see it."

"And I don't," he said bluntly. "I don't need to give the whole damn world any more reasons to pity me."

A muscle clenched along his jaw, and Sage felt immediately ashamed of herself for her selfishness at wanting to showcase her best work here.

Her motives weren't completely selfish, she amended. Yes, she was proud of her work on Wolf Ridge. This project, more than any other she had been part of, might help her begin to emerge from her father's huge and well-earned shadow.

It wasn't easy being Jackson Lange's daughter and trying to find her own way in the same field as one of the world's most brilliant architectural minds.

That was the very reason she hadn't taken Jack's surname, even after they reconnected. She still went by Sage McKnight, the name she'd always had. She didn't want to be known first as Jackson Lange's daughter, with the weight of all those expectations on her. She wanted to succeed on her own.

Beyond that, she was doing good work with Homes for All. She knew she was making a difference in people's lives, not only by changing minds about universal design but by changing lives.

Should she tell Jackson Lange that Homes for All was also the name of her foundation, funded by the ad revenue her videos generated online? The purpose was to help people who couldn't otherwise afford to make necessary changes to their living spaces when age or health issues impacted mobility.

No. She didn't want to guilt him into letting her invade his privacy by showcasing Wolf Ridge.

"Will you at least think about it?" she finally said. "You don't have to decide anything right this moment."

He shrugged. "I can think about it from now until Christmas. I won't change my mind. My house, my decision. You can take all the pictures and video you want for your own personal use but if you post them online, I'll sue your ass for breaking our nondisclosure agreement."

He wheeled away without another word, leaving Sage to gaze after him with helpless frustration.

She hadn't really expected any other answer, but she had *hoped*.

Her watch alarm dinged, and she glanced down at the reminder she had set. She was supposed to be at her mother's bookstore and coffeehouse, Books & Brew, in ten minutes.

She quickly shot a few more images then walked back out into the December twilight.

The house had an incredible view, Sage had to admit. The placement was one of the most appealing facets of the house and probably one of the reasons Mason Tucker had chosen to renovate this mountain estate rather than building new.

She could see the ski resort from here and even a glimpse of Hope's Crossing, where Christmas lights were beginning to wink and gleam.

She always forgot how much she loved it here. This property, yes. More than that, Hope's Crossing itself.

As she walked to her car, snowflakes danced on the cold air, floating gently to land on her coat.

She took a deep breath of mountain air. This was her home. No matter where else she traveled for Lange & Associates and with Homes for All, Hope's Crossing had her heart.

Though she was disappointed at Mason Tucker's response, she couldn't be too upset. She had an entire month ahead of her to be here, in the place where she loved and with all the people she cared most about in her life.

2

Mason

Sage McKnight was not happy with him.

Even ten minutes after they parted, Mason felt as if the echo of her annoyance seemed to hang in the air, along with the scent of new drywall and paint.

Her frustration was nothing new. Mason was fully aware he had been tough to work with through the entirety of this journey they had embarked on together nine months earlier.

He was a demanding client with very particular ideas about what he wanted in his house. This would be his haven, the retreat he and Grace desperately needed after the turmoil and chaos of the past two and a half years.

In all fairness, Sage McKnight seemed to perceive exactly what he envisioned for Wolf Ridge. She had come up with solutions to many problems he had never even foreseen, and she had a unique genius for taking his most abstract concepts and turning them into actual workable ideas.

Sage was excellent at her job, considered among the best around when it came to creating comfortable spaces for people of all abilities. He considered it a minor miracle that she hadn't backed out after working with him through the first round of blueprints.

Mason knew some of her frustration stemmed from his insistence in being part of every decision, large or small. He hoped she understood why creating the perfect house out of the style disaster that had been Wolf Ridge was so important to him.

He could control very few elements of his world right now. Hell, he could only control his legs about half the time. He couldn't bring back Shayla or their baby. He couldn't recapture his days as an All-Star catcher and cleanup batter on a Major League team.

Despite nearly thirty months of constant, intensive physical therapy, he could only take a few wobbly, uncertain steps at a time without using a walker or crutches.

Doctors had told him that at this point, his prognosis was unlikely to change significantly until major medical advances caught up with those suffering spinal cord injuries, or in his case, an incomplete SCI.

Mason knew his doctors considered it a miracle that he had survived at all. The fact that he had regained most of the sensation in his legs had astonished everyone. He knew that, just as he was doing his best to come to terms with the fact that he would never be the man he was the morning before the helicopter crash.

No, he corrected himself. He *had* come to terms

with it. He had switched to using the wheelchair more instead of always struggling to lurch around with the Lofstrand forearm crutches, hadn't he?

And nearly a year ago, he had hired Lange & Associates, and the very lovely Sage McKnight, to rebuild this house in Hope's Crossing in order to make it fully accessible for him.

While his life might feel in tatters, at least his house didn't have to reflect that.

He loved what they had created together here. He and Sage McKnight and Sam Delgado, his contractor. That didn't mean he was ready to show the world every detail.

He had turned down literally hundreds of interview requests since the helicopter crash.

He didn't feel any need to talk about it ad nauseam, and the world certainly didn't need to see the wreckage left behind.

As Mason made his painstaking way down the elevator, out of the house and across the circular driveway to the guesthouse, he had to admit Sage McKnight had been right about something she said earlier. The guesthouse was the least accessible structure on the property, with steps into the house, narrow hallways and small spaces.

He rose from his chair, gripping the railing hard with one hand while lifting the wheelchair along behind him with the other as he made his way up the stairs.

At least he had plenty of upper body strength.

29

He always had, mostly from growing up on a farm where hauling hay tended to build muscle early. The same muscles that had helped him have one of the best batting averages in the National League now came in handy pulling himself in and out of places when his legs decided not to cooperate.

He had almost reached the top when his mother opened the door to the two-bedroom guesthouse and peered out at him.

"I thought I heard something out here," Rebecca said. "Let me get the chair inside for you."

"I've got it," he said, exertion turning his voice more curt than he intended.

He saw Rebecca veil the soft concern in the blue eyes that matched his own.

"No problem," she said calmly. "Looks like you have it under control."

Ha. He didn't have *anything* under control, and they both knew it.

She stepped aside so he could make his ungainly way inside, using the wheelchair as a sort of support.

He rarely used the wheelchair inside this small house, simply because it barely fit through the regular-sized doorways and around the large western-style pine furniture that had been here before he and Shayla bought the house, years ago, shortly after Grace was born.

"Do you want the canes or the walker?"

"Neither," he muttered.

He never seemed to know what to say to Rebecca. The awkward dance he and his mother seemed to perform together hadn't become any easier since the crash, when she had inserted herself into his life against his wishes, during a time he had been too numb with physical and emotional pain to push her back out.

Rebecca desperately wanted a relationship with him now, in marked contrast to his first eighteen years, when she had been happy enough to pretend she didn't have a son.

He would have liked to shove her completely out now, but both of them knew he needed her help with Grace, as much as he hated to admit it.

"Crutches," he finally said. They were just out of reach of where he stood, leaning against the wall for support. She handed them to him and Mason made his lurching, unsteady way into the comfortable great room of the guest cottage, the large area that served as living, dining and kitchen.

Grace was curled up on the sofa next to the gas woodstove with a book on her lap and their six-year-old mini goldendoodle, Elsa, next to her.

They both looked up when he moved into the room, and the sheer joy on Grace's face at the sight of her broken-down father humbled the hell out of him.

"Hi, Dad!"

"Hey, kid. How was school?"

She shrugged. "Good, I guess. I was the first one done with my math worksheet. Again. And at recess I played football with my friend Nick and some other kids. I call it soccer but he says it technically should be called football."

"Did he?"

"Yeah. I played forward and kicked two goals, but it was no big deal."

"Two goals. That's a very big deal."

He eased onto the other end of the sofa and Elsa, the third female in his life who apparently thought he needed looking after, abandoned Grace to snuggle next to his hip.

The house smelled delicious, he had to admit, of roasting tomatoes and onions and peppers.

His mother, who had picked up and closed her apartment to come with them to Hope's Crossing entirely on her own accord, often threw something in the oven for them to eat.

He wanted to tell her to knock it off, that he wouldn't be manipulated so easily. But he had to admit, her taco casserole was scrumptious.

"It's not really that amazing," Grace said. "The goalie for the other team was Jayden Nuttall, and he was too busy playing on his phone to pay much attention to the game. A first grader could have scored against him."

That was a damning indictment, coming from a fourth grader like Grace.

"Anyway, Nick said he's on a soccer team that

32

plays indoors at the rec center. Don't you think that's weird?"

"Not really."

"He said I should sign up for it."

"Is that something you want to do?"

"If you think it's okay," she said, far too tentatively for his liking. She had played junior soccer back in Portland before the crash and had seemed to love it. For the past thirty months, their lives had been so chaotic, with surgery after surgery, that he was ashamed to realize he hadn't even thought about it.

"I'll talk to Nick's mom and dad about the indoor league," he said.

"Okay," she said happily.

The calf muscles in his right leg, the one he could feel most, suddenly started to spasm. He hitched in a breath, trying to hide it. He must not have succeeded. Elsa whined a little, nudging his leg with her nose, and Grace gave him a concerned look. "Your legs hurt, don't they?"

Always. He swallowed the word. "I'm good," he lied. "Smells like Rebecca has fixed something delicious for dinner."

"It's taco pie," Grace said. "I helped make it. And I made the salad."

"And you did a great job," Rebecca said, stepping forward a little, tall and elegant at just over fifty. "It should be ready whenever you are. You only have to take it out of the oven."

His mother gave them both a smile as she picked up her coat and purse from the back of one of the kitchen chairs.

"Grandma, you should stay and eat with us," Grace announced. "Shouldn't she, Dad?"

Mason wanted to say no, but it seemed graceless and ungrateful, when she had gone to all the trouble to fix dinner for them.

Rebecca looked at him with so much wary hope in her eyes, he couldn't refuse.

He forced a thin smile. His mother's presence in their lives, like it or not, seemed to be one more area he couldn't control. "Sure. Why not? You always make plenty."

"Thank you," she said, her voice soft. She took off her coat again and moved to the oven to take out the pan of bubbly goodness.

"It should probably sit for a few moments. I'll grab the salad and we can start there."

As she bustled around the small but efficient kitchen of the guesthouse, Mason wanted to shake his head at the surreal moment. If someone had told him when he was an angry teenager that some day his completely AWOL mother would be fixing him and his daughter dinner, he would have thought they were having delusions.

Shortly after he signed his first Major League contract at nineteen, Rebecca had emailed him in a tentative effort to reconnect.

Mason had treated her attempt at reconciliation

with disdain, telling her bluntly never to reach out to him again.

His mother hadn't wanted anything to do with him since handing him over to her own parents when he was three days old. He sure as hell wasn't about to open the door to let her back in, now that he had signed a multimillion-dollar contract and was gaining recognition on the ball diamond and off.

He shouldn't have been surprised when she hadn't heeded his wishes. Instead, Rebecca had tried to reach out and establish a relationship a few other times over the years—when the tabloids announced he and Shayla had married and again when Grace was born. Each time, Mason had been quick to shut her down.

After the accident, when he had been in the ICU fighting for his life and out of his head with the blur of pain and grief, Rebecca had shown up out the blue and moved into his house to help with a lost and frightened Grace, who had been staying with Shayla's devastated parents.

By the time he started to emerge from the haze of medication, Rebecca was firmly established in Grace's life, and the two of them had formed a relationship.

Rebecca had been there for Grace at a time when his daughter had desperately needed her. He couldn't deny that. He might not like it but how could he deprive his daughter of the relationship with her grandmother, when she had already lost so much?

As soon as he had been able to think beyond his own pain, he had done his best to put down ground rules. She could spend time with Grace when he wasn't around, but that was as far as he was willing to go.

To his great surprise, she had honored his wishes. He couldn't avoid seeing her occasionally, but he limited their interactions as much as possible and carefully maintained a polite, cool tone with her.

To his further surprise, when he announced six weeks ago that he and Grace were moving into the guesthouse of Wolf Ridge to oversee the last stages of the massive renovation project, she had quietly nodded and proceeded to find an apartment of her own to rent not far from Wolf Ridge.

He was still suspicious of her motives but no longer thought she was trying to cash in on his fortune. She had money of her own, apparently. Besides her own career as a showgirl and part-time model, she had been married twice, divorcing her philandering first husband, a real estate developer, and being left a wealthy widow by the death of her much-older second husband five years earlier.

Dinner was an awkward affair, at least for Mason. His mother and Grace seemed comfortable chattering about all kinds of things, from school to a movie they had watched a few days earlier to all the Hope's Crossing holiday events slated for the month.

Grace seemed especially excited about the upcoming Hope's Crossing Fire & Ice Festival, a one-night fundraiser when apparently everyone in town gathered to celebrate the opening of the town skating rink in a downtown park.

"It's cool because nobody knows when it will be until the day it happens."

"Like a pop-up town festival?"

"I guess," she said. "We can go, can't we? My friend Nick says it's the most fun ever."

Mason could hardly stand up. How was he supposed to ice skate?

"I'll take you, if your dad can't," Rebecca said quickly. "I love to ice skate, though I haven't been for years. I used to skate on a pond near the farm where I grew up."

Was that something Leland and Sariah Tucker would have allowed? Mason doubted it. That sounded entirely too much like fun. She probably went out on the sly, when she was supposed to be doing some of the endless chores required on a Nebraska farm.

He was mostly quiet, listening to them chat as he ate what was admittedly a delicious meal. Still, he was relieved when Rebecca finished, cleared away the dishes and excused herself.

She wanted him to forgive and forget. How could he? She had escaped her parents' cold, cheerless house as quickly as she could, running away with a boyfriend when she was sixteen.

And then a year later, boyfriend out of the picture now apparently, she had dropped off her innocent newborn son with those same parents she despised so she could return to her hard partying life and her search for fame and fortune.

He wasn't sure he could ever get over that.

Mason was breaking the cycle, though. He and Shayla had tried hard to create a warm, loving home for Grace, as they would have done the same for the unborn son who had died with Shayla.

He pushed down the familiar ache and focused on Grace's bedtime routine. After she showered and changed into her pajamas, they sat together in the living room, taking turns reading aloud from a book series she loved.

"So you know my friend Nick?" she asked when they finished the chapter.

You mean the one you mention about fifty times a day?

He nodded. "Sure. You guys seem to have a lot in common."

"Not everything. He's super funny and everybody likes him. He's really good at spelling and always wins the class spelling bees. But he's not as good in math as I am."

"Everybody has strengths. I wasn't good at spelling *or* math." Only sports. Baseball, basketball, football. He had been obsessed with all of it, to the dismay of his grandparents.

"You know how Natalia in the story was adopted? That's like Nick. He was adopted too."

"Was he?" Mason said. He had wondered. Nick's parents were Jackson and Maura Lange. Sage McKnight was their oldest daughter, separated by nearly two decades from her two younger siblings, Nick and Anna.

"Yeah. Except Natalia doesn't know her parents and Nick does. Well, his mom, anyway. He told me his mom and dad are really his grandma and grandpa but they adopted him when he was born."

Mason stared at her, his mind trying to process the unexpected information. "Is that right?"

She nodded. "And guess what? He told me his sister Sage, the nice lady helping us with our new house, is really his mom! Isn't that funny?"

Mason could think of other words besides funny.

"But Nick said she's not really his mom. His mom is his mom. Sage is his big sister, just like Anna and their other sister Layla, who died."

He didn't want to know this, information that linked Sage's experience to Rebecca's. The parallels were unavoidable. Nick was nine, like Grace, and he knew Sage wasn't quite thirty. So she must have had Nick when she was barely out of her teens, handed him over to her parents to raise and then blithely went on with her life.

He was suddenly glad he had never crossed the line and acted on the unwanted attraction simmering inside him for his architect.

"It would be weird to have a sister who is also your mom, don't you think?"

"Families come in all shapes and sizes. We've talked about that before."

"Sure. I know. I mean, my friend Benny back home had two moms and no dad. And my friend Julia doesn't live with her mom and dad, she lives with her aunt and uncle and cousins."

"That's right."

She looked at him. "We're kind of a different family too, now. Just you and me and Elsa. Oh, and Grandma."

He managed not to make a face at the addition. Rebecca was *not* part of their family, no matter how hard she might try.

He couldn't say that to his daughter. "The important thing is that everyone should have people in their families who love each other and take care of each other. Sometimes that comes from the family you were born into and sometimes it's the family you make through the other people you love."

She smiled up at him and leaned on his arm, this child who was everything to him.

Mason let out a breath. His resentment toward

his mother, his conflicted feelings for his architect, even his stupid aching legs weren't important.

His daughter was the only thing that mattered—Grace and the future he was trying to build for her here in Hope's Crossing.

3

Taryn

This was her birthday party and she was supposed to be happy.

Taryn Thorne looked around at all of her friends and family members gathered at Maura Lange's shop, Books & Brew, here to celebrate the happy occasion of her twenty-sixth birthday.

She knew she should be thrilled at all the attention, but somehow Taryn felt as if she had just been sucker punched.

She looked at Genevieve Caine, certain she must have misheard her friend.

"Are you serious? Charlie is here, in Hope's Crossing? Did he . . . just arrive?"

Her voice sounded faint, with a slight wobble, but she knew her friends and family were used to that. Her words often stumbled over themselves, especially when she was tired.

Genevieve apparently didn't notice. She popped a shrimp into her mouth from a tray carried by a passing waiter, really one of Maura Lange's bookstore employees. "I don't know. Five days, I guess."

Five days. Her best friend had been in town for *five days* and he had yet to reach out to her.

Taryn frowned. "Did he know about this?" She

gestured around to the red-and-purple birthday balloons festooning the seating area of the small coffeehouse attached to the bookstore.

"Yes," Gen said, her voice a little wary. "I mentioned it to him. He said he wasn't in the mood for a big crowd today and offered to stay with the kids. I'm supposed to tell you happy birthday from him."

Why couldn't he tell her that himself? Taryn had to fight a tangled mix of annoyance and hurt.

She wanted to drive straight to his house to tell Charlie off herself. Not only had he not bothered to come to her party, but he had been in town *five days* and hadn't once called or texted her to let her know.

What had she done to make him want to avoid her?

She thought she knew.

Charlie Beaumont, Gen's brother, had been her best friend forever. No matter where he had been in the years since he had left Hope's Crossing, they texted, talked on the phone or connected via social media at least two or three times a week.

Until about four months earlier, anyway. Things had been strained between them since the last time they had spent much time together, when he had come back to Colorado for a good friend's wedding in Denver and had asked her to be his last-minute plus-one.

Taryn's hand tightened on the stem of her champagne glass.

Every time she thought about that weekend they had spent together, she wanted to cry. She had been stupid and impulsive and had ruined everything.

She might have been able to fix things between them but then Charlie and Gen's father, William Beaumont, had unexpectedly passed away from a heart attack a month later. While Charlie's relationship with his parents had been strained at best, Taryn knew William's death had hit Charlie hard, especially as his mother had died of liver disease five years earlier.

How could Taryn be so put out about him not coming to a silly birthday party, when he was dealing with the loss of his only remaining parent?

"How is he doing after . . . everything?"

Genevieve shrugged, sadness clouding her lovely features. "You know Charlie. He keeps so much inside. He always has."

"Yes. I remember."

After his mother's death, which had occurred as Charlie was finishing his undergraduate work with the intention to soon start med school, his plans for his life seemed to shift. After her funeral, he had announced he was taking a job with The Sheridan Trust, an organization that built medical clinics and schoolhouses in poor villages throughout the world.

For the past five years, he split his time working for the foundation and running his own successful carpentry business in the deserts of southern Utah, where he could hike and bike and river run to his heart's content.

"This fits me better than being a doctor would have," he had told her once when he had stopped in town for a short visit between assignments. "I'm still helping people, but I don't have to deal with all the paperwork or the insurance companies."

"How long . . . will he be in town?" Taryn asked Genevieve now.

She shrugged. "Until he can sort through Dad's affairs and get the house cleared out and ready to sell. Dad kind of left everything in a mess. I'm afraid it's going to take Charlie weeks to sort through it all."

Weeks. Charlie planned to be in town for *weeks.*

She was going to have to face him at some point but she wasn't sure how, after the awkwardness of the previous summer.

She had seen him at his father's funeral, of course, but Charlie had been distracted and distant with everyone, not only her. While Taryn had reached out with words of sympathy, she also knew that wasn't the best time to try making things right again between them.

Not everything was about her, Taryn reminded

herself. Okay, this particular gathering of friends was intended to celebrate her birthday, making *tonight* and this party basically about her. But beyond tonight, the people in her world had their own lives, their own issues. Charlie might be one of her closest friends but he was also dealing with plenty of his own stress, coming to terms with losing his one remaining parent and their conflicted relationship.

She wished she could help him. That was the reason for her hurt, she admitted to herself. Charlie had been her rock since she was fifteen. Through all the dark, difficult days of her recovery, she had leaned on him, confided in him. Counted on him.

Now, when she could finally try to repay a little of that vast debt by providing comfort in turn to him, he seemed to have completely turned away from her.

She wanted to leave the party right that moment to confront him but of course she couldn't. All these people were here to celebrate her birthday. She couldn't simply walk away.

Soon, though. She would figure out a way to fix this. She had to.

For now, she needed to focus on all those who had made the effort to celebrate her birthday and kick off the holiday season together.

"And how are *you* doing?" she asked Genevieve. Her friend had also lost her father, though she wasn't alone like Charlie. Gen had her husband, Dylan, and their two children, with a third on the way.

"I'm okay. A little sad sometimes, but some of that might be pregnancy emotions. Anyway, the kids don't let me brood for long. Thank you for asking." Genevieve gave her a hug, something that would have seemed completely shocking a decade ago when the other woman had been the mean girl of Hope's Crossing.

Taryn always felt so bad for Genevieve and Charlie about their dysfunctional childhood, especially when she compared the Beaumont house with her own. She looked over at her father and stepmother, deep in conversation with Claire and Riley McKnight.

Brodie and Evie Thorne were deeply in love and had created a beautiful life together. They had three other children, two with special needs they had adopted as older children and one they had created together.

Taryn found their example of wedded and familial bliss both inspirational and more than a little intimidating. She wasn't sure she would ever be able to have what they did, a relationship filled with laughter, joy, meaning.

Sure, she dated, but no one ever quite seemed to be the right fit.

Taryn knew the reason for that. No one else interested her beyond a second date because she was in love with Charlie Beaumont and had been since she was fifteen years old.

She sighed, returning to the conversation with his sister. They chatted for a few more moments, then with other friends who joined their group. They were all discussing their plans for the upcoming holidays when Taryn spotted someone she hadn't expected.

Her lingering blues about Charlie and the distance between them seemed to lift, if only briefly. With a quick word to the rest of their group, she hurried to the newcomer.

"Sage!" she exclaimed. "I had no idea you would be here."

Sage McKnight gave her a tight hug. "I wouldn't miss it. How's the birthday girl?"

Hurt. Frustrated. Lonely.

She said none of those things. Instead, she reminded herself of the mantra that had helped her endure all the long months of rehabilitation.

Focus on what you have. Not what you've lost.

All these people had come out to celebrate her party. Okay, mostly because her friends and family were always ready for any excuse to celebrate, but she would be ungrateful to mope about the one person who had decided not to come, instead of having fun with those who had.

"I'm terrific," she said with a smile that almost

49

felt genuine. "Your mom really knows how to throw a party."

"Definitely."

"Are you in town long?"

"I'm going back between Christmas and New Year's."

"You'll be here with your family for Christmas. How wonderful! We should get together."

"Yes. Definitely!"

Sage was another friend who had moved away from Hope's Crossing. She lived and worked as an architect in San Francisco. Taryn sometimes felt like the whole world had moved on while she was still here in her hometown, living only a few blocks away from her family.

Why would she go anywhere else, though? Taryn loved Hope's Crossing. If she hadn't, she never would have taken a job as a guidance counselor at the middle school.

"Any new videos on your channel?" she asked. "I watch religiously, every time you post a new one. I loved that beach house you featured near Sonoma."

"Wasn't that gorgeous? I didn't want to leave the day we taped there."

Taryn loved watching Sage's videos. Her friend had a natural camera presence and an intricate knowledge about architecture and design. She was funny and warm, and people seemed to respond positively. Taryn knew her YouTube channel received hundreds of thousands of hits whenever she posted a new video. She even had a few in the millions.

"You have really created a niche for yourself, haven't you?"

"The whole YouTube thing has been a blast, something I never expected."

"Are you filming something in town while you're home?"

A dark shadow flitted across Sage's green eyes. "I'm not sure. That was the plan. I've been working on renovations to a house in town that I wanted to feature, but it turns out the owner is a bit . . . reluctant."

"Is it Mason Tucker?"

"I didn't say that! How did you know?"

Taryn smiled. "Lucky guess? Not really. Everybody in town is talking about that gorgeous house on the hill and I know Sam Delgado has been busy on it. Your mom told me you had designed the renovation. I know I'm not the only one in town who was hoping for a chance to see inside it when it was featured on Homes for All."

Sage sipped at a drink from a passing waiter, frustration evident on her lovely features. "No luck right now," she said. "I'm still working on it. Mr. Tucker is . . . very private."

Everyone in town had talked about that too. He seemed to go out of his way to keep his private life private.

Taryn knew more than most how he might be feeling. After the accident, she had wanted to hide away in her bedroom and never leave. Sage and Charlie and other friends—and of course her father and Evie—had pulled her out and back into the light.

"I'll keep hoping." Sage smiled. "If you have any free evenings, let's go out while I'm home so we can sit down and catch up."

If she had any free evenings. Right. Taryn had nothing *but* free evenings, unless she was babysitting for her siblings.

She was twenty-six years old as of today and had no social life to speak of because she was waiting for the one person who couldn't seem to be bothered to even come to her birthday party.

"Say the word. I'll make time."

Sage smiled and hugged her. "It's so good to see you, T."

"Thanks."

Sage's features grew pensive. "Now that I think about it, you might be exactly the person to help me. Don't be surprised if I use our time together to pick your brain."

"Ha. You should know by now that picking my brain will probably take you about thirty seconds," she joked. "And twenty-nine of those would involve working your way through all the random thoughts I have about who might win the current season of *The Bachelor*."

Sage made a face. "We both know better than that. From what I hear, you're the favorite guidance counselor of every student at Hope's Crossing Middle School. My niece and nephews all rave about how cool you are."

She might not have a YouTube channel watched by millions or a growing reputation as a brilliant architect, but she loved her job and felt like she made a difference to her students.

Sage's mother, Maura, joined them a moment later, hugging her daughter. "There you are. I was wondering when you would show up."

"Sorry I'm late," Sage answered. "You know how I can be on a project."

"Too well. You and your father are obviously cut from the same cloth." Maura reached out a hand to squeeze one of Taryn's. "Happy birthday, my dear."

"Thank you. And thank you for the party."

"It's our pleasure. I know you didn't want a party, but I'm so glad you let us have one for you."

"Twenty-six is an odd year for a big party, don't you think?"

"Well, this is the party your grandma wanted to throw last year for your twenty-fifth, but you were inconveniently in the hospital."

True. Taryn had needed another surgery on her knee that still caused her problems, never healing right after the crash.

Maura looked around. "I haven't seen Charlie yet. Gen says he's back in town for a few months. I thought for sure he would be here. You two are usually inseparable."

Maura went out of her way to be kind to Charlie, which Taryn knew meant the world to him. Charlie still blamed himself for being behind the wheel the night Maura's daughter, Sage's sister—and Taryn's best friend—Layla had died.

Taryn could feel a muscle spasm in her jaw and realized she was clenching her teeth. She forced herself to relax. "Apparently not. Gen said he didn't feel up to a big crowd tonight."

Maura looked concerned. "Poor Charlie carries more than his fair share of baggage, doesn't he?"

Taryn nodded, though she felt a pang, hoping she hadn't added to it by her actions over the summer.

4

Sage

Sage loved being back among friends and family in Hope's Crossing, some of whom she hadn't talked to in a few years. Nearly everyone embraced her warmly and seemed happy to see her.

She had worried a decade earlier that her choices would haunt her the rest of her life here in town. How foolish of her to be concerned about that.

Oh, she knew there were some who whispered about her behind her back, but they were inconsequential in her life. Most people didn't care that she had been pregnant, unmarried and barely out of her teens. The circumstances were different thirty years earlier when her mother had been pregnant with *her*. Then it had been a juicy scandal, with much speculation about who her father might be.

She finished the last bite of a piece of delicious birthday cake, made by Charlotte Caine Gregory who owned a sweet shop in town. She rose from her spot to throw away her napkin and paper plate when Genevieve Beaumont Caine, Charlotte's sister-in-law, moved into view.

Sage held her breath.

She never quite knew what to say to the other woman. Of all the people who had been most hurt by Sage's actions a decade ago, Genevieve topped the list.

She had apologized a long time ago for sleeping with Gen's then-fiancé and becoming pregnant with his child. Gen seemed to have accepted her apology and had certainly moved on with her life after dumping Sawyer Danforth, but Sage still couldn't help feeling anxious whenever their paths crossed in public.

They had both been different people all those years ago. Sage had been eighteen, grieving and lost after her younger sister died in the same tragic accident that had seriously injured Taryn Thorne.

Genevieve was very different these days from the woman she had been a decade ago. She had once been spoiled, self-centered, concerned most with appearances. If she hadn't known for certain her identity, Sage would never have associated that Gen with the glowing, smiling woman in front of her.

"Sage. Hi. Your mom was telling me you're back in town through the holidays. How wonderful that you get to be here to enjoy all the seasonal fun in Hope's Crossing."

"The timing was perfect. Since I had a gap in my schedule and a fairly flexible boss, I decided to come back and be on hand while the reno project on Mason Tucker's house wraps up."

"Oh, I love that house. I'm so happy someone will be living there full time. It's too beautiful for only a vacation home."

"It's quite close to your place in Snowflake Canyon, isn't it?"

"Yes. We can see it through the trees from our place. It's been fun to watch the progress. For a while there, Dylan was thinking you must have gutted the whole thing, from all the truckloads of scrap we saw driving up and down the mountain."

"Close enough." She was again so grateful Mason had chosen to renovate Wolf Ridge instead of starting over with a new build.

"I would love to see what you've done with the place. Are you going to feature it on your YouTube channel? Dylan and I watch every new video religiously."

She wasn't sure how she felt about Genevieve watching her channel, especially considering Past Gen had once called Sage a dumpy little troll.

Different people, she reminded herself.

"I don't have permission from the owner to feature it yet, but I'm still keeping my fingers crossed," she said.

"Oh, I hope so. Charlotte and Spence are close friends with Mason. They might be able to put in a good word for you."

"I might have to try that, if nothing else works. I would love the world to see what we've done there. Wolf Ridge is my favorite kind of project,

57

when I know I'm making a difference in someone's ability to fully enjoy their home."

Genevieve, who seemed to be extremely pregnant with what would be her and Dylan's third child, sipped at a glass that looked like it held sparkling water. "I've been meaning to ask you a question," she said.

Sage braced herself, wary suddenly. "Go ahead."

"Is it really true you funnel all the ad revenue from your videos to renovating homes for people with mobility needs?"

Sage shifted, fighting an old urge to bite her fingernails. "Who told you that?"

"Harry told me in confidence. He's so proud of the work you're doing."

Her grandfather. Naturally. Funny how he could be loose-lipped about everyone else's business but so protective of his own.

Of course, there were very few true secrets in Hope's Crossing. Except maybe the true identity of the Angel of Hope, the town's benefactor who made it a point of helping many people going through tough times.

"Yes. I realized the need for more homes that feature universal design during Taryn's rehab. That need only grows as people age."

"I love what you're doing. Dylan and I were wondering if you might consider going into partnership with A Warrior's Hope."

Dylan and Genevieve, along with several others

in town, worked closely with the organization that helped wounded veterans and their families draw closer together through mountain retreats and recreational activities like adaptive skiing and snowboarding.

A small village of cabins provided housing, and a few years ago her father had designed several other facilities for A Warrior's Hope, including state-of-the-art workout facilities and an indoor swimming pool.

"What kind of partnership?"

"Our program works beautifully but then our clients leave after a week or two and return to often completely inadequate housing situations. Many of them really struggle with housing that doesn't work for them now."

"That definitely can be a concern. I have come up with a few blueprints for some relatively inexpensive new construction homes that follow universal design principles. I'm happy to provide those for you to show your clients."

"That would be terrific!"

"I can also help plan renovations to existing homes. I'm happy to help your clients with either of those things."

"That would be perfect. Maybe while you're in town you could meet with our board to give us some guidance about where to start."

"Sure. I would be happy to."

"Thank you!" To her shock, Genevieve hugged

her and she couldn't help thinking again that this woman seemed completely different from the Gen Beaumont who had hated her so passionately a decade earlier for ruining her fairy-tale wedding.

An hour later, the crowd began to disperse, and Sage stifled a yawn from her long day of travel as she helped clean up the café area.

Maura came through with a garbage bag to collect discarded napkins and paper plates.

"Good party, Mom, as usual."

"Thanks." Maura gave a satisfied smile. "I'm glad we could celebrate Taryn's birthday, even if we're a year late for the twenty-fifth birthday we planned. We're all so fond of her. Taryn is our little town miracle, isn't she?"

"She might be the town miracle but she's mostly just Taryn. Our friend."

Maura's smile was a little wobbly. "Yes. Exactly."

Sage felt a pang, guessing her mother was thinking about Layla. Sometimes she couldn't believe her sister had been gone for a decade.

They both returned to cleaning up and were nearly finished when the bell jangled over the door and her father came in, followed by two school-age children.

"Sage!" Her baby sister, Anna, seven and missing her front teeth, rushed to her, wrapped her thin arms around Sage's waist and squeezed tightly. Nick followed close behind.

Her heart gave a little jolt in her chest, but she quickly hid her reaction.

"There they are. My two favorite trouble-makers!"

Anna giggled. "I'm not a troublemaker."

"Okay. My one favorite troublemaker. And his little sister."

"She's *your* little sister too," Nick said with a grin.

"Aren't we lucky?"

She hugged them both, and Sage felt that familiar tug on her emotions when Nick's arms also went around her.

She couldn't believe he was nine. Where had the time gone?

Now that he was growing older, she sensed a tiny, barely perceptible shift in his dealings with her. She wondered if maybe he wasn't quite as accepting of their unique relationship as he used to be.

None of that seemed apparent now. He appeared as happy to see her as Anna.

"Mom says you're going to be here until after Christmas."

"That's the plan."

"And you're going to stay in the apartment above the garage!" Anna added.

"Yes. I just hope I don't freeze in there."

"It's warm and toasty," her sister said. "But if you get too cold, you can always come sleep in my room. You can have the top bunk."

She smiled. "Thanks, kiddo."

Because of the wide age gap between them and because she had been away from Hope's Crossing creating her own life, she always felt more like the children's cool aunt than their older sister but was deeply grateful to have them in her life.

"Can we build a snow fort again?" Nick asked. "That was so fun last year. I can't believe we could make it so big without the roof caving in. And it lasted the whole winter. All my friends thought it was the coolest thing."

"Sure. We have plenty of time to build an even better one this year. It's all about where you put the support walls."

Who knew that all her years of training to become an architect would be so handy when it came to playing in the snow with her much-younger siblings?

Usually, her visits home were quick, frenetic affairs. A weekend here, three days there. It would be so lovely to have time to savor each moment with her family.

"Maybe we can do some skiing too. Dad tells me you guys are getting really good."

"Nick might be but I'm not," Anna said with a pout. "I always fall down when I try to turn."

"That is tricky. We can work on it."

Over the children's heads, she saw Jack approach Maura from behind, wrap his arms around her and kiss the top of her head. Sage pushed down the pang she always felt at the obvious affection between them.

She knew what that pang was.

Loneliness.

Since her parents had reconnected a decade ago, the two of them had become a team in every way. Watching them work together only seemed to reinforce how alone Sage was.

Oh, she had friends in the Bay Area and coworkers at Lange & Associates she liked and respected. Her partners on the channel, Anton James and his wife, Rachelle, were among her dearest friends.

She didn't have that one person she could count on always to have her back, no matter what.

Sage knew it was her own fault. She tended to choose poorly—usually men who weren't available, either emotionally or otherwise.

That had been clear when she had fallen hard for Sawyer Danforth, despite his long-standing engagement.

Two years ago, she had started to fall for a man she had dated for a few months, even though she knew he was moving permanently to work in Brussels and wasn't interested in a long-distance relationship.

The therapist she had seen the summer before

had suggested her childhood was responsible, that she purposely picked men she knew would never truly love her because she had been scarred by not knowing the identity of her father until she was nearly twenty.

She didn't know if that was the truth. She only knew that some part of her ached to have the same kind of soul-deep connection with someone that her parents shared.

She pushed away the familiar ache as she helped clear away the rest of the party debris.

"Thank you for your help," Maura said as she prepared to turn the lights off in the store.

"No problem. I'm happy I made it in time so I could be here tonight."

"So are we. We're glad you could stay for so long." Maura and Jack exchanged a speaking glance that again left Sage feeling a little excluded.

"I'll take the littles home, if you want to give your mom a ride," Jack said.

"Sure. No problem."

When they were in Sage's car driving toward her parents' beautiful home, located on a hillside in the historic part of town, her mom cleared her throat. "This is awkward, but I was . . . wondering if I could ask you a favor while you're home."

Sage blinked as her wipers beat away a light snowfall. Her mom rarely asked anything of her.

Sometimes she wished Maura would lean on her a little more.

"Sure. Anything."

"You might want to hear what I have to say first," Maura said with a short laugh.

"Unless you want me to a rob a bank or help you hide a body, I'm glad to help with whatever. And I could probably be convinced on the other things."

Maura was silent for a moment. "It's not quite that. But as you know, the dedication of the new museum in Rouen is in a week and a half. Your dad has been working so hard on the project, and it's a huge honor for an American to have been chosen to design it."

"Yes. It's absolutely gorgeous too, from the pictures and videos I've seen of the progress."

"I haven't been able to go to many openings for his projects, and I know this one is dear to his heart. After you told us a few weeks ago that your schedule had shifted and you would be here throughout the month, I had a crazy idea. I was wondering if I could ask you to stay with Anna and Nick so I could go with your father to France for the museum opening."

"Oh, Mom. That's a great idea!"

Maura looked flustered. "I know it's a lot to ask."

"Not at all! I would love to do it. You never go anywhere, just the two of you."

A big part of that was her fault. Sage's hands tightened on the wheel. Her parents hadn't even had a real honeymoon, because of her.

Jack and Maura had only just found each other again, after twenty years apart, when Sage had upended all their lives by announcing she was pregnant.

"When will you leave?" she asked now.

Maura looked relieved. "The event is scheduled for two weeks from today. Your dad was planning to be gone from December 12 to December 17. Five nights. Is that too many?"

"Not at all. It's not enough, if you ask me. You should stay as long as possible."

"I would love to, but five days will be enough, especially during this busy time of year. I'm not sure I can be away from the bookstore longer than that. Plus the kids have so many things going on that I would hate to miss. They're only nine and seven once. Are you sure? I don't want you to say yes if you have even a sliver of doubt."

She had a feeling her mother would need plenty of reassurance between now and when she finally stepped onto the plane in a week and a half.

"Absolutely positive. This will be great. Don't worry about a thing. The kids and I will have a blast."

"Oh, thank you." Maura gave a little laugh that sounded relieved and excited at the same time. "I can't wait to tell your dad I'm going with him."

Yes. Her parents were a team, connected by the love that had first grown between them when they were only teenagers.

While Sage might not have a special someone, at least she had her family. This Christmas she had the rare and lovely privilege of spending more time with them than she'd had in years, and she intended to seize every moment.

5

Sage

By the next morning, her assurances to her mother of the night before had begun to fade, sliding into self-doubt.

Had she really agreed to take charge of her siblings for nearly a week during the holidays?

The prospect suddenly seemed daunting. What did she know about caring for small children? Nothing. She had rarely even babysat when she was young, except for Layla, four years younger, and that always had been a blast.

She would be fine. She loved Nick and Anna and was sure they would have a great time together. Or so she tried to tell herself, anyway.

Her parents deserved a chance to get away, and she was happy her mom was willing to turn to her for help.

She had work to do while she was here, plans due for three clients, but she could do most of that work while Nick and Anna were in school or in bed.

Her parents weren't leaving for more than a week. With the idea of finishing as much of her work before then as possible, she focused all the next day on her to-do list. She was answering emails on her laptop when her phone beeped an incoming call. She saw on the screen it was Anton James, the producer who filmed and edited the videos for her channel.

"Hi, Anton."

"Hey, babe. You're on speaker. I'm in the car and Rachelle's here."

"Hi, Chelle."

"Hey there," Anton's wife said with her usual cheer. "How's it going in glorious Colorado?"

"Colder than San Francisco, I'm sure."

"I don't know about that. We've had bitter winds blowing off the bay all week. I can't seem to get warm anywhere. How's the fam?"

"Everyone seems to be good, but I haven't even been here twenty-four hours yet."

They chatted a few more moments before Anton got to the point of his call. "I wanted to let you know I've uploaded the finished video of that apartment in Los Angeles we shot last month to the server, if you want to take a look before I go live with it on the channel."

"I'll do that now."

"You don't need to right away. I wasn't going to post it until tomorrow. You can watch it later and get back to me."

Stumbling onto Anton and Rachelle and the production company they ran together had been one of the luckiest days of her life. Anton was brilliant both behind the camera and in the editing process. Over the past two years of working together, he and Rachelle had become cherished friends.

"That was a spectacular apartment," Sage said. "I'm sure the video will be great."

"Naturally, since I shot and edited it."

She heard the humor in his deep voice and could picture his dark eyes dancing. Anton was six-three, bald, Black and gorgeous. All of her girlfriends in San Francisco had crushes on him, but he was devoted to his wife of eight years. Rachelle also used a wheelchair, after a spinal cord injury from a diving accident when she was a teenager.

Anton's personal situation, married to someone with different mobility needs, gave him a passion and enthusiasm for the Homes for All mission, which came out in his work.

"That's not the only reason I called. We're trying to work out our schedule for the next few weeks. I got a couple of last-minute jobs, but you know you always take priority. I wanted to be sure to block off time for you before I work these other jobs into my schedule. When do you think Mason Tucker's house will be done so we can shoot there?"

She winced. She had gone straight to Taryn's party the night before and had totally forgotten to reach out to tell Anton what happened with Mason the day before.

"Um, we might have a problem there."

71

"Don't tell me the project is behind schedule."

"No. That's not it. If anything, the contractor thinks he'll be done early. The problem is with Tucker. He hasn't given us permission to showcase the renovation."

"Why not? I thought most celebrities loved this kind of thing."

"Mason Tucker isn't like most celebs. He is intensely private. Why else would he be renovating a house in the mountains, surrounded by nothing but trees?"

"Doesn't he realize what a huge boon this would be to Homes for All?" Rachelle broke in. "Any video of his home would be sure to go viral. I mean, the whole world is in love with the guy. Or at least the female half of the population, and probably a good percentage of the male half."

She absolutely wasn't, Sage told herself. Sure, she might be attracted to him, but she planned to keep that locked tight in the vault where she stored all her other inconvenient emotions.

"I think a viral video is exactly what he doesn't want."

"Everything about his story just screams public interest," Rachelle went on. "I mean, Major League baseball star survives a helicopter crash only to lose his wife, unborn child and his ability to walk and then spends the next two years fighting his way back. Everyone is dying to know how he's doing."

In addition to being a partner in the production company, Rachelle was a journalist for a news website in the Bay Area and was always talking about the power of stories. She helped write the loose scripts for Homes for All and was brilliant at highlighting the human-interest angles of all the homes they featured.

"I'm afraid the masses may have to find out about Mason in some other way, barring a miracle. I spoke with him yesterday about featuring the renovation on the channel and he was having none of it."

"Damn. I was looking forward to a trip to Colorado before Christmas," Rachelle said.

"You sure you can't change his mind?" Anton asked.

"I wouldn't hold your breath. I tried to take a few videos yesterday to document the progress on the remodel for my own records and you would have thought I was a member of the paparazzi, shooting pictures of him in the hot tub or something."

She didn't want to think about Mason, naked to the waist with all those chest and arm muscles gleaming, sliding into a hot tub.

"That is going to be a problem. We were trying to make a big splash during the holidays, when everybody's surfing the web instead of interacting with their families. You don't have much in the can that's seasonal, since we shot everything else in the summer between your trips overseas. Can you find something else Christmassy to upload in place of that one?"

"Good question. I'll give it some thought."

Maybe she could feature something with A Warrior's Hope, to show the good work they were doing to help veterans there.

"This doesn't help me coordinate my schedule much."

"I know. I'm sorry."

"How about this?" Rachelle interjected. "You know how much I've been dying to see this town you're always talking about. And what would be more fun than Colorado at Christmas? Why don't we plan on coming out anyway for the week before Christmas? A sort of working holiday. If you can convince the Mighty Tuck to let us film his house by then, great. If not, we'll either come up with something else or Anton can always just go shopping with me."

"Sounds like a plan," Sage said, though she suspected she would have little chance of convincing Mason of anything. He had been implacable in his opposition. "I'll work on finding something else for us to feature on the channel. Maybe I could organize a rehab project for someone in town while I'm here."

"You do realize Christmas is only a few weeks away, right?" Anton sounded doubtful. "How are you going to find a candidate, design the remodel and make it all happen in that short window?"

"Who knows? Stranger things have happened, especially here. Hope's Crossing is magical."

Throughout its history, the town residents had rallied around to help each other, any time tragedy struck.

"So you're always saying," Rachelle said. "I can't wait to see for myself."

"I know you'll love it. Oh, and don't worry about finding a place to stay. I'll talk to my grandfather about you staying in the penthouse apartment he keeps at the Silver Strike Lodge. It usually sits empty, unless he has VIP guests coming in."

"Sold!" Rachelle laughed. "Wow. It must be nice to be related to somebody who owns an entire ski resort."

"Most of the time," she said. She did adore her grandfather and knew he had a soft, gooey marshmallow heart, despite his reputation for being hard and irascible.

"Sounds good," Anton said. "I have another job that won't be done until Tuesday, the twentieth. We can fly out that night, spend four nights there and still fly back Christmas Eve to spend the holiday with Rachelle's mama and sister."

"Thank you. You are the best."

"And don't you forget it," he said, with that deep laugh she loved.

"If we're heading to the mountain, I think I

need a new parka," Rachelle said. "Baby, we better head to the mall."

Anton gave a moan, though Sage could tell his heart wasn't in it. Rachelle had the man wrapped around her finger.

"Sounds like we have to go," he said. "See what you can do about working on Mason Tucker. Try a little of that famous Sage McKnight charm on the man. He won't know what's hit him."

"I'll do my best," she promised, though she wasn't hopeful.

As far as Mason Tucker was concerned, Sage had less charm than one of the support beams at Wolf Ridge.

6
Mason

His architect was invading his space, and Mason couldn't figure out how to avoid her.

Bad enough he had dreamed about her every night for the past three days, since their last interaction.

Now here she was in his bedroom.

He stopped his wheelchair in the doorway, wishing he could slip away undetected and roll on back down the hall.

He had lost the ability to sneak around when his stupid legs stopped working right. It was hard to tiptoe out of a room using a wheelchair.

Still, it was worth a shot. He did his best, but his wheels squeaked a little on the hardwood flooring of the hallway and she and Sam Delgado both turned at the sound.

"Hey, Mason," Sam said in his usual friendly tone.

He froze and, feeling foolish, switched directions and rolled through the wide doorway, with its pocket door that opened and closed with the push of a button.

He loved everything about this room, from the wide windows overlooking the Silver Strike ski resort to the huge closet with automatic height-adjustable racks to the private, secluded deck.

That had been another of Sage's ideas, adding the deck and the hot tub accessed by a lift so he didn't have to climb in and out with only his upper body strength and one leg that only cooperated half the time.

There was a larger spa on the lowest level of the house as well as a sauna, and a pool that was half indoor and half outside, all easily accessible for him.

He loved that area of the house as well as the fully equipped home gym, but he had a feeling this deck would become his retreat.

Would he think of Sage when he used the hot tub?

With the dreams he had been having about her, he wouldn't be surprised.

He didn't want to think about her at all. He wanted Sage out of his head completely, the sooner the better.

"Hi," Sage said. Her posture seemed to straighten almost imperceptibly, as if she were nervous about seeing him.

He hadn't exactly been cordial the last time he saw her, when she had stopped by a few days earlier after arriving in town. Had he been that intimidating?

"Sam was just showing me how well the automatic clothing racks work in the master bedroom. It's brilliant! Better than I hoped."

"Yeah. Too bad I don't have many clothes. I'm

going to use about a quarter of that space, mostly with sweats that don't really have to be hung on hangers."

"Maybe someday you'll have a partner who is a clotheshorse," Sage said.

No chance in hell. He wasn't going to open himself up to that kind of raw pain again. He had no desire to explain any of that to Sage McKnight so he only shrugged.

"Sam was also telling me you made the teak table outside by the spa."

"It was some half-finished project I had lying around the house in Oregon. I decided it would fit just right in that nook next to the lift and would be a good place to put my towel."

"It's perfect. I'm impressed."

He shrugged. "I'm no great woodworker, but I've always liked working with my hands."

Her gaze flickered down to his fingers, resting on the hand rims of his chair. He saw something flare in her eyes, something he didn't know quite how to interpret.

He felt a sudden fierce ache of hunger for Sage, with her big green eyes and her lush curves and her fast, always spinning brain.

He did his best to push away the ache by focusing on something inane, the batting averages of everyone on the team with him during his rookie year.

He hadn't been with a woman in two and a

half years, since his wife died. It was easy to tell himself he wasn't ready, but he was increasingly beginning to wonder if he ever would be.

What woman would possibly want to take him on now?

"We're still on schedule to be done by Christmas, right?" Sage asked the contractor. "It seems like there's still a lot to do."

"Mostly finish work. Little details here and there. We're in the home stretch."

"Everything is better than I imagined," Sage said. "You and your crew have been brilliant, Sam."

The older man smiled at her. When she beamed back at him, Mason felt a little twinge of jealousy but he quickly pushed it away. For one thing, he had no right to be jealous of anyone Sage smiled at. For another, after working with the man for the past nine months, he knew Sam was thoroughly devoted to his wife, Alexandra—who happened to be Sage's aunt.

"I had a good plan to work with. And it helps that Mason knows what he wants."

About the house, anyway. The rest of his life, he had no idea.

This house and the move to Hope's Crossing had occupied so much of his attention for nine months. Now that it was reaching completion, Mason knew he had to figure out where he was going to go from here.

The owner of his old team had reached out to him, asking if he might be interested in doing some color commentary for their games. While he loved baseball and missed it with a ferocity that startled him, he couldn't drum up much enthusiasm for watching his former teammates on the field, enjoying the sport that was forever out of his reach.

He spent most of his time working with his investment team and the foundation he and Shayla had started when they first married that provided sports equipment to underserved communities.

"Have you seen the sauna downstairs since the crew finished installing it yesterday?" Sam asked.

"Not yet."

"I'm heading there now, if you want to check it out with me," Sage said, her cheeks a little rosy.

He didn't. But he had no good excuse to avoid it, and he also didn't want to give either her or Sam the impression he was afraid to spend time with her.

"Sure. Let's go see it. You can take the stairs and meet me there."

"I want to try the elevator, if it's okay with you. Sam was telling me how smooth it is. I'd love to see for myself."

The residential elevator was convenient, but it was also small. He could reach out both arms from his chair and touch the sides. Both of them in the elevator car would be a snug fit.

He wanted to tell her it wasn't at all okay, that he didn't want to be that close to her, but of course he couldn't.

He pushed the button, which was at the perfect height for him in the chair. When the doors slid open, he gestured for Sage to go in first.

As he expected, it was a tight fit. He could smell the citrus-sweet scent of her, like lemon cake and springtime in the middle of a December day.

"This really is an amazing house," she said as the doors noiselessly closed behind him. "Without a doubt, this is the most gorgeous project I've ever been part of."

"Not just part of," he said gruffly as the elevator quickly moved them to the lower floor. "It's all down to you."

"That's a bit of an overstatement, since Sam and his subcontractors have done all the heavy lifting."

He had to give credit where it was due. "Maybe. But none of it would have happened without your vision. I was almost convinced I should sell the place and start over with a new build until you convinced me we could make all the necessary changes here without substantially changing the footprint or losing the view."

She looked startled and touched, which made

him feel more than a little guilty that he hadn't expressed that enough to her.

He had been so busy trying to pretend he wasn't attracted to her that he probably came across as a difficult jerk.

"Thank you," she said, her voice soft. "It means a great deal for you to say that. I'm very proud of Wolf Ridge. I've worked on other new construction projects perhaps of the same caliber that included a few universal design concepts, but I find something so unique and exciting about taking the good bones of an existing house and building something that works better for the owner."

"You have certainly done that," he said, his voice gruff. "Grace and I are both excited to move in."

Her smile tested all his best intentions, right then and there.

"Oh, I can't tell you how happy that makes me. Thank you."

His dreams of the night before filled his mind, hot and erotic. Tangled sheets, tangled limbs, tangled mouths.

He took a deep breath, hands tight on the hand rims of his wheels. He shifted the chair, trying to shift his attention just as abruptly as he rolled toward the sauna.

After a moment, she followed him past the swimming pool, still empty.

"I love this part of the house," she said. "That pool turned out better than I dreamed."

"Me too. I expect Grace and I will spend a lot of time down here."

He and his daughter both loved swimming. Mason always had, harkening back to the days when he would sneak out of his grandparents' farm to meet friends and play in the small lake near their property.

He loved it even more now. In the water, he felt free, without all the limitations he had on land.

Before Sage, this pool area on a lower level of the sloped property had been dark and gloomy, with a low roof and only a few windows. She had suggested the retractable glass roof.

He couldn't wait to be swimming with snow falling on the roof or on a summer night where he could open the roof to the stars glittering overhead.

"I love this space," Sage said. "If I lived here, I would probably spend every available moment here."

He could easily picture her too, soft and delicious as she sliced through the water.

He wheeled toward the sauna with a little more force than strictly necessary as he did his best to blink away the image.

The wide wooden door of the sauna swung open with a button, and Mason gestured for Sage to go in ahead of him.

She looked around at the pale wood walls and the small control panel next to the bench.

"Oh wow. It's so clean and restful in here."

Mason grabbed his forearm crutches from their holder on his chair, rose to his feet and made his ungainly, awkward way to the bench so he could show her some of the state-of-the-art features of the sauna.

"I can use it from my wheelchair or using the bench. All the controls are at midlevel, within easy reach. I can also run things with my smartphone, which is nice."

"Oh, that's terrific. I can imagine it will feel so good to come in here on a cold night."

"I expect it will."

Demonstration over, he started to stand but the forearm crutch he had taken off to show her the controls slid to the wooden floor of the sauna. Sage immediately stepped forward to grab it for him and lift it back to him.

"I don't need your help," he snapped.

She froze, her cheeks turning rosy. "Sorry. If it looks like someone needs help, my automatic reflex is to step in. It's tough for me to ignore."

His protest had also been an automatic reflex, one he regretted now. He had to stop being so touchy.

"I get that. While I do appreciate the intent, I have to figure out how to do as much as I can on my own. Most of the time, I won't have people around to open doors for me or pick up a crutch that I drop."

"That makes sense."

To Sage's credit, she never treated him with pity or tried to coddle him, like so many others did.

He made his way to the chair, sat down and then reached behind him to return the crutches to their holder. It was a complicated, ungainly process, making him wonder again if he would be better off choosing one or the other. Either use the wheelchair all the time and give up his dream of trying to regain some semblance of his old life or forgo the wheelchair and use the crutches, no matter how awkward and slow it made him.

Instead, he had adopted this weird hybrid form of mobility. For now, it was the best he could do.

He didn't expect that all the therapy components he was adding to Wolf Ridge would change his life in some radical way, especially after thirty months of intensive rehab, but none of it could hurt.

As if by tacit agreement, he and Sage both moved back toward the elevator. When they were once more on the main floor of the house, she gave him a careful look.

"I'm a little afraid to broach the subject," she said, a little breathlessly, "but I was wondering if you have given any more thought to what we talked about a few days ago, about allowing me to feature Wolf Ridge on my YouTube channel."

He raised an eyebrow. "I didn't realize there was anything more to think about. I've already given you my answer."

Her disappointment was palpable. "That's it? You won't even consider it?"

Mason was surprised at the guilt washing over him like heat coming off the sauna walls. Why should he feel even a moment's regret? Yes, she had done a wonderful job designing his house, but he had paid her handsomely for her effort. Beyond that, he didn't owe her anything.

"I did consider it. For about five seconds. That's all it took for me to know I would rather have every one of my fingernails yanked out than have my privacy invaded by some camera crew."

"It wouldn't really be a crew," she protested. "Only me and one other person behind the camera, my good friend Anton, who also edits the videos for me. That's it. Homes for All is a pretty lean team."

He would rather have his fingernails *and* toenails yanked out one by one than admit to her that he had watched every single video on her channel over the weekend, late at night in his room after Grace was in bed.

While the houses were beautiful, Sage was the real draw. She had a warm, genuine presence on-screen and a way of articulating architectural concepts that made them fascinating.

She should be hosting a show with a much wider audience, though judging by the view counts on her videos, she had plenty of reach.

"You wouldn't even have to be here," Sage told him now. "I mean, obviously it would be better if you were, but I can completely show the house without you."

"No."

She sighed. "Why are you so stubborn about this? Your house is beautiful."

"It is. And it's my house. Not some showplace."

"I would think you would want to show that off to the world."

"You would be wrong, then."

"Most people have no concept of all the things in an ordinary home that can make the day-to-day activities of someone using a wheelchair difficult, if not impossible. Of course, Wolf Ridge is far from an ordinary home. But the whole goal of my channel is to show that all homes, from starter places to luxury mountain estates, can be made usable by people of all abilities. I want to show the average viewer how considering a few design principles from the outset of a new build or in a redesign can pay huge dividends in the future."

"Why are you so passionate about this?" He had wondered that for a long time.

A curious mix of emotions crossed her expressive features, and she said nothing for several seconds. When she finally spoke, her voice was low, as if she didn't trust herself to be able to speak in normal tones.

"When I was eighteen years old, in my freshman year of college, my younger sister was killed in a car accident."

The grief in her voice was a painful echo of his own, the constant companion that had lived in his chest since waking up after the helicopter crash and finding out he was the lone survivor. That Shayla, their unborn son and his pilot and good friend Cal Hernandez all hadn't made it.

He didn't have the monopoly on pain. Others had deep wounds on their hearts, empty holes they had learned to either skirt around or jump over in order to go on.

"I'm sorry," he said, his voice gruff. "That must have been tough."

"It was. It still is. I miss her every day. For a long time, my family was only the three of us. My mom, Layla and me. She was my best friend."

At the slight tremor in her voice, he wanted to pull her into his lap and wrap his arms around her and kiss the pain away.

He didn't. Of course he didn't. Still, he might have offered some kind of gesture of comfort, but she seemed to shake off her sadness.

"In the same accident, my sister's friend was also seriously injured. Taryn Thorne suffered head and spinal injuries and was in a coma for weeks. When she came out of it, she required extensive rehabilitation. She used a wheelchair for months after the accident and for the first time, I became aware of how most houses simply aren't set up for those with different mobility needs. Not only wheelchair users either. I'm talking about older people or those who might be recovering from an accident or surgery."

"So you decided to become an architect to solve all the world's problems." While he spoke in a light tone, he found her commitment and passion sweet. Touching, even.

"Not quite," she corrected him. "I had already decided to become an architect."

"Following in your father's footsteps."

Sage gave a little laugh. "You'd think so, wouldn't you? But I didn't know my father was an architect at the time."

At his baffled frown, she shrugged. "It's a long story. I didn't even know his name, let alone his occupation, until I had already started school with plans to become an architect. I guess maybe a love for building things was in my blood or something."

He was more than a little uncomfortable to realize they shared that unique background. He also hadn't known his father's identity until later in life, when he was finally able to pry a name from Rebecca.

Joe Abbott, she had told him with reluctance. The internet had filled in the gaps, providing enough information about the man that Mason wasn't a bit sorry he had never met him. Abbott had been arrested multiple times for an assortment of violent crimes and had ended up dying in a prison yard fight in Kentucky about fifteen years earlier.

Sage had received a love of architecture from her father, even before she had known his identity. Mason could only be glad he hadn't inherited anything from his father, except maybe his dark hair.

"It's really funny how life works out," she went on. "Long before I knew my father was the great Jackson Lange, I decided I wanted to be an architect. From the time I was about eight, I used to design and build elaborate dollhouses out of cardboard boxes for me and my sister."

What had she been like as a child? He could guess she had been smart, inquisitive, creative. Probably a handful.

"After Taryn was injured, I became fascinated with the idea of making homes usable by all the inhabitants, no matter age or physical abilities. One of my professors called it inclusive design. I like that much better, actually, but most people know what I'm talking about when I say *universal design*. My website is all about spreading that message to as many people as possible."

"I admire your passion," he murmured. "You obviously care about your work."

"I do," she said, her voice barely above a whisper.

They gazed at each other and something seemed to sizzle between them, something fragile and new and delicious. For a moment, the air felt as thick and as sweet as pulled taffy.

He wanted to kiss her.

The urge was so strong, he had to grip the hand rims of his chair tightly to keep from reaching from her.

Where the hell had that come from? Probably those completely inappropriate dreams of the night before.

Did it matter? He *wouldn't* kiss her, no matter how much he might want to.

A noise at the front door jolted him back to his senses and an instant later, he heard Grace calling him.

"Dad! Where are you?"

Mason inhaled a breath, trying to gain a little equanimity again. "In the kitchen," he called.

Grace came running in, her color rosy and her eyes bright with excitement, followed by his mother.

"Dad! Guess what! We're doing a Christmas play at school about the Nutcracker, only without the dancing, and I got the part of Clara, even though all the girls in class tried out for it."

"Clara! That's terrific."

He needed to put away this ridiculous attraction

to Sage McKnight and focus on the only thing that really mattered. Grace.

"Christmas is only a few weeks away," Mason went on. "That doesn't give you much time to practice."

"I know, but Ms. Suarez said we won't have a lot of lines. It will be mostly the narrator and then the whole class singing. Will you come see me?"

"I wouldn't miss it for anything," he declared.

He hugged her, so grateful again that he had this bright, cheerful child to center him and shake him out of his frequent bouts of self-pity.

This move had been exactly what they both needed to heal, to regroup, to start over.

His mother, he saw, had greeted Sage while he was talking to Grace. The two of them were engaged in a cordial conversation. Judging by the way Rebecca was gesturing to the kitchen, they must be talking about the house.

Seeing them together was yet another reminder that he couldn't possibly be attracted to Sage.

She had given birth and dropped her son off with her parents, as Rebecca had done thirty-four years ago. If he couldn't forgive his own mother, wasn't he being hypocritical to ignore the same act from Sage?

Grace chattered about the play for a few minutes more before her attention was drawn back to the two women.

"Hi, Ms. McKnight."

Sage gave her a warm smile. "Hi, Grace. Congratulations on being Clara. I'm sure it will be a wonderful show."

"Nick is my best friend. He gets to be Herr Drosselmeyer!"

"How terrific! I will definitely go see that."

"I love our house," Grace informed her. "It is the coolest. I can't wait to move in."

"It *is* pretty cool," Sage agreed.

"Do you know what my favorite part is?"

"Your bedroom, with the built-in reading loft and all those bookshelves?"

"No, even though that's supercool. No. It's the pool. I *love* it. I can't wait to go swimming. Dad said they're putting water in it soon, and it might be warm enough to swim before Christmas! Maybe Nick and Anna can come over and go swimming with us."

"I'm sure they would love that."

For all her warmth, Sage seemed distracted, her gaze meeting Mason's, then shifting quickly away. Did she sense how much he wanted her? If so, no wonder she looked like she wanted to flee.

"I'm afraid I need to run," she said, confirming his suspicion that she couldn't wait to leave. "It was great to see you again, Grace. Rebecca, it was lovely to meet you."

"Yes," his mother murmured. "I've been wanting the chance to meet you, after I've heard so much about you from Mason."

Had he talked about Sage at all to his mother? He couldn't imagine why. Now Sage gave him a sidelong look and he could feel his face flush.

"Thanks for the tour," she finally said.

He nodded, not trusting himself to say anything else.

What would he say, anyway?

Kiss me.

He stayed quiet, watching her grab her coat and head for the door.

Sage McKnight was as beautiful and as bright as a Christmas star and just as far out of his reach. He needed to remember that and focus on his daughter and this house and the life they were building here.

7

Taryn

Hope's Crossing was about to have a killer snowstorm.

Monday afternoon, three days after her party, Taryn slid into her small SUV after school as the first gentle flakes began to float from the sky.

Oh, they were pretty now, all wispy and soft as they settled onto her windshield. The dark clouds overhead and that unique smell in the air, fresh and woodsy, told her this would not be a light storm. No doubt she would have to shovel off several inches from her driveway by morning.

Her back gave a sympathetic twinge, almost a premonition, and Taryn sighed. She loved her little cottage in an older neighborhood of Hope's Crossing, a two-bedroom starter her dad had bought years ago as an investment, before house prices started going through the roof.

When she had taken the job in town, Brodie had asked her if she would like it. He'd wanted to give her the house as a gift for her college graduation, but Taryn had refused. She had mortgage paperwork drawn up and paid him diligently on the first of every month.

She had a feeling her dad was merely keeping those payments in an account he would one day sign back over to her. He was pretty stubborn that way. Still, she needed to pay her own way, to stand on her own two feet.

Her dad—and, really, everyone else in town—coddled her too much. She was a grown woman, not poor Taryn Thorne, who had to relearn how to walk and talk and feed herself.

As much as she adored her snug house, during the wintry months, she couldn't help sometimes wishing she lived in one of the condo developments in town where someone else would be responsible for clearing snow.

Shoveling was good exercise, she reminded herself as she pulled out of the school parking lot after waving to a couple of students waiting at the town bus stop.

Over the years, her dad often stopped by to shovel for her and had even sent a worker from his various businesses a time or two.

Taryn was always quick to set him straight.

While she knew he was only acting out of love and concern for her, Taryn fiercely prized her independence, probably because it had been so hard-won.

After the accident, everyone in town seemed to want to wrap her in cotton batting and protect her from anything else bad happening in her life.

Her father had wanted her to stay close to go to college, but Taryn had insisted on going away to school. She had picked somewhere warm and sunny and many hours away, the University of California, Santa Cruz.

Coming back to Hope's Crossing after graduation had been a difficult choice.

On the one hand, she loved it here and couldn't really imagine building her future anywhere else. On the other, she still sometimes felt smothered by the concern of those very friends and family members she had missed so much while she was away at school.

Taking a job at Hope's Crossing Middle School still felt like the right choice for her life, even if that meant shoveling Colorado snow at 6:00 a.m. so she could get her vehicle out of the driveway and make it to school.

She headed toward her house but when she reached her street, she slowed slightly at her driveway. On impulse, she drove on, through snowflakes that were now coming faster against her windshield.

She was meeting Sage later at the Center of Hope café in town for dinner, but that gave her barely enough time to take care of something else.

Her palms felt sweaty on the steering wheel as she headed up the hill toward the exclusive neighborhood where the Beaumonts had lived.

She had given Charlie long enough. It was time to figure out why he was avoiding her.

This neighborhood always seemed quiet, filled

with huge ski properties owned by celebrities and East Coast financiers who were seldom in residence. At the top of the hill on a large parcel of property was a house that conversely seemed both out of place and as old and settled as if it had been there forever.

She had always liked Beaumont House, as Charlie's mother had so pretentiously called it. Constructed of light gray stone quarried in Texas, the house was built to resemble a huge French country estate, with a hipped roof and arched windows flanked by heavy shutters.

For her faults, Laura Beaumont had good taste. The house really was beautiful, even if it looked like it belonged in the Loire Valley instead of the mountains of Colorado.

That still didn't excuse Laura for what she had done to her children. Taryn wasn't sure she could ever forgive the woman for the completely unreasonable expectations she had placed on both of her children.

Genevieve, at least, had managed to shed the wounds of her childhood to build a happy, fulfilling life with Dylan, but the verdict was still out about whether Charlie could ever completely heal.

She drove through the open wrought iron gates and pulled up to the house. As soon as she stepped out of her SUV, she heard the sounds of squeals and children's laughter, not at all what she might have expected in this empty mansion.

Curious, she followed the noises around the side of the house. Through the fluffy snowflakes, she spotted two giggly children pelting snowballs at a tall man with sun-streaked brown hair.

Charlie was grinning back at the children, who happened to be his eight-year-old nephew, Finn, and five-year-old niece, Addie.

She had a feeling he was letting the children win, since he was covered in snow and they weren't.

"You can't hit me, Uncle Charlie," Addie sang out, dancing around in the snow like she was a prizefighter.

Charlie threw a snowball that whizzed past her head, confirming her suspicion that the fight was rigged. Charlie used to have unerring aim as a pitcher on the high school baseball team. He wouldn't have missed unless it was on purpose.

"You're too fast for me," he replied.

Addie giggled and ran behind the artful landscape rock where her brother was scooping more snow for snowballs.

Oh, her heart. If she wasn't already head over heels for Charlie, she would have fallen for him in that moment, as she watched his sweetness with his niece and nephew.

Before she could make her presence known, the sliding door opened and Genevieve Caine stepped onto the patio.

"Kids, you need to come in and get out of your

snowsuits. We have to leave for piano lessons in a few minutes."

The children both moaned in protest but before they could answer, Gen spotted her.

"Taryn! Hi! I didn't know you were here."

Charlie whipped his head around. If she hadn't been looking, she might have missed the way his eyes lit up when he saw her, an expression he quickly veiled.

"I drove up and heard the warfare going on back here. How are you feeling?"

Genevieve made a face and patted her protruding abdomen. "This kid is going to be a champion soccer player. Either that or an Irish step dancer. My ribs feel bruised from all the kicking going on in there."

Taryn felt a sharp ache under her own breastbone. Would she ever know that feeling? She loved her students, but she was beginning to think about having children of her own.

She was only twenty-six, she reminded herself. She had plenty of time.

"I would love to chat but we really do have to run. Time got away from me this afternoon."

"No problem," Taryn said as Genevieve ushered her still-protesting children inside. Soon she was alone with Charlie, snow dusting his hair and clinging to his long lashes.

"So," she said abruptly. "The rumors are true, then. You are back."

He wiped snow off his jeans. "Apparently. Hey, Tare."

She frowned. "Don't you *Hey, Tare* me. I'm not happy with you."

"Uh-oh. What did I do now?"

"From what I hear, you've been back in town for a week and you haven't bothered to reach out to me yet."

Guilt flashed briefly in his eyes as he brushed the last of the snow off his parka then headed for the house. "I've been busy."

"Too busy to reach out to your best friend?"

Or was she still his best friend? After that wedding this summer, she wasn't sure. Had she ruined everything?

"I've been meeting with attorneys and Realtors nonstop since I hit town. This is the first chance I've had to get out of the house in a week, only because Gen stopped by to grab a few photo albums and needed me to get the kids out of her hair for a minute."

Charlie loved being outside. She knew he would much rather be skiing, hiking or snowshoeing through the backcountry than trapped in meetings with attorneys as he worked through his father's estate.

He hadn't always found comfort being outside, but something had shifted during the nine months he had been serving his sentence in a juvenile detention facility.

He had been seventeen, nearly eighteen, and she had been so afraid he would be sentenced as an adult after pleading guilty to impaired driving in the accident when they were kids.

Thinking about his incarceration always filled Taryn with a vast guilt, even after more than a decade. He should never have been locked up. Yes, Charlie had been driving on those snow-slick roads the day of the accident. And yes, he had been drinking and his blood alcohol was over the legal limit. But he had only had a few beers after she and their other friends had pressured him to join them and basically made it impossible for him to refuse.

She hadn't served a day in jail, even though the accident was as much her fault as his.

She pushed away the past. She had learned a long time ago that she couldn't dwell on that night or she would sink into depression and regret.

"Did you even intend to let me know you were back in town?" she asked when they were in his parents' huge kitchen, with its marble countertops, massive Wolf cooktop and Subzero refrigerator.

Her two-bedroom cottage would fit nicely in this space, with room to spare.

"Eventually," he said as he reached into the cupboard for a glass and filled it with water from the sink. He filled a second glass of water for her and handed it over without asking if she wanted it. She took it from him, grateful to have something to hold on to as he continued. "Like I said, I haven't had a chance to do much yet. With my schedule so packed, I didn't see the point in reaching out until things settled a little."

"Since when does reaching out have to have a point? I get that maybe you were too busy to come to my party, but you could have at least texted to say *happy birthday*. That takes all of ten seconds."

"You're right," he said after a pause. "I should have. That was wrong of me. I'm sorry."

"So. Why didn't you?"

He sighed. "It's been a rough week. Not just going through the house and packing things up but . . . everything. You know how hard it is for me to be back in Hope's Crossing, after everything that has happened. I guess some part of me wanted to hunker down and not talk to anybody but Gen."

She told herself she shouldn't feel hurt. He had lost both parents in only a handful of years and now had the responsibility for managing all of William Beaumont's tangled business affairs.

But they were friends. Or at least she thought they were.

"How long are you in town?"

"I freed my schedule for about a month. That should give me enough time to clear up most of the estate issues and get the house on the market.

Gen's due right after Christmas so I'll stick around at least for that."

A month. Would he have tried to avoid her the entire time?

What did she expect? The last time they had seen each other, not counting his father's funeral when he had been distant and grieving, she had basically thrown herself at him.

"I'm sorry I didn't text you the day I rolled into town. I should have."

"It doesn't matter. I forgive you."

"Thanks." His dry tone almost made her smile, even as she worried their friendship was dying.

"How's What's Her Face?" she asked. Last she knew, he had been dating a real estate agent from Texas who had relocated to his Utah desert town. Lindsay something or other. Taryn had met her briefly over a Zoom conversation in the spring, and the woman had been gorgeous. Tall, slim, perfectly put together. And nice too, with a warm drawl and friendly blue eyes.

Taryn had hated her on sight.

She wasn't sure whether to be grateful or upset that Lindsay had a European cruise scheduled with her family during that weekend in August when Taryn had helped Charlie out of a bind.

As if he were remembering as well, Charlie didn't meet her gaze, suddenly inordinately interested in his glass of water. "I wouldn't know. We broke up months ago."

When, exactly, *months ago?* Did it have anything to do with that night?

"Too bad," she lied. "I'm sorry. She seemed nice."

"She was."

Taryn and Charlie had a great time together during the wedding ceremony for his friend. She remembered having to actually bite her lip to keep from laughing too much in the chapel.

The whole wedding festivities had been fun, from blowing bubbles at the bride and groom as they hurried out of church to making jokes about the pretentious meal during the wedding dinner.

That weekend had been the longest period they had spent together in a long time, and Taryn had loved every moment.

During the reception, though, everything seemed to change. They had been having a great time on the dance floor with the bride and groom and Charlie's other friends. During the few slow dances, she had danced with several of his buddies, until finally she had ended up with Charlie.

He had held her as the music shifted and Taryn, a little tipsy and a lot in love, had rested her cheek against his chest, letting the thrill of the moment carry her away. When the music ended, she had lifted her gaze to his. The tenderness in his expression had stolen her breath.

Kiss me.

She had actually blurted the words out. The look in his eyes had changed in an instant, becoming dark and hungry.

A few moments later, as the wedding festivities were wrapping up, Charlie had taken her back to their floor of the hotel. Outside her room, she had fumbled with the key, her heart pounding. This was it, she remembered thinking. After all the years she had hoped for this moment, maybe they were finally going to act on the heat that had been simmering between them for years.

Kiss me.

This time, instead of only saying the words, she had wrapped her arms around him and lifted her mouth to his, needing him more than she had ever needed anything in her life.

He had kissed her with all the heat and hunger she dreamed about . . . for about three minutes. And then, when he set her away from him, his expression had been shuttered, any hint of desire completely wiped away.

"It's late," he had said. "We're both not thinking clearly. Let's forget this ever happened."

After a hurried good-night, he left for his own room without another word.

Taryn had cried herself to sleep that night, aching for Charlie and wishing she could make him see her as something more than poor, sweet Taryn.

"It was inevitable," he said now with a casual

shrug. "Lindsay wanted a house, kids, the picket fence. All the things that aren't in my plans."

"I hate when you say things like that."

"When I state the truth?"

"When you make excuses," she answered tartly.

Charlie had told her often that he didn't intend to have a family. His own had been so dysfunctional, he didn't see how he could ever have a successful long-term relationship.

She always pointed out that Genevieve had grown up with the same parents and she and Dylan seemed to be deliriously happy together.

She strongly suspected Charlie's real reasons went deeper than growing up with an alcoholic mother and a distant, workaholic father.

Everything came back to that night a decade ago. Charlie carried a heavy load of guilt over Layla's death and Taryn's life-threatening injuries. She suspected he didn't think he deserved a happy life, especially when Layla's life had ended before it really began.

That was the reason he worked for The Sheridan Trust half the year, out of some need to atone.

She had no idea how to convince him he couldn't put his own life and happiness on hold out of guilt.

He cared about her. She had always known he did. That fleeting, tender look during that dance at the wedding only confirmed his feelings ran deeper than mere friendship.

He wanted her to be happy. How could she prove to him that she would only be truly happy if he finally allowed space for love to bloom between them?

He was here for a month. Could she prove to him in that time that he was all she would ever want? She had to try.

She let out a breath, her nerves tingling. "Do you remember the promise you made to me when I saved your butt this summer?"

She thought she saw something hot spark in his gaze, but he looked away before she could be certain.

"Not word for word."

"I do. You promised me that if I spent a very boring weekend making conversation with people I didn't know, you would be forever in my debt and would do anything I asked to pay me back."

The wedding hadn't been boring. Far from it. But a promise was a promise.

"I don't believe I would make such an open-ended promise."

"Yet you did. Don't try to get out of it now. Time to pay the piper, Chuck."

He made a face at that particular nickname that he hated. "How?"

"Nothing too stressful, I promise. I need a date Friday. You."

"A date for what?" he asked, suspicion crackling through the question.

"I have to chaperone the ninth grade Christmas dance Friday night, and I need somebody big and tough and scary to help me keep the ruffians in line."

"I can't imagine anything I would enjoy less than chaperoning a middle school dance. I hated them even when I *was* in middle school."

"Too bad. You owe me, buster. Remember how I talked to Jason's great-uncle for a whole half hour about his colonoscopy? And I even danced with his creepy cousin, who tried to drag me into his multilevel marketing scam. All for you."

He sighed. "What time?"

Relief left her almost giddy. "Apparently a few freshmen still have an early bedtime, so the dance runs from seven to ten. I need to be there a little after six to make sure the chairs are set up and supervise the dance committee as they finish the decorations."

"Do I have to wear a tux?"

She had to smile. "No. Jacket and tie are sufficient, if you have one here."

"I can probably rustle up something."

"Great. Since I asked you, I'll pick you up at quarter to six."

"Funny, I don't recall any asking happening here."

She shrugged. "I was never very good at promposals."

"Promposals?"

"You know. All the elaborate ways teenagers ask other teenagers to go to dances with them. Like when Casey Phillips rented a skywriter to ask Bianca Waterson to the prom. Or when Violet Martin filled Ben Garcia's pickup truck cab with balloons and he had to pop them all to find the note inside one asking him to the Valentine's dance."

"We're not teenagers anymore."

His abrupt words made her heart hurt.

"True. This is strictly to repay a debt. So Charles William Henry Beaumont. Will you go to the Hope's Crossing Middle School Christmas Dance with me as a chaperone? If you play your cards right, there might even be a cookie or two in it for you."

"Oooh. I don't know how you could possibly make that offer any more appealing."

She bit her lip before she could blurt out that she would even let him make out with her in the back seat of her car. That would likely have the opposite effect.

"Fine," he finally said. "I'll drive, though. I'll pick you up in time to make it by six."

"Thank you."

On impulse, she reached out to hug him, as they used to do all the time. He hugged her briefly, then stepped away, leaving her feeling empty and sad and not sure how she could possibly break through his stubborn shell in only a few weeks.

8
Sage

Sage paused outside the Center of Hope Café in downtown Hope's Crossing on Monday evening to stomp the snow off her boots and shake her coat.

Snow had been falling steadily for the past few hours. While it was a pain to drive through, she couldn't deny it gave the downtown a magical, fairy-tale look, coating everything in sight a gorgeous white.

Warmth washed over her as she walked inside the always-busy restaurant. Delicious smells made her stomach growl, apple pie, chicken soup and some kind of roasting potato.

She scanned the diners and immediately spotted Taryn at one of the tables by the front window. Sage waved and headed toward her friend.

"Sorry I'm late," she said as she slid into the chair opposite her friend. "It's snowing, which means traffic is crazy with tourists who have no idea how to drive in it, then I ended up having to park miles away. I swear downtown is busier every time I come."

"The town is in the process of building a new parking garage about a block east of your mom's store. That should help ease the congestion downtown a little."

"I hope so." She pulled off her coat. "I'm so happy you could find time to have dinner. I know how busy you are."

Taryn made a face. "Am I? During school hours, yes. After hours, not really. I hang out with my family, go to the movies with friends, maybe hit the town on the occasional weekend. This week, the only exciting thing on my plate is the freshmen Christmas dance on Friday. That should tell you all you need to know about how exciting my social life is at the moment."

Sage gave her friend a steady look. "Why is that? You could date anyone in town you wanted."

Taryn shrugged. "Maybe I don't want to date anyone in town."

Who did she want to date? Sage suspected she knew the answer to that. For a long time, Sage had thought Taryn might be interested in Charlie Beaumont as more than just a close friend.

Charlie appeared to have grown into a good person who spent his life helping others. She had to respect his journey, especially given how entitled and spoiled he had been as a teenager.

Sage and her mom had forgiven Charlie a long time ago for being impaired behind the wheel when he was seventeen, with such deadly consequences.

She wasn't, however, convinced he had ever forgiven himself. Or that he ever could.

"Have you ordered yet?"

"No. I've only been here about five minutes. Soup of the day is chicken enchilada."

"Oh, that sounds good."

Their server, a young woman Sage didn't know, approached the table to take their order only a moment or two later. Sage and Taryn both ordered the soup and salad combo.

"So," Sage said after the server had left, "how are your students?"

In Hope's Crossing, the middle school made up grades seven through nine, with grades ten through twelve going to the new high school. To Sage, middle school seemed like stressful years but Taryn was completely in her element.

Her friend smiled. "Pretty wonderful, actually. I love them all, even the troublemakers. Maybe all school guidance counselors should have once been troubled teens themselves. It certainly helps me understand some of the things they're facing, maybe a little better than some of the other teachers on the faculty who act as if they never made a bad decision in their lives."

"Everyone has made bad decisions. If someone tells you they haven't, they're either lying or they haven't admitted it to themselves yet."

"True enough. How's the architecture world these days? Your mom tells me you've been living in Singapore for a few months. What was that like?"

"Amazing." She was telling Taryn about the project she had been working on there and a few of the people she had met when she spotted through the front windows a woman using an electric scooter, trying to make her way through the snow. She was followed by a girl with long dark hair who looked to be about fourteen, carrying a large flat box.

A moment later, they came into the café. Sage swiveled to watch them.

The woman had deep circles under her eyes and her coat hung on her frame, as if she had lost weight recently.

As if sensing her gaze and her interest, the girl looked toward their table. When she spotted Taryn, she gave a small smile and lifted her fingers in a wave.

"Who is that?" Sage asked.

Taryn's features softened with affection. "One of my students and her mom. Chloe and Lynette Greene. Lynette is starting up a home-based business making gluten-free cookies and brownies. Chloe told me she's been helping make deliveries in the evenings to some of the local restaurants. Dermot must be offering them here at the café."

Sage had to smile. That sounded exactly like something Dermot Caine, married to Taryn's grandmother, would do. He was always looking for another lost soul to rescue. Sage knew that he still came into his café nearly every day, though he had to be pushing eighty by now. She could only hope she would be half as energetic when she was his age.

Always interested to see how people with mobility challenges navigated the sometimes difficult spaces of the world, she watched as the woman talked to one of the servers and the girl handed over the box of goodies.

The girl said something to her mom, who followed the direction of her gaze and then smiled and waved at Taryn as well. A moment later, the girl came over to their table while her mother was still busy talking to the staff of the restaurant.

"Hi, Ms. Thorne," Chloe said, her voice quiet and her eyes shy.

"Hi, Chloe. It's great to see you. Do I dare hope you've delivered some of your delicious chocolate chip cookies?"

"Yes. Fresh out of the oven about twenty minutes ago. They might still be warm," she said eagerly.

"We'll definitely have those," Sage said, smiling as well.

Where the mother's coat was too large, Sage couldn't help noticing the girl's looked a size too small and the raggedy tennis shoes she wore were soaked through, completely unsuitable for trudging along snowy sidewalks.

"This is my friend Sage McKnight," Taryn said.

"She has come back to town to visit her family for the holidays."

"Hello. It's nice to meet you."

"My pleasure," Sage said honestly, ideas already beginning to spin through her head.

She had no idea what the family's situation might be, but they might be ideal for a project sponsored by Homes for All.

They chatted with the girl for a few more moments, with Sage growing increasingly excited, until Lynette waved to her daughter in a let's-go sort of gesture. Chloe gave them an apologetic look. "Looks like my mom's done. I better go. See you tomorrow, Ms. Thorne."

"Bye, Chloe. Have a good evening. Make sure you work on that history homework."

"Do I have to?"

"Only if you want to pass."

Chloe made a face but rushed away to help her mother with the front door.

After the server brought their salads, Sage decided to pick Taryn's brain.

"She seems like a nice girl."

"Very nice. And smart too, when she has time in the evenings to do her homework. She's got a tough load."

"I don't think I know the family. Have they been in town long?"

Sage shook her head. "Only a few years. Lynette's aunt lived in town. Suzanna Beaton."

"Oh, I remember her. She lived close to our old place near Sweet Laurel Falls. On Balsam Lane, wasn't it?"

"That's right. Suz left her house to her niece when she died, so Lynette and her husband brought their three children here. Chloe and two cute younger brothers, Liam and Sean. Their dad took a job managing one of the hotels, then about six months ago he was driving home late one night when he was T-boned by a drunk tourist who sped through a stoplight. He died instantly."

Her heart seemed to squeeze with sympathy. "Oh. Poor things."

Taryn nodded. "It just doesn't seem fair. Chloe is such a sweetheart and so is her mom. Lynette has multiple sclerosis that was in remission when they moved here but now isn't. She has really struggled since her husband died."

They might be perfect candidates for Homes for All. Sage knew she couldn't take away the pain of losing a husband and father or the fear of dealing with a serious condition. But maybe she could do one small thing to make life seem a little brighter for this family.

"I suddenly have a crazy idea," she said to Taryn. "I can't pull it off myself, but if you think it might work, I can probably come up with a team of people to help me."

This was Hope's Crossing, a town that had its very own Angel of Hope.

Taryn looked intrigued. "This seems to be my day for crazy ideas," she said after a moment. "Go on. Tell me more."

While they ate salad and the deliciously thick, creamy soup perfect for a December night, Sage told Taryn about the organization she had started through her YouTube videos, about the foundation's mission and some of the other projects they had completed.

"What do you think? Would the Greene family be good candidates?"

"They would be perfect," Taryn said, her voice soft and her eyes moist. "I worry so much about Chloe. As her mother's condition has become more limiting, Chloe has taken on more and more responsibilities. And Lynette seems more worn down every time I see her. This might be exactly what they need to help them through this first holiday without their dad."

"I'm a stranger," Sage said. "Lynette won't know what to think if I show up at her door on my own with such an outlandish idea. They know you and I get the feeling Chloe, at least, trusts you. Will you help me convince her mom to accept some help?"

"Take it from me, sometimes taking help from others is harder than facing obstacles on your own."

"I know. But you also know sometimes we all need someone to lend a helping hand."

Taryn nodded. "I don't know if she will listen to me. I'm willing to try, though."

A half hour later, the two of them stood on the doorstep of a charming stone cottage a few blocks away from Sage's childhood home, the little house Maura had purchased after divorcing Sage's stepfather.

From the outside, this cottage looked a little rundown, with flaking paint on the wooden shutters and a sagging rain gutter on the attached garage.

Four steps led up to the front porch, with no ramp. How did Lynette manage it?

Perhaps, like Mason Tucker, she could take some steps but needed the electric scooter to help with balance and endurance issues.

As she and Taryn walked up the steps, Sage's mind whirred with possibilities. She could add a ramp along the side of the porch. Or maybe inside the garage, so Lynette could make it from her car to the house easily.

She did not know what the inside of the house would show. Maybe all of this was for nothing and Suzanna had already remodeled the house to make it more accessible in her older years. If so, she would thank the Greene family for their time and look elsewhere for another project.

As Taryn rang the doorbell, Sage felt a flutter of nerves. The woman very well might tell them they were crazy. Sage couldn't blame her. How would she react if some stranger came bursting into her life, ready to turn things upside down right before Christmas?

Chloe answered the door and looked shocked and a little scared when she saw her guidance counselor standing in the doorway.

"Ms. Thorne. Hi. Is, um, something wrong?"

"No. Nothing's wrong. My friend Sage and I would like to talk to your mother. Is she available?"

"She's in the kitchen. I think she's taking out a batch of cookies. Come in."

She let them inside to a narrow hallway. Through a doorway into a small living room to their right, Sage could see a rather scraggly fresh-cut Christmas tree, decorated with an assortment of handmade ornaments and a popcorn garland.

The house did have lovely bones. The woodwork was beautiful and she could imagine that in the daytime, sunlight would stream through the south-facing windows.

The kitchen was large but rather old-fashioned with dark cabinets and avocado-colored appliances. It smelled seductively good, though, of chocolate and flour and butter.

Lynette Greene was using a walker for support as she transferred cookies from their baking pan to a wire cooling rack. She blinked in shock when she saw them.

"Taryn. Is everything okay?"

"Yes. Fine. I didn't have the chance to introduce you two earlier when you were at the café. This is my friend Sage McKnight, and, well, she has a proposal for you."

Lynette frowned in confusion. "Hello. Nice to meet you, Sage. Which branch of the McKnights do you belong to?"

"Maura is my mom. She owns the bookstore in town."

"Oh, of course. I know Maura."

"And Jackson Lange is my father."

"Yes. Would you . . . like to sit down? Chloe, will you grab plates for our guests and a few of these cookies?"

"This is your business. We didn't come to eat the inventory!" Taryn exclaimed, even as she eyed the cookies with undisguised longing. They had been in such a hurry to leave the café, they hadn't ordered dessert.

"You can have some of the discards. They're still good, even if they're broken."

By now, two younger boys, one about eleven and the other maybe seven, had joined them in the kitchen. They looked so much like Chloe, they could only be her brothers.

"Can I have a broken cookie?" the younger of the two asked.

"Yes. One each. Then you need to go pick up the family room and put your video game controllers away so I don't roll over them."

The boys snatched up cookies from a small pile that obviously contained the imperfect ones, then chased each other down the hall.

"How can I help you?" Lynette asked.

Taryn pointed to Sage as if to say, "Take it away."

"Mrs. Greene, I know this is going to come out of the blue but please hear me out before you answer, okay?"

The woman frowned. "Okay," she said slowly.

"If you know my parents, you probably know my father is an architect."

"Yes. Only one of the best architects in the world."

Sage felt the same sharp thrill of pride she always did when talking about her father's work. She could still remember how astounded she had been to find out the brilliant Jackson Lange was her father.

"I'm also an architect, though certainly not at the level my father is."

Yet, she added silently.

"My specialty is universal design, of new builds and renovations. Inclusive design is another term for it. I especially love taking homes that are not accessible to everyone and making them work much more efficiently for those who live in them."

The woman's mouth tightened briefly, as if with a spasm of pain, then she mustered a smile. "That must be rewarding for you."

124

"Very much so," Sage said, though that was a vast understatement. "While most of my work is focused on designing homes and businesses, I also have a YouTube channel called Homes for All where I explore innovations in universal design."

"Oh wow. That might be why you seem familiar. I think I've looked at a video here or there."

"I love raising awareness of some of the obstacles people face in using their own homes."

"That sounds like a very worthy project. But what does it have to do with me?"

Sage chose her words delicately. "I would love your help, actually. I have been working on a project here in town I hoped to feature on my channel, but I'm afraid the homeowner is not very enthusiastic. That leaves me needing to come up with something else within a very short window of time."

"Okay," she said slowly. "I'm sorry. I'm still not sure what that has to do with me?"

"This is a terrific house, in one of my favorite areas. My mom and I lived only a few blocks away for a lot of my youth. As I look around your home, I can see a few areas where accessibility might be a problem for you. The entrance out front, for instance, and the higher kitchen island and countertops, out of reach for someone using a wheelchair or a scooter."

Lynette looked away. "Things haven't been too

bad yet. I can still take a few steps and stand for short periods of time, as long as I have my walker close by."

"That's great. Really great. I hope that state of affairs continues."

Oh, this was so awkward. She suddenly wished she had never started this.

Over the past few years, Sage had developed an application process for the dozen or so projects that had been funded and designed through Homes for All. This was the first time she had ever offered to make changes to someone's home without that person coming to the foundation first.

Struggling for words, she finally decided to be blunt. "This home works for you now. But what happens when it doesn't?"

Lynette's mouth tightened. "I'll probably have to sell the house and relocate. I don't want to have to move the children again now that they're settled in school here, but the real estate market is impossible in Hope's Crossing."

That truly was one of the problems with towns that became tourist draws. Housing prices climbed so much that the average family couldn't afford to buy locally and the rental market could be even worse, especially for those who had mobility challenges.

"This is a great house," Sage said. "It could still work perfectly for you, with a few modifications. Would you consider letting me design and implement a few changes that I know would make life easier for you? You would have full approval and input on anything my foundation would ultimately do."

Shock widened the other woman's eyes. Sage thought she saw a little glimmer of hope flicker there before resignation pushed it out.

"I'm sorry," she said in a quiet but dignified tone. "This is not a great time for me, financially, to jump into a renovation project."

"You don't understand," Sage said quickly to assure her. "You wouldn't have to pay for a thing. The cost of the renovation would be completely covered by the show."

In the unlikely event that the Homes for All budget couldn't cover the entire cost of a project, she knew she could probably persuade the Angel of Hope to come out of retirement to help.

"Are you serious?" That hope began to flicker a little more brightly.

"One hundred percent covered, I promise. I'm thinking we start with the kitchen and a ramp and see if we have time to adapt a bathroom for you. If not, we could do that after the first of the year."

The other woman looked stunned. "I . . . I need to think about this. I can't simply hand my house over to you for some YouTube channel. It's all I have now."

"Of course." Sage should have known she was asking too much. Her spirits fell. Helping the woman had seemed the ideal project, with Mason Tucker being so obstinate. "I should tell you we're in a bit of a time crunch. I would love to get started as soon as possible and wrap up the kitchen at least before Christmas."

"I use my kitchen for my business. I can't just . . . just stop everything and let you take it over right when I need it most, during the holiday season."

Sage winced at her own thoughtlessness. "Oh, right. I should have thought of that."

Her mind raced. "What if I can find an alternative kitchen for you to use temporarily while we're busy here? My aunt Alex owns a couple of restaurants in town. I know at least one of them, not far from here, Mabel's, is only open for breakfast and lunch, so it's empty every afternoon and evening."

"That's when I do most of my baking, when Chloe is available to help me."

"We can make it work, I promise. I know the kitchen at Mabel's has a couple of lowered workspaces and front controls on one of the ovens. We could easily move all your baking supplies from here to Mabel's. It might not be ideal, but after a few weeks, you can move back here and have a kitchen that works much better for your needs."

Lynette wore the suspicious expression of someone who had seen life pull the rug out from under her too many times. "Why me? Why are you doing this? What's the catch?"

"No catch. I promise." On impulse, Sage moved forward and placed a hand over the other woman's. "Please, Mrs. Greene. You would be doing me such a favor if you let me do this. I can't even tell you how much you would help me. When I saw you tonight in the café, working so hard to take care of your family, I had the very strong impression we needed to do this. You're the perfect person for Homes for All to help in Hope's Crossing."

The woman's fingers trembled under Sage's hand. "I'm not good at accepting help."

"I totally understand that." Taryn suddenly spoke up from across the table. "I know more than I would like about taking help from other people. It goes against the grain, doesn't it? We all try so hard to be independent and self-sufficient, but there is no shame in leaning on someone else when we need to."

Taryn gave the woman a reassuring smile. "You really would be helping Sage out if you would let her do this for you. And her work is amazing, believe me."

Lynette swallowed and Sage could tell she was waffling. "My condition is degenerative," she said, her voice low. "I know it's only a matter of time before I'm not going to have any choice. Either fix this place or move. It would be . . .

129

really great if we didn't have to move again. I have a little money set aside I could use to help buy some of the materials."

"No need, I promise," Sage said. "Is that a yes, then?"

After a long pause where Sage held her breath, the woman finally nodded and Sage wanted to give high fives all around, her mind spinning with possibilities.

"Would you mind if I come back tomorrow morning to take some measurements and snap a few pictures? I would do it now, but I don't want to barge in and take over your entire evening, especially after I've just given you a shock. I'm sure you need time to process. It won't take me long. Maybe a half hour."

"I don't mind if you do it now, if that's easier. We were only hanging out, experimenting a little with recipes and doing homework."

"Perfect! Taryn, do you mind being my lovely assistant?"

"Sure."

For the next half hour, Sage and her friend took photos and measurements of the kitchen from every angle. She was grateful she had brought her notebook along so she could sketch some ideas.

After the kitchen, with Lynette's permission, they walked through the other public spaces of the house as well as the woman's bedroom and en suite bathroom.

The house was graceful and lovely, though built in a different era without any thought toward accommodating those with mobility challenges. Still, Sage could envision how much better it could work for Lynette and her family with a few relatively easy updates.

Their tour also gave her a good sense of Lynette's decorating style, a charming mix of traditional and farmhouse that was warm and inviting.

After Sage promised Lynette she would be back the next day as soon as she could arrange a time with a contractor to take a look at the project and give her time estimates, Sage and Taryn said their goodbyes and headed out into the snow again.

While they were inside, Lynette must have sent her boys out to brush the still-falling snow off Taryn's car. They were busy shoveling the sidewalk in front of the house now, lit by the moonlight, the streetlamps and the glow from all the colorful Christmas lights in the neighboring yards.

"Wow. That was exciting," Taryn said as she waved to the boys and backed out of the driveway. "Do you really think you can renovate a kitchen before Christmas? That's less than three weeks. It's impossible, isn't it?"

Her shoulders tightened with self-doubt. Could she pull it off? She now would be in the middle of a major renovation, in addition to trying to finish Mason's house on schedule, juggle her other work long-distance *and* take care of Nick and Anna while her parents left town.

So much for her relaxing holiday in Hope's Crossing!

"It definitely will be a push but it's doable."

Barely.

"This is something everyone in Hope's Crossing would love to get behind. I'm sure we can get a crew of people up here at a moment's notice to do whatever you need," Taryn said. "You know how people are in town, especially if you can get your aunt Claire on board."

Sage had to smile at that. Claire McKnight, married to her mother's younger brother Riley, was a force to be reckoned with. When she put her mind to things, she did not rest until the job was done.

Claire was one of those people who was always looking for a way to help someone else. She would love to participate in this renovation.

This would work, she thought with growing excitement. Sure, Sage would have loved to show her internet audience the massive renovation at Wolf Ridge, with all the technical innovations and luxurious features, but the Greene project would have heart, emotion and holiday cheer.

She would simply keep her fingers crossed that she could pull it off.

9
Taryn

Taryn had no idea how Sage would accomplish an ambitious home renovation in such a short window of time, but she greatly admired her energy and enthusiasm for an idea that had bloomed from nothing to full glory over the course of a single evening.

By the time Taryn drove the fifteen minutes from the Greenes' house to the downtown parking lot where her friend had parked before dinner to pick up her car, Sage had already arranged for Sam Delgado, the best contractor in Hope's Crossing, to oversee the project. She had also made arrangements with him to meet at the Greenes' house first thing in the morning and confirmed the time with Lynette.

Sage was still wrapping up the details with Sam when they arrived at her car so Taryn turned her vehicle engine off and waited patiently until her friend ended the call, content to watch the snowflakes piling up through her windshield.

"I'm so sorry. This isn't the way you planned to spend the evening," Sage said after she hung up.

"It was perfect," Taryn said. "I'm excited to be part of it."

"Thank you again for introducing me to

Lynette. I am so happy we saw her tonight in the café."

"You're doing a good thing for a family in crisis. I hope you know I'm here to help in any way I can. I'm not great at construction, but I can make phone calls or organize volunteer teams or whatever you need."

"Thank you," Sage said. "I will definitely take you up on that."

"You might want to reach out to Charlie Beaumont," Taryn suggested, trying to keep her voice even. "This kind of thing is right up his alley. He's used to building things quickly and efficiently through his work for The Sheridan Trust, and he's a whiz at carpentry."

"That is a great idea!" Sage exclaimed. "I'll let Sam know. But isn't Charlie busy dealing with his father's estate?"

"Yes. Probably."

"Still, it doesn't hurt to ask him. I can reach out if you don't have time."

"I'll talk to him. I'm seeing him Friday but since we're on a short clock, I'll try to reach out earlier than that."

"Thanks, Taryn. You're the best."

After she made sure Sage's vehicle would start, never a sure thing when cold weather could drain batteries, Taryn finally took off for home, anxious to see her fur babies.

Except for a few moments between talking to

Charlie and leaving to meet with Sage, she had only been home briefly all day.

She yawned as she neared her house. It was nearly nine. The middle school started at eight so she tried to be in her office no later than seven fifteen, in case any students needed to reach out to her.

She was debating with herself about whether to shovel now or in the morning as she pulled onto her street.

The decision was taken away from her. As she drove up to her little house, she saw that half the driveway was already cleared and someone was busy shoveling the rest.

Her heart gave a sharp kick when she recognized the man wielding the shovel.

What was he doing here?

She hit the remote on her garage. As the bay door opened, Charlie turned to face the road, his features clear in her headlights.

She pulled into the garage, climbed out of her car and picked up her own snow shovel, propped against the door.

"You didn't have to do that," she said as she stepped out of the garage, shovel in hand.

"I was driving past on my way back from the grocery store and saw that nobody had been by yet to clear off the snow. I wanted to be done before you got home."

"Thank you," she said, not trusting her voice

135

to say more than that. She loved his concern on her behalf; she only wished it wasn't borne out of guilt and pity.

He gestured to the shovel in her hand. "Put that away. I've got this. It should only take a few more minutes."

"You saved me an hour of work. I'll do the steps and the walkway. It's the least I can do."

"Taryn. I've got this," he repeated. "You shouldn't be out in this snow."

She planted the shovel in the deeper snow on the grass. Nobody would dare treat *Sage* like she couldn't lift a shovel. Her friend plowed forward to take what she wanted, while Taryn sometimes felt like a passive observer in her own life.

"This might surprise you to know, but I am not completely helpless. In fact, I actually live a fully independent life. These days, I can dress myself, feed myself, go the store without supervision. I have a job. I drive a car. I am also fully capable of shoveling my own damn driveway when the need arises."

He blinked at her vehemence. "I never said you weren't capable."

"You didn't need to say it."

"I was only trying to help."

"I appreciate that. I do. But I hate when you and everyone else act like I'm made of glass and will shatter into pieces if you look at me wrong. I appreciate your help on the driveway. I will take the steps and walkway," she said again.

After a pause, he shrugged and returned to shoveling.

"That should hold you for a bit," he said when he finished. "You'll have to give it another go in the morning."

"Thank you. I appreciate your help," she said, trying to sound gracious instead of combative.

Being out in the snowy night for even the short time it took her to clear her porch and the walkway had cooled her down, and now she felt silly for her outburst.

Charlie leaned on his shovel, protected from the snow in the small covered walkway between her garage and her house. "What are you doing out so late? Hot date?"

She made a face. "Oh yes. That's me. Hot dates every single night. Not enough days in the week to fit them all in."

He didn't seem amused by her light tone. "Anybody I know?"

She sighed. "Yes. Sage McKnight. We went to the Center of Hope to catch up. Afterward, we went to the house of a friend of mine. She's having some health problems, and Sage wants to remodel her house to make it more wheelchair accessible. Before Christmas."

He shoved his baseball cap back an inch or two. "Before Christmas? That's impossible."

"She seems to think it's not. I'm supposed to

ask if you might be available to help, considering that's basically what you've been doing for the past few years for The Sheridan Trust."

He gave a short laugh. "Not really. I build medical clinics and schoolhouses in developing countries. That's not quite the same as remodeling a house."

"The concept is the same. Hurry in, do the job and get out again. Right up your wheelhouse."

The bitterness in her voice seemed to come out of nowhere, to her dismay. She should be used to Charlie moving in and out of her life. He had been doing it since he was released from youth corrections.

"I know you're busy, but if you have any spare time, I know Sage would appreciate it. Sam Delgado will be the contractor on the job. I'm sure he would love your help."

Charlie had worked with Sam during the summers after he was released from youth corrections and then later, when he would come home from college.

She had always figured he worked construction mostly to annoy his parents, who would have preferred their Golden Boy to spend his summers lounging by the pool or hobnobbing on the golf course with William Beaumont's business associates.

"I'm up to my neck in estate details and trying to get the house ready to sell," he said.

138

"I know. I wouldn't ask unless the need was urgent. Maybe you can squeeze out a few hours here or there to help out. Anything will be appreciated."

"I can probably help out a little," he said after a moment. "It might be good to have something else to focus on. I'll give Sam a call, see what he needs."

"Oh, thank you." To make up for her annoyance of earlier and as a gesture of appreciation for his work clearing her driveway, she gave him a hug, like she had done a thousand times since they were kids, as she had done earlier that day.

Their hugs were different now. *He* felt different. Stiff and unwieldy. It was like hugging a traffic pylon. He stepped away quickly, leaving her chilled.

"Have a good night."

She didn't expect to, after this awkward encounter. The glow from being involved in a project to help someone deserving had floated away like the snowflakes.

"You're still going with me Friday, right?"

She thought for a moment he was going to back out. He finally nodded. "Sure. Acne and hormones and awkward teenagers. I can't wait."

"Thanks. I'll see you then," she said.

She returned her shovel to its spot and hurried into the house, her heart aching. Normally, she would have invited him in and they would have stayed up all night talking and laughing and enjoying each other's company.

In one night over the summer, everything had changed, and she was terrified she would never be able to fix it.

10

Mason

He didn't want to be here.

As Mason maneuvered through the crowded park in his custom all-terrain wheelchair, he was certain everybody was staring at him.

From furtive glances to outright stares, he could feel their looks burning under his skin.

This.

This was the reason he had avoided going out in public much since he and Grace moved to Hope's Crossing. He knew people recognized him from his days as a professional athlete, and he hated seeing the pity in their eyes.

He wanted to grab his kid, climb into his SUV and drive back to the guesthouse at Wolf Ridge. He was stuck, though, with no escape in sight.

What else could he do? Grace had come home from school, bubbling over with excitement about the Fire & Ice Festival, the pop-up event she had told him about the other day, held on one day only, with no advance notice.

The festival was to celebrate the opening of the town's free outdoor ice rink, created each year by the fire department in one of the city parks.

Apparently this was a grand event, a spontaneous celebration that only happened when the weather was cold enough. Townspeople had been awaiting the announcement with great anticipation, at least according to all the other fourth graders at Hope's Crossing Elementary School.

When it was finally cold enough for the ice to be maintained, the town held a big celebration and everyone came out to skate at the event, which doubled as a fundraiser to help the local food bank.

"All my friends are going, Dad," Grace had informed him as soon as she came in from school. "I really don't want to miss it. Please can we go?"

"I can take her, if you want," his mother had offered again.

In order to avoid the staring crowds, Mason had been tempted to accept Rebecca's offer. A moment's thought changed his mind. He and Grace were trying to make a home here in Hope's Crossing, the new start they both needed after the pain and loss of the past two and a half years.

What would be the big deal about taking her to a town celebration? Everyone would be focused on the skaters, not on him.

He should have known better. The moment he rolled away from the SUV and into the crowd, he was aware of the stares and the murmurs.

He knew it was the novelty that drew people's attention. He had only been here a few months and had basically kept to himself. Once he put more effort into participating in the ebb and flow of the town, people would become used to seeing him among them. It wouldn't seem like such a big deal whenever he showed up somewhere.

On the other hand, Hope's Crossing was a tourist town. There would always be visitors who didn't know he lived here now. Mason had known that was one of the things he simply would have to accept when he decided to renovate Wolf Ridge.

He couldn't leave the park now, as much as he might want to, especially when Grace simply glowed. She smiled widely as they made their way toward the skating area, draped with strings of colored lights and ringed by fires glowing in metal barrels all around the edge of the rink.

"Should we find somewhere to sit?" Rebecca asked.

Yet another thing he couldn't seem to control. Even after he insisted he could take his daughter, Grace had invited her grandmother to come with them. Mason couldn't come up with a good reason to refuse.

"Sure," he started to say, but Grace's excited squeal cut him off.

"Hi, Nick!" she greeted the boy her age who came racing toward them wearing a stocking cap that had to be about eighteen inches long. "I made it! I told my dad we had to come because all my friends would be here. I can't wait to ice skate. It's my very first time!"

"You never skated before?"

She shrugged. "I think I did once when I was really small, but I don't remember very well."

Mason remembered. When Grace was about three, he and Shayla had taken her to New York for the holidays and had made the obligatory stop at Rockefeller Center. None of them was any good at ice skating, but Shayla still took about a hundred selfies to remember the moment.

"Are you here all by yourself?" she asked her friend with a curious look.

He shook his head. "No. I could never come by myself. My dad isn't here, but my mom is and so are my sisters. My mom was talking to one of her friends and Anna, Sage and me were about to get hot chocolate when I saw you and came right over to find you. Do you want some hot chocolate? We have room at our table."

"Can we, Dad?" Grace asked.

His first instinct was to tell her they should hurry to rent some skates so she could spin around on the ice a few times and they could go home.

The words died when he saw her bright features. They had come here and gone to all the trouble of finding a parking place. Why not let her savor the event?

"Sure," he said. "You guys go grab a seat and I'll get in line."

"I can do that," Rebecca offered.

"I've got it."

"How are you going to carry them back?" she asked, giving the chair a pointed look.

Damn. He always seemed to forget he needed both hands on the hand rims of the wheels if he didn't want to end up going around in circles.

"I'll figure something out. I can hold them on my lap."

She looked like she wanted to argue but since Nick and Grace were already racing toward a picnic table near one of the fire rings, she nodded and hurried after them.

Why was he always such an ass to his mother?

He didn't like that part of himself, the hurt kid who lived inside him and couldn't seem to forgive the past.

Every night, he told himself he would try to drop some of his defenses around her. Then the next time he dealt with her, all the old feelings of rejection and resentment would swell.

He needed to let it go. She was trying now. Why couldn't that be enough?

He was still wondering as he wheeled to the hot chocolate kiosk, housed in a tiny camp trailer that seemed too small for a human to stand upright. A woman wearing elf ears and a striped elf costume was taking orders.

Mason rolled to the back of the line of about six or seven people. The guy in front turned around and did a double take. "You're Mason Tucker," he said, as if telling Mason something he didn't already know.

"Yeah," he answered, wishing he had worn a balaclava instead of a beanie so he could have hidden his identity.

"Man, the Mighty Tuck. I saw you hit that 3-run homer in game five of the World Series in Portland. Freaking unbelievable. It was the single best day of my life. Except the day I got married and when my kids were born," he said quickly when the woman beside him gave him the stink eye.

Even in his previous life, he had never really known what to say to people who wanted to talk about the glory days with him. It was all far more awkward now, given his current physical condition. "It was a pretty good day for me too."

The guy looked at the wheelchair, and Mason could see his expression twist into a familiar one of pity. To Mason's relief, he didn't offer any platitudes.

"You can go ahead of us, if you want," his wife said.

"I'm good. I don't mind waiting," Mason said as the line moved forward a little. "Are you visiting the area?" he asked politely.

"No. We're locals. Not a lot of tourists come to the Fire & Ice Festival unless they stumble onto it. The town doesn't advertise it except by email to the residents," the man said. "I'm Bob Coleman, by the way. This is my wife, Jan. We're kind of your neighbors. Our house is at the base of the mountain."

"Nice to meet you both," he said. While they chatted about inconsequential things, he was vaguely aware of someone coming up behind him to stand in line but he didn't turn around, busy listening to Jan Coleman tell him she had served on the school board for ten years and had just been elected to another term.

The woman stopped in midsentence, catching sight of the person behind him. "Sage! Hi. I didn't know you were back in town."

Mason whipped his head around and found his too-lovely architect standing behind him.

"Hi, Jan," she answered with a bright smile. "I'm here until after Christmas, working on a few projects in town."

"Including my place," Mason said.

"That house is gorgeous," Jan gushed. "I've always said so, haven't I, Bob? I would love to see inside. Hey, here's an idea. Wolf Ridge would be perfect for that YouTube channel of yours, Sage. We subscribe and watch every episode, don't we?"

"Every one," her husband agreed.

Mason tensed, half convinced this had all been a setup to persuade him to change his mind.

147

One look at Sage's embarrassed features told him otherwise. To his relief, a young child he assumed was a grandchild hurried over to the pair and gripped Bob's hand, distracting both of them.

The line moved forward at an excruciating pace and Mason knew he would be rude not to talk to Sage, especially after all she had done on his house.

"Exciting night, isn't it? Grace is over the moon at coming out to skate with all her friends."

"I always love the Fire & Ice Festival," she said. "It's hard to bring the locals together in a town like Hope's Crossing when we have about three times as many tourists as year-round residents during the winter months, but this is one event that seems to do that. Everyone in town gets into the spirit of things. It doesn't feel like the holidays until the ice rink is open."

He had to admit it was a festive scene, with those colorful lights, Christmas music coming through speakers set up around the rink and those flames flickering in the night.

"We saw Nick when we first got here," he said. "He rushed right over to say hi to Grace."

"They've become pretty good friends, haven't they?"

"Yes. He seems like a good kid."

He wanted to kick himself as soon as he said it, remembering she was Nick's birth mother. Did she find it awkward to discuss him? She didn't seem to.

"He is," she answered. "He's always looking out for others. He and Anna both are becoming wonderful humans. Does Grace have skates of her own?"

"We have to rent some, if there are any left."

"There should be. Plenty of people only skate for a few minutes and then call it good."

While he was talking to Sage, he realized with some surprise, either other people seemed to stop staring at him or he ceased to care.

He liked the way Sage McKnight met his gaze directly, instead of looking at the chair or above his head like so many people did. He also never saw pity in her eyes.

The line moved forward as Bob and Jan reached the window and ordered ten hot chocolates. Either they had a serious cocoa addiction or they were ordering for a group, probably including the young boy who had stayed with them in the line.

"I still can't believe it's already December," Sage said. "What holiday traditions did you have when you were living in Portland?" she asked.

"My wife, Shayla, handled all of that." He felt the familiar sting of loss, but it was more like a sharp jab instead of gouging pain. "She was always into Christmas. Most years she liked to spend the holidays at home with her family, who had a place on the Oregon Coast, and then we would take off between Christmas and New Year's to spend a few days somewhere with just us and Grace. Usually somewhere warm, if we could, but sometimes we came to our place here."

"The holidays must be tough on you and Grace both."

This time her features did show sympathy but he knew it was for his grief, not for his current physical condition, which he deeply appreciated.

"You could say that. We haven't really had the chance to have a good one for a few years. The first year after the crash, I think we were both kind of numb. Last year, I ended up needing emergency surgery right before Christmas. Grace had to spend Christmas with her aunt and uncle. My late wife's sister and her husband."

Rebecca, by then a fixture in their lives—like it or not—had wanted to come stay at their house while he was in the hospital so Grace could have Christmas in her own place. Instead, Mason had insisted his daughter once more go with Shayla's family to Cannon Beach. It had seemed important at the time, but now he knew it was a decision he had made as much to punish Rebecca as for the sake of tradition.

Lord, he could be an ass.

"I promised her this year would be different. My natural instinct is to become a hermit and hunker down on the mountain, but I can't do that to Grace."

"You're a good father." She looked at him, eyes sparkling, and Mason suddenly felt breathless. He told himself it was the cold December night, even as some part of him knew it was because no woman had looked at him like that in a long time.

He looked away to see Bob walk off with two drink holders, each with four hot beverages, while Jan followed him holding two cups.

Steam curled off the cups, rich and chocolatey. With the snow lightly falling and the laughter of the skaters, the night seemed suddenly magical.

Mason gripped his hand rims and wheeled forward. It was his turn next, but the elf in the cocoa trailer automatically directed her smile to Sage, standing behind him.

"May I help you?"

Sage pointed to Mason. "He's next."

"Oh. Sorry." The woman flushed. Mason wanted to tell her she wasn't the only one who did that. In his limited experience over the past thirty months, he had noticed people either genuinely didn't see him or subconsciously assumed everyone using a wheelchair should be treated like a helpless toddler.

"Sorry. How can I help you?"

"I'll take three hot cocoas, one with marshmallows and extra whipped cream."

"Right away, sir."

After he paid for them, she bustled around

preparing the drinks, inserting the cups into a cardboard drink holder, which she slid out the window toward him.

Mason lifted them down onto his lap, hoping like hell he didn't burn anything down there.

"Those are going to spill all over the place while you roll over the bumpy grass," Sage said. "If you give me a second to grab my order, I can help you carry them to your family."

He wanted to argue, as he had with Rebecca. He didn't need help with every little thing.

On the other hand, she was right. He had to wheel the chair over bumpy snow and icy sidewalks. It wouldn't be a smooth ride, under the best of circumstances.

"Fine. Thank you." He added the last as an afterthought, then wheeled away from the counter, the scent of chocolate wafting from the cups in a delicious cloud.

Sage joined him shortly. "Okay. I can take yours now."

"Thank you," he muttered again.

"You're welcome." She stood next to him so she could reach for the drink holder and Mason had a sudden wild urge to toss the hot cocoa into the snow and pull her into his arms instead.

She made her way through the crowd, and he gripped his rims and wheeled along next to her, not an easy task as it was always more cumbersome for him to slip around people.

"You're pretty good on the snow and ice," she remarked. "I'm impressed."

"This one is my outside chair. The tires on it are more all-terrain than some wheelchairs, plus it has a power assist motor if I need help over grass or gravel."

"Which I'm going to guess you rarely turn on."

He felt his mouth split into a smile. "Am I that transparent?"

"After nine months of working with you on Wolf Ridge, I think I know a little about how your mind works."

He doubted that or she wouldn't be walking so calmly next to him, with no idea of how much he wanted to touch the soft skin of her cheek or taste that little pulse in her neck.

"I forget how difficult the average park can be to navigate for someone using a wheelchair, with all the different surfaces. Grass, gravel, sidewalk, dirt."

"I'm sure you think about it more than most people or you wouldn't have made a career out of focusing on universal design."

"I suppose."

He remembered what she had told him about her reasons for starting on this career, about losing her sister and her friend who had been seriously injured.

He hadn't asked how the story ended, he realized.

"How is your friend now?" he asked.

She looked puzzled. "Which friend?"

"The one who started you on your journey to promote universal design? The one who was injured in the accident with your sister?"

She hesitated and then pointed toward the skating rink, where a pretty blond woman was smiling as she skated with an older man and a boy a few years older than Grace. She seemed wobbly, but no more than anyone else on the ice.

"That's Taryn, with her father, Brodie, and brother. Anthony has low vision. Brodie and Taryn's stepmother, Evie, have adopted two children with special needs and then they have one together, a little girl who is five."

"That's a houseful."

"Yes. They're quite amazing. And Taryn is doing great. She's a counselor at the middle school and lives here in Hope's Crossing. She still has some lingering issues with balance, and occasionally when she's tired, her speech can falter a little but unless you know her well, most people wouldn't notice. She's really made a remarkable recovery."

"That's great."

She sent him a swift look, and he was hoping he didn't reveal any of his dark feelings.

He knew everyone had their own path through recovery from traumatic injuries, spinal cord or otherwise. One of the toughest things for him during rehab had been seeing a few people who had seemed much worse off than he at the beginning regain the full function that still eluded him.

Where was his miraculous recovery?

Oh, he knew his doctors said it was a miracle he survived the crash at all, especially when Shayla and their pilot hadn't.

And, yes, at first doctors had told him to be prepared that he likely wouldn't ever stand or walk again. Mason had worked his ass off to prove them wrong, then had to face the grim reality that while he technically could walk, it would never be easy or comfortable and he was much more mobile in a wheelchair. He wasn't a quitter but he was a realist.

He had some sensation in his legs and all his internal parts worked as they were supposed to, thank the Lord. Things could be so much worse.

He tried not to be bitter. He was alive. Grace had one parent, at least. He would continue trying to be the best father he could, even if that meant he had to accept help to carry a cup of hot cocoa to his daughter.

11
Sage

Sage felt like she had been handed a precious gift. Mason Tucker was letting her help him.

It wasn't much, only carrying a couple of hot beverages for him, but at least he was letting her do *something*.

They reached the picnic table a moment later to find Grace was chattering away with Anna and Nick while Rebecca and Sage's mother talked together.

The next few moments were a flurry of distributing drinks and throwing away the cardboard drink holders.

"Thanks, Sage," Nick said, snatching his away and taking a big swig that made him gasp. "It's hot!"

"That's why they call it hot chocolate," Anna retorted.

"Thank you," Rebecca said, taking an insulated cup from Mason. "I can't remember the last time I had hot cocoa. I forgot how delicious it is. The perfect thing for a cold night."

"You're welcome," he answered, voice gruff.

Sage was a little surprised to see his mother there. Over the past several months of working with Mason, she had received the distinct impression from a few things he had said that he and Rebecca weren't exactly close.

Sage wasn't sure why. She found the woman friendly and warm.

"We should get you some skates," Mason said.

"Grandma already rented them for me and even put them on when you were in line. See?" Grace held out her foot, where she wore skates covered with blade protectors.

"Thanks," he said a little stiffly to his mother, who gave him a small smile and returned to sipping her cocoa.

The children seemed eager to get out onto the skating rink. They each finished only about half their drinks.

"Can we go out now, Mom?" Nick asked.

"You don't want more than that?" Maura asked.

"We'll have it after. I bet skating will make us thirsty."

"Probably," Grace agreed.

"It's fine with me, if you think you're ready."

"I'm ready," Anna said, jumping up from the picnic table and nearly falling in her skates.

Nick and Grace stood up, equally as wobbly. "How about I give you a helping hand to the ice?" Sage offered.

She held hands with Grace on one side and Anna on the other. Nick held his younger sister's hand and with much giggling, they traversed the fifteen feet to the rink, where the children took off their blade protectors.

"When you're ready to come off the ice, sit right here and I'll bring your boots over," Sage said.

"Thanks." Nick gave her a quick, casual hug that made a lump rise in her throat, then all three children staggered out to the ice, holding each other for balance.

She watched for a moment to make sure they could stay up then returned to the table, where Mason was silently sipping his cocoa while Maura and his mother seemed to have struck up a friendship.

"Rebecca, you really need to come to one of our book club meetings at the store," Maura said.

"I would like that," she said with a smile.

"What kind of books do you like to read?"

Trust her mother to turn the conversation to books. Maura was a true bibliophile. She was able to keep her bookstore thriving in an age when many independent stores were struggling, mostly because she had loyal customers that she knew well. Maura always stocked the books they wanted, not only the popular bestsellers.

"I like anything. Mysteries, romance, literary fiction. Whatever grabs my attention."

Maura smiled. "Now you're speaking my language. I love eclectic readers."

"You love all readers," Sage said.

Her mother shrugged. "True. What's not to love?"

"To be honest," Rebecca said, "I was never much of a reader until about six or seven years ago. I suppose I never had much time for it."

"What changed?" Maura asked.

Rebecca shifted her gaze to Mason with a look of such naked longing, it made Sage's throat ache. "I was going through a rough time. A period of reinvention, I guess you could say. I got out of a bad relationship, went through rehab and tried to clean up my act. Books became my salvation. My best friends, in many ways."

Mason sipped at his cocoa, looking uncomfortable at the revelation.

"You definitely need to come to our book group meetings," Maura declared. "We already had this month's, technically, which was a birthday party for one of our members. But January's will be the second Wednesday. I'll get you the info about what we're reading."

"I would like that," Rebecca said. "I haven't had much chance to meet many people in Hope's Crossing since I've been here."

Maura suddenly waved at another group sitting a few tables away. "There's some of my family members, a couple of my sisters, Angie and Alex. You should meet both of them. Angie is on the city council, and Alex owns a couple of restaurants in town. Brazen, which is high end, and Mabel's, which is only open for breakfast and lunch."

"I've eaten at both of those restaurants. Their food is delicious."

"Make sure you tell Alex that. Come on, I'll introduce you. Sage, we'll take the kids' boots closer to the rink so you don't have to get up."

Few people could say no to Maura. Rebecca was no different. With a rather helpless look toward Sage and Mason, she followed Maura to the other table, leaving the two of them alone.

Or as alone as they could be surrounded by about four hundred other Hope's Crossing residents.

They watched the children on the ice, now skating with such glee that Sage was almost tempted to grab some skates herself and join them.

She wouldn't leave Mason on his own, though. Instead, she gave him a sidelong look. "So. What's the story with your mom?"

He stiffened. "I don't know what you mean. What story?"

Sage immediately regretted her question. The fissure between him and Rebecca was none of her business. "Nothing. I shouldn't have asked. Never mind."

Flames flickered over his features, set in a hard frown. "No. I'm curious. Why do you ask about my mother?"

"Really, it's none of my business. Things seem

a little tense between the two of you. I could be completely misreading the situation, though."

She thought for a moment he wasn't going to answer her, but he finally glanced over at Rebecca, who was chattering now with Sage's aunts and her mother.

"You're not," he finally said. "Things have been tense between us my whole life. Rebecca didn't raise me. Actually, I saw her only a few times until I was eighteen or nineteen. Even after that, she hasn't really been part of my life until the past few years."

"What about your dad?"

"Dead. He was never in my life. From what little I know about him, that's a blessing. I only know my mother was a runaway who gave birth to me when she was seventeen. One day she showed up back at her childhood home with a new baby. She handed me to her parents and went back to her party life."

The story felt all too familiar to her. She looked across the ice at Nick, laughing as he helped Anna back to her feet.

Oh, poor Rebecca. Sage felt an instant bond with the woman. She knew exactly how it felt to be pregnant, alone and afraid.

"That must have been so hard for her."

He stared at her. "Hard for her? If it was, she never showed any sign of it. She walked away and didn't look back. Once I signed a Major

162

League contract and was making some money, of course she came back and wanted to forge a relationship with me."

The bitterness in his voice made her wish she could hug him. How painful for him, to carry the belief that his mother only wanted a relationship because of his bank balance.

"It wasn't hard for Rebecca," he went on in that same harsh tone. "Not for a minute. She didn't give me a second thought after dropping me off at the very home she herself couldn't wait to leave. A home focused on Bible-thumping and sanctimony instead of affection and kindness."

Some of the sympathy she felt for him must have shown on her face. He broke off with an oath.

"Sorry. I shouldn't have told you all that. But you did ask."

"I did."

She was glad he'd told her, actually, touched that he trusted her enough to let her inside that far. She had a feeling he didn't reveal this to many people.

"I'm surprised you have Rebecca back in your life at all, if you're so angry with her."

He made a face. "Not by choice. When I was in the hospital after the accident, she rushed in to help with Grace, relocating from California to be closer to us. I was in no state to argue at the time. By the time I could think straight again, it was too late. Rebecca and Grace were already close. What was I supposed to do? Grace had already lost her mom. I didn't have the heart to take her grandmother away, as much as I might have wanted to. So here we are."

Oh. Sage's throat closed and she had to blink back tears, her emotions a tangled mess. She felt deeply for all of them. Grief for poor Grace, losing her mother, sadness for Rebecca and the choices she had made and a deep respect for Mason, who had emerged from what sounded like a tough childhood to become a decent person who cared deeply for his child.

What a good man he was, to allow Grace to forge a relationship with Rebecca, even if he couldn't quite manage one on his own.

"She followed you here."

He nodded. "She's renting a place in those apartments on Skyline Drive."

Not living with him, as huge as Wolf Ridge was? She could understand, she supposed, why Mason needed distance from his mother.

"The only thing I can say in her favor is that she seems to be a much better grandmother than she ever was a mother."

She saw Rebecca, now on the outer edge of the skating rink, cheering on Grace, Nick and Anna. So much pain in the world.

"I'm sorry I poked at old wounds."

"It's not a wound. Not anymore. I might have

been angry and hurt when I was a kid but now I'm . . . indifferent."

If she were Rebecca, she would find his indifference so much worse. The hard set to his features contradicted his words, though. He wasn't indifferent toward his mother or he wouldn't have spoken with such bitterness.

"From the outside," she ventured, "it seems as if Rebecca might be trying to atone a little for the choices she made when she was a frightened seventeen year old in an impossible situation."

He gave her a steady look. "Like you were with Nick?"

All the air seemed to leave her lungs. How did he know about that? Nick, probably, through Grace.

Did Nick tell everyone about their relationship?

She could feel her face heat, which infuriated her. She wasn't ashamed of any of her choices.

"Yes," she said quietly. "I was a little older than your mom. I was nineteen and a sophomore in college when I found out I was pregnant. It was the year my sister was killed, when grief and pain were leading me into all kinds of questionable life decisions."

She vividly remembered that time so many Christmases ago, when she had been terrified to even tell Maura she was pregnant, especially after Jack reentered their lives.

"I have no regrets. Not one. During the pregnancy, I was pursuing adoption, agonizing over giving up my child, and trying to find the perfect couple for him when my grandfather Harry suggested my parents should adopt Nick. For a hundred reasons, it immediately felt like the right decision."

"Right for whom?"

"All of us, especially Nicky. I was a single mother, twenty years old by the time I had him, with only a year and a half of college under my belt and no relationship at all with Nick's father. I had no way to provide for him, though of course my parents would have helped. That way didn't seem fair to any of us. My parents, on the other hand, were and still are deeply in love, completely committed. Most importantly, they had love to spare. So they became his parents and I became my son's older sister instead."

Had it been easy? Hell no. There had been many nights she cried herself to sleep, hugging a pillow instead of the baby she had come to love so much, once the shock of her pregnancy wore off.

She couldn't regret it. Nick had a wonderful life with her parents and Anna, and Sage knew she was extraordinarily fortunate to be able to stay in his life and still have a loving relationship with him.

"Do I wish things could have been different?

Sometimes. Would I change anything I did nine years ago? No chance. Nick has been loved every single moment of his life, by my parents and by me."

Her voice softened. "I'm so sorry you didn't have that. Every child deserves to be loved."

"I survived."

He did more than that. He had become a wonderful, loving father. She didn't know how she knew, but Sage was suddenly certain he had been a wonderful husband as well.

What would it be like to be loved by a man like Mason?

Her chest ached with a deep yearning that shocked Sage to her core. She was still grappling with it when the children hurried over, skates in their hands and boots on their feet. Maura and Rebecca followed close behind.

Grace headed straight to Mason and leaned over the side of the wheelchair to hug her father. "That was so much fun!" she exclaimed. "I fell like a hundred times."

"It looked like you were having a great time," he answered.

"You should come out and skate," Grace said to her dad.

"Grace," Rebecca admonished, inclining her head to Mason's wheelchair as if to point out her statement had been insensitive.

"What? There's a kid out there in a wheelchair,

167

and his sister is pushing him around. They're both having a blast. If I had your chair to hold on to, maybe I wouldn't fall so many times."

"Maybe another time," Mason said.

Sage was suddenly quite certain that as much as he loved his daughter, he would rather be hog-tied and dragged down Main Street than find himself being pushed around the ice by his nine-year-old daughter in front of the whole town.

"Okay," Grace said happily. "Maybe we can come later this week."

"We'll have to see."

"I'm freezing now," Nick announced. "Is my cocoa still hot?"

"Yours is that one," Sage said, gesturing to the one beside her at the table.

"Finish your cocoa," Mason said to Grace. "Then we should probably hit the road. You have school tomorrow."

"Oh. Do we have to?"

"I'm afraid so."

"We're leaving too," Maura assured her, which seemed to mollify the girl.

"Thanks for letting us share your table," Rebecca said. "Your family is wonderful. I loved them all."

"We did win the family lottery, didn't we, Sage?" Maura said.

"Definitely," she said, sad for both Rebecca

and Mason, both raised without love, when she had been blessed with so much.

She only wished Mason could remember that his mother had endured the same cold childhood he had and had become a warm, kind person who loved her granddaughter and clearly wanted a relationship with her son.

12
Taryn

As Taryn waited for Charlie to pick her up Friday evening, she felt as giddy as when she had been a ninth grader herself, going to her first dance.

Anticipation seemed to sparkle through her veins like seltzer.

Yes. She was perfectly aware she was being ridiculous. Charlie was her friend. A friend who seemed determined to keep their relationship platonic.

Did she really think one middle school dance could change that?

Her dog Jacques, an old man at thirteen now and moving with aches and pains, came up beside her and nudged her hand with his nose. She adored this dog with all her heart and knew she had a limited time left with him.

He officially had been certified as an emotional support dog after her accident, but he hadn't needed certification for her to give him most of the credit for pushing her back to health.

He had some health issues, and her heart ached to know the time would come soon to let him go. Not yet, though. She would worry about that later. Her other dog, Yvette, wagged her tail. Yvette was a small, feisty mixed-breed spaniel, a rescue Taryn had adopted as a puppy to keep Jacques company while she worked after she moved back to Hope's Crossing.

"You guys can't go with me tonight. I'm sorry," she said to them. They both looked sad but returned to their favorite spot, nestled together on the sofa they had claimed as their own.

A few moments later, headlights shone into the room and the dogs perked up and went to the door. Anticipation swirled through her, sweet and rich.

Along with it, though, was a frisson of anxiety.

Why wouldn't he open his heart to the feelings she knew he had for her?

She had been wearing her own heart on her sleeve when it came to Charlie since she was fifteen and he was helping her learn how to walk and talk again.

If he wasn't going to let their relationship ever shift from friends to something more, Taryn knew at some point she was going to have to move on. She could not spend the rest of her life waiting for him.

Her accident had taught her that life was a precious gift, meant to be opened and savored, not tucked away on a shelf, waiting for something that might not ever come.

She wanted a family. Children of her own. A relationship like her father and Evie had, filled with joy and support and love.

She was only twenty-six, but many of her

friends and fellow teachers her age were already married and had children.

She had told herself she would give Charlie this holiday season and that was it. If he continued to insist that their relationship remain platonic, she would have to carefully tuck away her love for him so she could make room in her heart for someone else.

She didn't want to, but she also didn't want to live in this limbo.

Maybe everything would change tonight.

Or maybe not.

The doorbell rang. With fingers that trembled a little, she shrugged into the white faux fur cape she had bought to go along with her tea-length silvery blue dress and opened the door.

The dogs' tails wagged like crazy when they saw him, and Jacques was trembling with excitement. They loved him as much as she did.

"Hey there, guys," he said, reaching out with one hand to try giving them both some love. The other hand, she realized, was holding a corsage.

He looked up to smile at her, and Taryn had to catch her breath. He had always been gorgeous to her but something about him right now, wearing a bespoke gray suit and a tie that perfectly matched his blue eyes, made her toes curl in her strappy shoes.

He had also shaved off his beard. She hadn't seen him clean-shaven in forever.

"Wow," he said. "You look like an angel who just fluttered down from the top of the tree."

She wasn't sure whether to be moved by his words or annoyed. Part of their problem was that he had always put her too high on a pedestal.

"Thank you. But you, of all people, know I'm no angel, Charlie."

He looked as if he wanted to disagree but to her relief, he only held out the corsage. "This is for you."

"Thank you. I didn't think to get flowers for you."

"Well, I figured you missed a few dances in high school. Let's call this a makeup."

It was always there between them, the reminder of the accident, and how she missed nearly a year of school during her recovery and had to have tutors and homeschool to catch up so she could graduate with her class.

He held out the corsage, which was fixed to a band to wear on her wrist.

"Why don't we take it with us? I'm afraid my cape will smash it."

"Okay."

"You look great too," she said, to cover the sudden awkwardness. "Is that the suit you wore to Jason's wedding last summer?"

She chose her words deliberately, to remind him of how much fun they'd had together and of that stirring moment they had shared on the dance floor and the kiss that came after.

"It's the only one I have. Not much call to wear suits when I'm pounding nails in the jungle somewhere or hanging cabinets in the desert."

He had created a good life away from Hope's Crossing, spending a good part of it traveling around the world helping others. She respected and admired him for it, even as she wished he could find the self-fulfillment he sought here, with her.

"Are you ready to go?"

"Yes. I only need to settle the poochies."

He watched, features impassive, as she petted Jacques and Yvette and told them to be good.

"I can't believe Jacques is still going," Charlie said as they walked out into the night and she closed the door behind her. "He must be at least a hundred and fifty in human years."

"He's thirteen. That makes him about eighty-five. He's old but still gets around."

If she lost both Charlie and Jacques in the new year, how would she make it through? She didn't want to think about it.

"I'm going to the middle school, right?" he asked as he drove away from her house.

"No. Sorry. I forgot to tell you. Our PTA president is the events coordinator at the Silver Strike resort and she was able to reserve their small ballroom for us."

He nodded, though he didn't look thrilled as he turned in that direction.

"How many kids are you expecting?"

"The ninth grade has about two hundred students. We expect about a hundred and fifty to come to the dance. We'll see, though. You'll probably see Dan Salazar. He was a few years ahead of us in school."

"I remember Dan. He was a good guy."

"Still is. He's one of the PE teachers and the freshman football coach. He's also the other faculty chaperone tonight. Some parent volunteers will be there too."

They talked about others they went to school with while Charlie drove up the canyon toward the ski resort.

When he passed the spot of the accident, Charlie grew silent, eyes focused on the road. Taryn said a prayer for her friend, as she always did when she passed the tree, with a small silver plaque erected years ago.

The moment cast a pall over them both, but Taryn told herself she wasn't going to let that ruin the night. Only a few moments later, they approached the beautiful Silver Strike ski resort, luxurious and tasteful against the steep mountains at the end of the box canyon.

"You can park in the event parking," she said.

Charlie nodded and drove around to the vast parking lot on one side of the large ski lodge and hotel complex. He found a place close to the door, then walked around the car to open her door.

"It might be icy. Let me help you," he said, reaching for her arm.

She slid out, wishing for her comfortable boots instead of the heels that perfectly matched her dress. On the other hand, Charlie might not have gripped her arm so tightly if she weren't wearing silly little heels.

She was not about to complain. This was everything she hoped would happen. She wanted to force Charlie to see her in a different light, to make him finally acknowledge the feelings that had been simmering between them forever.

"Beautiful night, isn't it?" She lifted her face to the sky. Hope's Crossing was a Dark Sky community, which meant all outdoor lighting needed to point downward instead of spilling light pollution into the sky. As a result, the stars here were always so spectacular.

Even with dark clouds gathering overhead, stars poked through the gaps like bright gems on velvet.

A few stray snowflakes fluttered down, landing on her cheeks and her furry cape. Charlie wiped one way from her forehead, and Taryn fought the urge to nestle against him and stay right here in the parking lot forever.

"I'm guessing we're supposed to be heading

toward the door with the balloons around it," he said.

She followed his gaze and saw the middle school decorating committee had festooned one door with an archway of red, green and gold balloons. She could see more balloons inside.

"Good guess," she said with a smile. "Let's do this."

As the two of them walked toward the building, her arm still caught in his supportive grip, Taryn savored his touch as she soaked up the heat of his hard muscles against her.

"Do you chaperone a lot of these dances?" he asked as they headed toward the balloon arch.

"We don't have many dances. Only about one a trimester. It's not like the high school, where sometimes it feels like the PTA wants to throw a dance party every other weekend."

"Anything to keep the kids out of trouble."

He said the words lightly but she didn't miss the grim undertone.

They had been the troublemakers, she, Layla, Charlie and their other friends. They had too much time on their hands, too much disposable income to buy alcohol and marijuana, too much resentment toward their parents for trying to mold them all into people they didn't want to be.

That night had followed several days of mayhem, a rampage of vandalism, trespassing and outright theft.

They had all made mistakes during that time. Each of them had paid a steep price.

Layla had suffered most, of course, losing her life and her future. Taryn had faced a daunting rehabilitation. Charlie hadn't been seriously injured in the accident, but he had lost his freedom for nearly a year. Beyond that, he had lost less tangible things. His reputation, but most of all his self-respect.

She squeezed his arm, wishing she could convey again that he needed to forgive himself if he wanted to go on to have a good life.

Maybe inviting him tonight had been a terrible mistake and would only serve to remind him of that night neither of them could forget.

Too late now. They were here and she had a job to do. As soon as she hung her coat in the small closet outside the venue, Dan Salazar—as gorgeous as a Latin pop star and very happily married, to the dismay of most of the ninth-grade girls who had crushes on him—hurried over.

"Hey, man. Good to see you," he said, greeting Charlie with a handshake before turning to greet Taryn with a harried sort of look.

"We've got a problem," he announced unceremoniously.

She raised an eyebrow. "Already? There aren't even any students here yet except the planning committee."

"And therein lies the problem. Ashley P., our

venerable dance committee co-chair, broke up with her boyfriend yesterday. Well, he broke up with her, anyway."

"I hadn't heard that bit of gossip, but I can't say I'm completely surprised. Colton Samuels is the biggest flirt in the school."

"Right. And he apparently flirted his way into a new girlfriend, the other co-chair of the dance and Ashley P.'s previous best friend, Ashley L."

"Oh dear. Awkward."

"More than awkward. It's getting ugly. The Ashleys just had a screaming fight while they were supposed to be helping set up the tables and chairs. I was afraid they were going to start throwing punches and pulling hair any minute so I separated them. Ashley P. burst into tears and ran into the ladies' room a few minutes ago. You should, uh, go talk to her."

Why did she always get assigned the hard jobs? Maybe because her job was a guidance counselor, and Dan's job was to blow his whistle while kids ran around a track.

She gave Charlie an apologetic look. "Sorry."

He made a little shooing gesture. "Go. I'll be fine. I can finish setting up chairs and tables with Ashley L."

"Thanks. I'll find you when I'm done."

By the time she calmed the other Ashley down, no easy task, and convinced her not to let Ashley L. and Colton ruin the event she had worked so hard to organize, Taryn was already exhausted. The two of them returned to the ballroom to find the perimeter lined with chairs and small café tables, and a few other students had started to trickle into the dance. Most were standing in small groups or clustered around the refreshments table.

She found Charlie talking to Dan and his pregnant wife, Lucia.

"Ready to get the party started?" Dan asked when Taryn approached them.

"As I'll ever be."

"I'll let the deejay know."

A few moments later, the thump of bass rang through the ballroom and the first brave students, from the drama and debate club, headed out onto the dance floor.

The demands of chaperoning kept her busy at the start of the dance, first intercepting and heading off a fight before it could begin between a couple of feuding basketball players and then sitting at the entrance to make sure only ninth graders and their guests came in.

After the flow of arriving students trickled off, she traded places with one of the parent volunteers on the dance committee so she could monitor the situation at the refreshments table.

Charlie seemed to find plenty to do. He helped when one of the streamers fell down and he even danced once with Nadia Ali, another member of the faculty who taught French and geography at the school.

Nadia was a year older than Taryn, Charlie's age, and had also gone to school with them. Nadia and Charlie had been friends for a long time and Taryn had always considered her a friend too, but as she watched them dancing and laughing together, Taryn was suddenly aware of a possessive streak she never realized she had.

At least he seemed to be enjoying himself. She didn't see any of the tension she usually sensed in him at various Hope's Crossing social events.

Her path finally intersected with Charlie's when she headed over to grab a drink of water from the refreshment table at the same moment he carried in another tray of star-shaped sugar cookies supplied by one of the local bakeries to replenish the supply.

"There you are," Charlie said with a wry smile that made her heart pound. "This is the single strangest date I've ever been on, especially considering I've only exchanged a few words all evening with the woman who brought me."

"Sorry about that. I should have expected all the drama. It's middle school. Kind of goes with the territory. Thank you for your help. Our PTA president was telling me you've been invaluable at keeping the table stocked with refreshments."

"That isn't an easy task when you're talking

about ninth graders. I swear one kid ate a dozen cookies by himself."

He gestured with his head toward Tommy Rocco, slumped into a chair in the corner and looking a little green.

"You two should get out there and dance together while you have the chance. I can handle the refreshments table for a few minutes," Nadia suggested, and Taryn decided not to hate her after all.

"Shall we?" Charlie asked, holding out his hand to her.

Her pulse seemed to accelerate as he led her out to the floor. They only fast-danced for a minute or two before the deejay shifted the music to a mellow love song.

Around them, the students were pairing off, most with that uncertain hesitancy she found endearing.

She glanced over toward the deejay and saw Nadia walking away with a satisfied smile. Oh yes. She definitely didn't hate her friend now.

Charlie wrapped an arm around her waist and pulled her closer and she slid an arm around his neck, wishing she could sink against his muscular chest and stay there all evening.

At least she could hold his hand for a few moments, and she could feel his other hand around her waist. He was an excellent dancer. She had known that about him from the few times they danced in high school and had been reminded over the summer at his friend's wedding. She would guess that was a byproduct of all those dance lessons his mother required him to take.

She didn't want to think about Laura Beaumont right now, for multiple reasons. Mostly because it always made her sad for Charlie, wishing he could have had a childhood that hadn't been defined by his mother's alcoholism as well as her pretensions and social climbing.

"Are you having any fun at all?" she finally asked.

"More than I expected," he admitted. "I quite enjoyed confiscating a vape pen from a couple of guys."

"My hero," she said.

She spoke the words in a light tone, but they made his jaw tighten as they moved around the dance floor.

Why couldn't he see himself the way she did? As a good, honorable man who worked hard for those in need and always tried to help others? No matter how much evidence to the contrary, Charlie seemed to think the choices he made as a seventeen-year old kid had to define him.

She spotted a familiar girl standing with a few friends in one corner. "There's Chloe Greene. I've been meaning to ask how things are going with the project at her house."

"Oh, right. Chloe. She helped us rip out the

cabinets yesterday. She looks different with her hair up like that."

"How is the project going?"

"Fast. Sage delivered plans to Sam Tuesday, the day after you two looked at the house. Demo's been done to the kitchen and we're doing the bathrooms tomorrow. We should be ready to start installing cabinets Monday."

"Do you really think it's possible to finish before Christmas? I feel so bad about turning Lynette's world upside down during the holidays."

"Sage and Sam are both determined. I'm only the hired help."

"Except nobody's paying you."

"That's true."

They lapsed into silence, and for a few moments, she simply savored the moment, wondering if she would ever have the chance to be in his arms again.

All too soon the dance number ended and a fast dance started up again. She reluctantly slid away from him. "Thank you. I should probably get back to the chaperone thing."

This wasn't at all like that magical wedding over the summer, she realized. She had responsibilities here that went beyond dancing with the man she loved. How foolish she had been to expect things might be different. If anything, their relationship seemed more strained, especially with this new tension between them.

As he returned her to the refreshments table, Taryn had to fight down a sudden ache in her throat. She was going to lose him. She could feel their friendship slipping away, and she had no idea how to grab on to it.

She tried to turn her attention to her duties and was busy pouring some of the spicy wassail into insulated cups when Chloe came over, shifting and looking nervous.

"Hey, Ms. Thorne."

She smiled at the girl. "Hi. Would you like some wassail?"

"I guess."

She took a cup but didn't seem in any hurry to leave. Taryn had enough experience to know when a student wanted to talk to her but didn't know where to start.

"Are you having fun?" she asked gently.

"Um, sure," she said, which Taryn was 100 percent certain was a lie.

"Is something wrong?" Taryn prompted.

After a moment, Chloe looked around to make sure no one was within earshot before she lowered her voice, so low Taryn could hardly hear her. "I really hate to be a narc but I . . . I thought you should know. A couple of kids just headed out to the parking lot, and I heard one of them say he brought a flask of his dad's Jack Daniel's from home."

"Did he?"

She wasn't at all surprised. Though the students in the ninth grade were only fourteen to fifteen years old, Taryn knew some already had substance abuse issues.

She had been fourteen when she smoked her first joint at a party.

"Please don't tell anyone I told you. It's just . . . my dad was killed by a drunk driver, and alcohol abuse is kind of a thing with me. I know they won't be driving, but still. If they have no problem breaking the rules and drinking at a ninth grade dance, it's only a matter of time before they get behind the wheel. I just . . . thought you should know."

Taryn hugged the girl. "You did the right thing, Chloe. Thank you for telling me. I'll take care of it."

"You won't tell anyone I told you, will you?" she asked nervously.

"Told me what?" Taryn said with a reassuring smile, then she turned and headed for the door.

This was one of the toughest parts of her job. She loved helping students think about future careers, directing them to mental health resources if they needed it, working through scheduling problems with classes.

She didn't enjoy having to be the hammer and enforce the rules.

She looked around for Coach Salazar, who was

very good at handling rule-breaking students, but she couldn't immediately find him.

She was tempted to take Charlie with her for muscle if she needed it but quickly abandoned the urge. Despite what she had told him, she really hadn't brought him along to perform bouncer duties.

With resignation, she grabbed her fluffy soft cape from the closet and headed out to the parking lot.

At first, she couldn't see anyone but then she spotted two boys loitering between rows of cars.

Her heart sank. Jake Marshall was constantly in trouble. His father, a former Olympic skier, was operations manager at the ski resort and Jake was the quarterback of the ninth grade football team. Between those factors, Jake seemed to think he deserved special privileges.

Her dad would have called him a cocky little jerk. Or worse. Taryn tried to remind herself there were plenty who thought Charlie was just like him at this age.

The other boy was Carter McClain, smaller in stature and not as athletic but every bit as arrogant.

She headed over to the pair. When they saw her, Jake shoved something in the inner pocket of his suit jacket.

"Hey, guys. What's going on? It's cold out here. The party's inside."

"We're not doing anything wrong," Jake said quickly. Too quickly.

"Yeah," Carter chimed in. "We were just super warm in there and came out to cool down."

"What's in your pocket?" Taryn asked Jake.

"My pocket?" Jake asked, playing dumb.

"Yes. The left breast pocket. I saw you stowing something there as I came over. Can I have a look at it?"

"It's nothing. Just my phone."

"You brought two phones? I can see the other one sticking out of your right pocket. Have you been drinking? If I'm not mistaken, I smell whiskey."

"You can't smell it," Carter said. "There's no way she can smell it, dude."

"Shut up," Jake muttered to his friend.

"Open your coat," Taryn ordered, wishing she were in the halls of the middle school in one of her badass power pantsuits instead of here in flimsy heels and a ridiculous faux fur cape.

"You don't have to do it, dude," Carter said, clearly appointing himself Jake's legal representation. "She doesn't have a warrant."

"A, I'm not a police officer. And B, yes you do. When you bought the ticket for the dance, you and your parents both signed a form stating that you understood the rules and agreed to follow them, which included not bringing any alcohol or other contraband items to the dance. You

189

also agreed to be subject to search if any of the faculty at the dance suspect you broke that agreement. I know what I saw and also what I can smell. Please don't make this harder than it has to be."

"Make me." Jake drew himself up, and she was suddenly aware he was several inches taller and at least seventy pounds heavier. He also had no respect for authority or the adults in his life.

She didn't think he would attack her, but she couldn't be completely certain.

She should have looked harder for Dan.

"Don't make another choice you're going to regret," Taryn said.

"She can't do anything to us," Carter said. "Come on. Let's go back inside."

They turned to go but before they could take a step, a tall, dark shape appeared out of the darkness.

Charlie.

Relief washed over her. She could fight her own battles and figured the threat of suspension or expulsion eventually would have won the day, but she was suddenly deeply grateful she wouldn't have to take on both boys by herself.

"Is there a problem here?"

"No. We're fine. Aren't we, Jake? You were about to show me what you put in your inside jacket pocket."

He hesitated but even with his judgment

impaired, he apparently decided he didn't want to risk messing with Charlie.

"Fine," he snapped. He opened his suit and she could clearly see the top of a silver flask there.

"I found it out here on the ground," he claimed, adopting an innocent expression that didn't fool her for a second. "Carter and I were discussing whether we should turn it in to the hotel front desk or to Coach Salazar."

Did they genuinely think she would buy that? "Why don't you give it to me and I'll take care of it?"

"You don't trust me?" Jake asked.

She held out a hand, and after a moment, he all but shoved it at her. What a coincidence that the flask he found on the ground happened to have his initials, which were his father's as well, etched in the silver in a stylized monogram. JM for James Marshall and Jake Marshall.

"Thank you," Taryn said. "Why don't you head back inside for now? I'll talk to Coach Salazar. I'm sure he'll be interested to see it."

He and Carter both looked at each other, and she could tell it was beginning to sink through their bravado that they were in big trouble.

The young men gave her a look of loathing and then went back inside, leaving her with Charlie.

"What was that all about?"

Taryn sighed. "That was Jake Marshall. His older brother, Tony, went to school with us."

"Ah."

Tony Marshall had been an entitled brat and his brother was following in his footsteps, unfortunately.

"You don't seriously believe they found that on the ground, do you?" His scornful expression perfectly matched how she felt about the situation.

"Not for a second. Nice try. We have a mandatory suspension policy for any student who brings a banned substance to a school event. Jake knows that as well as I do."

"What will you do?"

"I have to tell the administration and he'll likely be suspended. It won't win me any popularity contests with Jake or his family, but it's my job. I have to do my best to keep my students on track."

"Can you really do that?"

"Who knows? Carter and Jake are both headed off the rails. Maybe this will be a wake-up call."

"But you doubt it."

Apparently, he knew her well. "Some students don't want to listen," she said, though Carter and Jake and their issues seemed far from her mind. How could she think straight with Charlie standing so close to her, his body heat drawing her like an open fire?

"Kids are going to do what they want, no matter how hard the well-meaning adults around them try to keep them on track."

"You make it sound like my entire career is a big waste of time."

"It's not. I admire what you're doing," he said, his voice low. "You're dedicated and passionate. Probably exactly what most of these kids need. There will always be outliers. Like Jake and Carter. Like we were."

"That gives me hope. I guess it's my destiny to serve the students at Hope's Crossing Middle School while you're out there helping the world. Thanks for the pep talk."

On impulse, she reached up on her toes and kissed him on the cheek. He made a small, strangled sound. His gaze burned into hers and she wanted to sink into the emotions there, tenderness and affection and what she was almost certain was hunger.

"Charlie."

Kiss me.

She didn't say the words this time, but surely he could see how much she wanted him to.

She was certain he would. His mouth moved toward hers and she held her breath, her heart pounding.

At the last instant, just before he would have finally crossed that invisible barrier, as he had the night of the wedding, he seemed to yank himself back to safer ground. He stepped away.

"We, um, should probably go inside. It's cold out here."

She told herself she was glad he had stopped. She didn't really want to kiss him in the parking lot of the Silver Strike where anyone could see them. She had responsibilities to her students.

Would they ever find the perfect moment, with Charlie so determined to push her away whenever she tried to move things to a different level?

"Yes. You're right. Since there are no more errant teenagers out here in the parking lot, I guess my work here is done," she said, trying for a light tone.

Inside, she had to shove down tears. She was suddenly certain she was pounding her head against a wall. Or at least against one very stubborn man.

Maybe he only needed time.

She sighed inwardly as she followed him back to the ballroom. She had been telling herself for about five years now, that when he was ready, Charlie would open his heart to her.

She was beginning to fear that day would never come.

13

Sage

Her mother was having a hard time leaving, as Sage fully expected she would.

"You'll remember that Anna has to sleep with a night-light, and Nick doesn't like onions on anything, right?"

"You wrote everything down. The schedule for the week, the homework they each have to do, their medical insurance and permission-to-treat forms. Also, you'll only be in France, not on a deserted island with no cell service."

Her mother looked embarrassed. "I know. It's harder than I thought to leave."

"We'll be totally fine. You guys go and have a wonderful time together."

"I'm not sure I remember how to do that," Maura admitted with a rueful laugh.

"Then it's high time you do. You don't need to worry about anything here. We're going to have a great time. We've already got all kinds of plans for what we'll do while you're gone, don't we?"

She sent a speaking glance toward Anna and Nick, who both nodded vigorously.

"Yep." Nick gave his mother a mischievous

195

look. "Sage promised we can have ice cream for breakfast every day, go to McDonald's every night and stay up late to watch scary movies, even when it's a school night."

"Yeah," Anna added, playing along. "And she said we don't have to do any homework either."

"Yep. That's exactly the plan," Sage said, biting down laughter as her mother's eyes widened with alarm.

"That's it," Maura said, setting her slouchy purse on the table. "Your dad can go to the dedication gala in Rouen on his own. I should stay here."

"You totally should not," Sage said. "You need to be there for Dad. This is a big deal for him."

Now it was Nick who looked alarmed. "You can't stay home. We were kidding."

"Yeah. I didn't even want ice cream for breakfast," Anna claimed.

"Anyway, Sage is probably way more strict than you are."

"Probably?" Sage asked.

"Definitely," he said with a grin.

Maura picked up her bag again. "I know I'm being silly. You'll be fine. You're more than capable. It just seems like so much to ask of you this time of year, when life feels so busy. You've got your channel to promote, the renovation of the Greene family's house and finishing the project at Wolf Ridge."

"Yes. All of which I can do around the kids' schedules. You have to go. I have been looking forward to this. We've got all kinds of fun things planned, don't we kiddos?"

Anna nodded. "We're going to have a blast!" she said.

Maura still didn't look convinced when Jack came in a few moments later looking handsome and distinguished.

"Are we ready?" he asked.

"As ready as I'll ever be, I guess," Maura said.

"Thanks again for doing this, Sage." Jack hugged her.

"It's my pleasure," she said again. "Now go, before I change my mind."

After hugs all around, her parents finally left to drive to Denver for their flight. When their car pulled out of the garage and backed out of the driveway, Sage watched them go then closed the door, nerves suddenly jumping through her.

Taking responsibility for two young children seemed easy in theory. Now that she held their safety and well-being in her hands, she wasn't sure why she had ever agreed.

She turned back to Anna and Nick, who were watching her carefully.

"Okay. I guess it's time for breakfast. What kind of ice cream goes best with oatmeal?"

The children giggled, which pushed away her

lingering nerves. She intended to consider this bonus time alone with Anna and Nick a precious Christmas gift and would try to savor every moment.

14
Mason

As he wheeled into the elevator that would take him to the basement, Mason couldn't help remembering the last time he had been here, when he and Sage had shared the tight confines and he had fought the fierce urge to kiss her.

He was spending entirely too much time thinking about the woman. He had found it annoying before, how often she would pop in and out of his thoughts. After the Fire & Ice Festival, she seemed to have taken up permanent residence in his head.

The woman fascinated him. She was brilliant at her career, passionate about inclusion and accessibility. She also seemed to love her family and her community.

She showed a warmth and genuine care for everyone in her circle. Including him. Through-out the design process, he knew he had been demanding and difficult, but she had treated him with patience and unfailing kindness.

He didn't want to think of Sage a dozen times a day. How could he avoid it, though, when he saw her mark everywhere in his new house?

He saw her in the bright, open feel, the creative use of industrial design elements that somehow merged perfectly with nature to bring the outside in, in a hundred clever small touches that would make life easier for him, both when using his wheelchair and when he was moving around with the forearm crutches.

Under her direction, Wolf Ridge was becoming the perfect house for him and for Grace.

The elevator reached the lower level, and Mason wheeled toward the exercise room off the pool area.

The room featured state-of-the-art exercise equipment, plenty of storage and a cushioned floor that would be easy on joints while still allowing him to maneuver easily through the room when using the chair. It also featured a separate HVAC system with extra ventilation so he could control the heat independently from the rest of the house and keep it warmer or colder, depending on his needs.

Sage had really thought of everything.

When he entered, he found Sam Delgado installing various hooks to a huge beam that bisected the room and also ran down the sides. The hooks would hold exercise straps.

"Hey, Mason," the contractor greeted him with a smile.

Mason gestured to the ladder and the drill. "I thought you were the boss. Don't you have guys who could do that?"

Sam smiled. "Sure. But everybody else was a

little busy today on another project so I figured I would try to wrap up a few odds and ends over here."

"Thanks. I appreciate it."

Recommended by Sage, Sam had been fantastic throughout the whole renovation process and had become someone Mason respected and considered a friend.

"This won't take me long. We're almost there in this part of the house. This is going to be a great space. Maybe I'll have to come use it on the days I can't get to the gym."

"You're always welcome," Mason said gruffly. "It's the least I can do. I know I've been a pain to work with."

"Compared to most of my clients, you've been a breeze, believe me."

"Everything has turned out so much better than I hoped."

Sam smiled. "It's a great house. I've loved bringing it back to full glory. I'll be sorry to move on. We have a few more details to finish, but we should be wrapping everything up by the weekend."

"Perfect. That's what I came over to talk to you about. I just got off the phone with the designer. Jean-Paul wants to have all the furnishings delivered Friday and staged over the weekend. I told him I would get back to him after I make sure that still fits with your schedule."

"Should be great. You'll be happy with Jean-Paul. He knows what he's doing."

Jean-Paul Boucher apparently worked regularly with Lange & Associates and had been another provider recommended highly by Sage. His ideas for the furnishings and accessories seemed to jibe exactly with what Mason envisioned. He didn't really have a strong opinion about that part and with Jean-Paul, the process had been simple and straightforward, which he appreciated.

"You've been terrific," Mason said. "I'm really grateful with how quickly you've been able to complete the project."

"I'm glad you're happy with it so far. We're not done working together. We still have the guesthouse."

"Right. Any idea of a time frame for that?"

The space where he and Grace lived now would also receive the same treatment as the main house, a rethinking and reconfiguring of the entire space. When it was done, the guesthouse would boast two bedrooms, two bathrooms, a gourmet kitchen and a private balcony that opened to a view of the valley below them.

"I would like to say we can start immediately, but Sage has kind of commandeered our time for this week and next. We might not be able to start demoing until after the holidays."

Sage again. Every time he tried to push her out of his head, she somehow wriggled her way back.

"What kind of project?"

Sam looked over his shoulder. "You can ask her yourself. Speak of the devil."

Mason whirled around in time to see Sage striding in wearing ankle boots, jeans and a soft sweater that perfectly matched her eyes.

And since when did he notice when a woman's wardrobe coordinated with her coloring?

His hands suddenly felt sweaty, not a good thing when he needed a decent grip to wheel around.

"Oh. Hi."

"Do I want to know what you were saying about me?" she asked, slipping out of her wool coat and draping it and her colorful scarf over the very expensive custom exercise bike his physical therapists recommended.

Sam gave her a teasing smile. "I was complaining about you poaching my time, diverting my crew so I have to delay working on Mason's guesthouse until the new year."

Sage winced. "Sorry. Totally my fault. That's what happens when my ideas get away from me. But you really don't have to divert your *entire* crew. We have plenty of volunteers offering to help."

"It should only be a small delay. We'll get on it right after the holidays."

"What's the project?" Mason asked again, curious despite himself.

Sage shifted, looking uncomfortable. "A widow in town has had a tough break. Her husband was killed by a drunk driver over the summer and left her alone with three kids."

"That's tough."

"Yes. Lynette has some health issues and currently depends on a scooter to get around. We're trying to do some renovations to her house to make it more accessible. The kitchen, bathroom and entrance to the house."

"Right," Sam said dryly. "Only the kitchen, bathroom and front entrance. No problem."

"When did you start?"

"What day is it? Monday? Technically, a week ago. I did the design Tuesday and Sam and his team started ripping out cabinets the next day."

"Wow. You don't mess around."

"This is a much smaller project, for one thing. For another, I have many volunteers lined up. Lots of people want to help. Hope's Crossing is like that, always ready to help when one of our own needs it. I hope this will make Lynette's life a little bit easier."

"Sounds very kind of you and the town."

She sent him a sidelong look. "Full disclosure, I should probably tell you my motives aren't completely pure."

"No?" He wasn't sure he wanted to think about *Sage* and *impure motives* in the same sentence.

"I do want to help Lynette and I'm so happy we can. But I'm also documenting the renovation for my YouTube channel."

She met his gaze steadily. "As I can't video Wolf Ridge while I'm in Hope's Crossing for the holidays, I had to find something else to feature on my channel."

"Sorry," he muttered. To his surprise, he found he wasn't completely lying. He *was* a little sorry he had said no to her.

He still didn't want the whole damn universe looking inside his house. But he couldn't blame Sage for wanting to show off her work to the world, and he didn't like being the one to deprive her of the chance.

"It will be fine. Good, actually. This is a great human interest angle, with the whole town coming together to help one of our own."

"How is it being funded?" he asked.

She glanced at Sam as if for guidance. He pointed back at her. "Most of the contractors and subcontractors donate their time, and we use a lot of volunteer labor," she said, clearly hedging.

"But you still have overhead, don't you?"

She looked embarrassed, for reasons he didn't quite understand. "Yes," she finally said. "All of the revenue from my channel is funneled back into a foundation, Homes for All, which I then use to fund renovation projects for people with mobility needs. I also have a few healthy

205

endowments from local sources. Namely my grandfather. Harry Lange."

"Only because he's a sucker for you," Sam said with a raised eyebrow.

Now he really felt like a jerk for turning down her request to feature his house. "I can write you a check too. It sounds like a good project. Hope's Crossing is my town now, and I want to do my part to help the people who live here."

He had more money than he could ever spend from his ridiculously high salary and endorsement deals from his time in the Major Leagues. He wasn't as frugal and penny-pinching as his grandparents—this luxury home was certainly proof of that. But Mason had protected his wealth through a combination of wise money management and canny investments. He also believed firmly in giving back and took every opportunity to donate generously.

She looked startled at his offer. "That's very kind of you. Thank you. I'll let you know if we run into any problems."

He could still donate to her foundation, even if she didn't need backing for the Hope's Crossing project. Mason was about to ask for more information about where to donate when Sam's cell phone rang.

The contractor excused himself and left the workout room to answer the phone.

"Did you need to talk to Sam about something?"

She held up the rolled tube in her hand. "I just have new blueprints for the Greene project for him to look over. A few changes I made to the bathroom reno. Nothing major." She hesitated. "And, okay, I also wanted to check on the progress here to make sure everything is ready for Jean-Paul and his crew this weekend."

"Sam assures me it is." He shifted in the chair, uncomfortable from more than simply the usual pressure points. "Why didn't you tell me your YouTube revenue goes to a foundation that helps people with mobility needs?"

"I guess I didn't want you to feel undue pressure to agree to something you really didn't want to do."

He did feel pressure, though. Guilt seemed to seep through him.

"I wish you'd told me."

"Would it have made a difference?"

He didn't have a chance to answer before Sam returned. "I've got to run. They've got a problem with the countertops for Lynette's house so I've got to go sort it out. I can come back later to finish up."

"No need," Mason said. "If you don't mind leaving your tools, I can do this. Looks like you're almost done, with only the lower hooks on the wall to secure."

"I hate to leave you with it."

"I can stay and help," Sage offered. "I have a

little time this afternoon. Between the two of us, it shouldn't take long."

"You don't have to but it's your house. Knock yourself out."

Sam's phone rang again, and he sighed as he reached for it on his way out the door.

Mason was suddenly uncomfortably aware that he was alone with Sage. The scent of her, citrusy and sweet, teased his senses. "I don't really need your help. This is a one-person job."

"I want to help," she protested. "I don't have the chance to play with power tools very often."

Would she have offered to stay and help if he wasn't in the damn chair? Mason doubted it. He wanted to tell her he didn't need her pity. He needed . . . something else. Something he didn't want to think about.

"Fine," he muttered.

Every time she moved, he caught that scent of vanilla and lemons, so delicious he had a sudden craving for lemon pound cake from one of his favorite restaurants in Portland.

The first time he tried it, during his rookie season, he thought it was the best thing he'd ever tasted. He had nearly licked the plate clean.

Would she taste like that pound cake?

He had a fierce need to find out, one he quickly suppressed. His body stirred to life anyway, and for once, he was grateful he was sitting down, where he could conceal the unwanted response.

His legs might be unreliable at best, but the rest of him was fine. After the crash, he had been so numb that he hadn't cared. But he was a man, and he couldn't help the vast relief the first time he woke up with a morning erection after the accident.

Right after the relief had come a complicated mess of emotions, especially deep grief.

Shayla was gone. Thinking about being with another woman had left him wracked with guilt, even as he felt more than a little sadness that that part of his life was over now. What woman would want to take on the physical wreck he was now?

"Tell me about your wife," Sage said.

He stared, forgetting what he was doing in his shock. Through the process of designing the renovation to his house, he had sometimes felt as if Sage could see into his soul to know what he wanted even before he did.

Did she know he was thinking about her and sex and guilt, all at the same time?

He looked away. "What about her?"

"What was she like? What first attracted you to her?"

He didn't want to talk about his late wife while his body was responding to another woman entirely.

She had asked, though, and he didn't want to brush aside the question. Over the past week or so, Mason had realized he was coming to see

Sage as a friend. Yes, he was attracted to her, but he liked her too. Friends shared with each other.

"She was sweet and generous," he finally said. "She was also patient. I suppose she had no choice about that one. I didn't make life especially easy for her."

"In what way?"

"Professional athletes often don't make the greatest partners. We're inherently self-absorbed and tend to have egos commensurate with our talent."

"You were very good, weren't you?" she said softly. "The Mighty Tuck. My dad showed me some clips of you at bat. You didn't mess around."

He felt a deep yearning for the game he had loved so much. He could almost smell the stadium crowd, the new-mown grass, the leather and metal and sweat of his catcher's mask.

He missed it almost as much as he missed Shayla.

He could have baseball back again, though. He could always coach or become a commentator, but neither of those held much appeal to him.

He also had Grace to consider. She needed him home with her, not chasing after a time he could never recapture.

"I loved the game," he said. "Except when I had to leave my family for long stretches of time. The baseball season basically lasts from February spring training until October, which meant I was only half there for much of the year."

"How did you meet her?"

Despite the pang of grief, he had to smile at the memory. "Blind date. She almost walked out when she found out who I was and what I did. Her dad was a high school football coach in Oregon. Still is. She had sworn she would never date an athlete."

She arched an eyebrow. "You must have really swept her off her feet to make her break that kind of vow."

"I don't know about that. I was twenty years old, raised in a very strict household where I had barely even gone on a date. I didn't exactly have a lot of game back then."

"Unlike now, when you go all out to charm a woman with your wide variety of scowls and monosyllabic conversation."

Her tart tone surprised a laugh out of him. Her eyes widened slightly, as if she was surprised at the sound. Did she think he didn't have a sense of humor? Probably. He hadn't exactly been a bucket of cheer for a while.

"Yes. I've always found general surliness makes for a winning strategy."

She shrugged. "One might think that would be a turnoff for most women. Somehow on you it works."

He was uncomfortably aware of a sharp ache

inside, a need buried so deeply, he didn't even want to acknowledge it.

He yearned and he didn't want to. He covered it with another of his patented frowns. "You don't have to patronize me."

"Patronize you?" Her eyes widened further. "Is that what you think I was doing?"

"What else? You're not the sort who would find it amusing to make fun of me."

She gave a short laugh. "I hate to break it to you, Tucker, but you still don't have game, especially if you can't tell when a woman is attracted to you."

The moment seemed to stretch between them as hot blood rushed to parts of him that had been cold for a long time.

Damn her for making him feel when he didn't want to. "I know exactly what I have to offer a woman right now," he muttered.

She made an exasperated sound, hands on her hips. "I don't think you do."

"What is that supposed to mean?"

She gazed at him for a few seconds, shook her head as if trying to talk herself out of something, then, before he realized what was happening, she leaned down and kissed him.

At first, he froze in complete shock and couldn't seem to grasp a single thought.

She made a soft sexy sound and before he quite realized it, he had grabbed her and pulled her against him and was kissing her back, tangling his mouth with hers.

How had he forgotten the magic and wonder of kissing a beautiful woman? Of feeling her breath mingle with his, her lips soft and warm as she brushed them against his mouth?

His body surged to life again, and he wanted desperately to pull her across his lap and fill his hands with her skin, her softness, her curves.

They kissed for what felt like forever but was probably only a few delicious moments.

This was a mistake.

The voice in his subconscious started poking at him, strident and sharp and inescapable.

Sage McKnight was not a woman a man could kiss and then forget. Every time he saw her now, he would remember this moment.

She was his architect and they still had to work together. Beyond that, she had deep roots here in Hope's Crossing. He couldn't avoid her, even if he tried.

How was he going to go back to a polite relationship after he had licked the corner of her mouth, felt her hands in his hair and her breasts brushing against his chest?

All of that resonated in his psyche on one level. The rest of him pushed it away, too lost in the scent and taste and feel of her.

Surviving a helicopter crash had taught him life was fragile, ephemeral. Perfect moments like this should be savored, not ruined by self-doubt and regret.

There would be time for all of that later. For now, he wanted to glory in the pulse of his blood, in the dance of her mouth against his, in this life-affirming surge of heat that reminded him that he was still very much a man.

15
Sage

She had made some pretty grievous mistakes in her life, but as Sage wrapped her arms around Mason Tucker's neck, she had the fleeting realization that this very well might be the biggest.

She had no business kissing him, surrendering to the attraction that had been simmering on a low burn inside her for all the months they had worked together on his home.

Mason Tucker was not the man for her.

It had nothing to do with the fact that he used a wheelchair, though she would guess that would be the first thing some other women might use as an excuse.

She personally didn't care about that, especially having witnessed firsthand the deep, admirable bond between her friend Anton and his wife Rachelle. They made it work, facing challenges together.

No, the fact that he used a wheelchair seemed inconsequential to the other truth resonating through her. Sage suddenly knew in her heart that if she gave in to these feelings she had been nurturing inside all these months, she would wind up devastated.

Mason wasn't open to love. He had showed that in a hundred small ways.

Sage felt as if she had spent her entire life chasing after unavailable men who would never fully allow her into their hearts.

She was doing it again now with Mason.

She didn't want to think about any of that. Not now, when this gorgeous man was kissing her like she was all he had ever wanted.

She had never known this kind of all-consuming hunger, this deep ache that left her trembling and unsure and feeling as if her body wasn't her own.

What was she doing? This wasn't her. She had learned her lesson and no longer let her emotions or her needs control her, especially not after the disastrous events of a decade ago.

She had been a heedless, naive girl who had thought she was in love with the handsome, charming Sawyer Danforth, and her thoughtless behavior had significantly altered numerous lives.

Genevieve Beaumont's planned marriage would have been the society event of the year. Instead, she had broken her engagement to Sawyer Danforth and had been bitter and angry at Sage for a long time because she slept with Genevieve's fiancé.

Of course, years later Gen would thank Sage for being the catalyst for her to finally become a strong woman who made her own choices in life and didn't care what anyone else thought about them.

Instead of marrying the well-connected Sawyer, Gen had fallen in love with a wounded, angry bear of a man, Dylan Caine, who clearly couldn't be more enamored of his lovely wife.

That wouldn't happen for Sage, with Mason, for a hundred different reasons.

He was also her client. Kissing him like this was not only foolish to her own heart but, more to the point, was blatantly unprofessional.

She slid away a little, feeling disoriented as the room seemed to spin wildly.

To her shock, Mason looked dazed, his pupils wide and unfocused. She felt exactly the same, as if all she had known and wanted out of life had suddenly been tossed outside into the Colorado snow.

They gazed at each other, their breathing ragged and short.

She didn't know what to say. How could she explain the wild impulse that had driven her to kiss him? She certainly couldn't tell this man that she had been attracted to him since the moment they started working together and had been fighting that attraction just as long.

She had to say something. They couldn't continue staring at each other like this, with the taste of the other's mouth on their lips.

Finally she cleared her throat. "You've got more game than apparently either of us gave you credit. I might be able to feel my toes again in three or four hours."

"Well, that makes one of us," he said, his voice so dry it took her a moment to realize he was making a joke of her thoughtless words.

How on earth was she supposed to resist this man?

"Sorry. That was a dumb thing to say, wasn't it?"

"You would be amazed at how many turns of phrases revolve around mobility. It doesn't bother me."

"I'll try to be more aware of my word choices."

"I'm not the word police. Someone can tell me to take a hike without me being upset because I no longer can do that." He gave her a probing look. "Why didn't you tell me to take a figurative hike just now?"

"I kissed you, remember?"

"I don't think I'll be forgetting anytime soon," he murmured.

"For the record, you have plenty to offer a woman, Mason," she said, her voice low. "You're a great father, a loyal friend, good with your hands."

He gave her an arch look and Sage could feel herself flush. "With tools. Carpentry. Oh, you know what I meant."

She hadn't seen him smile very often. The effect of it was devastating.

"I also think any woman would admire how you have allowed your mother to have a relationship with your daughter, despite your lingering childhood pain, because you know it's in Grace's best interest."

He looked as if he wanted to argue that point but held his tongue.

"That's all very nice. Thank you. Except you forgot one fairly important thing." He pointed with both hands to the wheels of his chair.

She frowned. "The fact that you use a wheelchair won't stop any woman in her right mind. If I were in the market for a relationship right now, believe me, we would be rolling around on that mat over there."

His blue eyes darkened with desire again, and he gave a rough laugh. "If I were in the market for a relationship, we might not have made it that far."

Sage discovered she adored this side of him, playful and sexy. She wanted to bask in it like a cat seeking out every patch of sunlight for a nap.

"I know why I'm not in the market for a relationship," Mason said. "But why aren't you?"

She thought about making some stupid, flippant excuse but he seemed genuinely interested. She figured she owed him at least the truth. "Many reasons," she answered. "For one, I travel too much. Who has time for a relationship when I'm rarely in the same place for a month at a time?"

"Are you sure you're not running away? Which, by the way, is another phrase you probably shouldn't say to someone in a wheelchair, if you're keeping track."

"Thanks for the tip," she said, startled to find herself enjoying the conversation almost as much as she had the kiss.

"Maybe I am running away from deeper relationships," she admitted. "I tell myself I'm in the season of my life when I need to focus on my career to make my own mark, but I would guess it's safe to say I carry a fair bit of baggage from my past."

"From Nick's father?"

She couldn't believe she was having this conversation with Mason Tucker, of all people. She rarely even talked about this with her mom and her close friends.

"Some. Which is ridiculous, really. I know that. I was a silly starry-eyed girl at a vulnerable time in my life. I thought we were in love. For him, I was just a friend with benefits. And not even a very good friend, since he cut off any contact after we . . . were together."

"He sounds like an entitled jackass."

She laughed. "A very good description. He's now a state legislator so he probably fits right in with all the other politicians. How did we get on this topic?"

"You started it by kissing me."

She wanted to do it again. Too bad she didn't have all afternoon to spend here in this cozy workout room, laughing and talking and kissing.

Something niggled at her subconscious, something important she needed to remember.

In an instant, the world outside this room intruded and Sage gasped and looked at her watch. "Oh no! It's nearly three. I have to go. I can't believe I lost track of time."

"What's the rush?" he asked, as if he didn't quite believe her.

"My parents flew to Europe today, and I'm in charge of Nick and Anna until Friday. I told them I would pick them up after school, which gets out in fifteen minutes."

"You can make that."

"I hope so. This does not bode well for the rest of the week, if I'm failing the very first task as their caregiver."

"You'll be fine. Relax. What could go wrong?"

"Please don't say things like that. I'm nervous enough about being in charge. I can think of a million things that can go wrong."

"Good luck then."

She hesitated, knowing she had to leave but unsure quite how to say goodbye. With any other friend, she might kiss them on the cheek, but she had a feeling that wasn't a good idea with Mason. She might end up kissing him passionately again, and she definitely didn't have time for that.

"Bye," she said, suddenly feeling awkward and even a little shy.

"See you."

And that, she thought a moment later as she hurried out to her car, was why mixing business with personal was a really lousy idea.

16
Taryn

When she pulled up to the Greenes' house after school on Monday, Taryn instantly spotted Charlie's pickup parked along the road in front of the house.

Butterflies danced around in her stomach, and she thought about turning around and driving back down Balsam Lane.

She hadn't seen him since Friday night, when he dropped her off at home after the dance and she wasn't at all sure she was ready for another encounter.

In a grim repeat of what had happened at the wedding the previous summer, Charlie had walked her to the door of her house and waited until she unlocked it. With a veiled sort of look, he said a quick goodbye and then turned around to hurry back to his truck without even one of their customary hugs.

It was as if that moment in the parking lot didn't exist, as if he hadn't nearly kissed her.

For years, she had yearned for Charlie to take their relationship from friendship to romance yet he stubbornly refused.

Maybe he didn't feel the same.

Perhaps it was past time she faced cold, hard

truth. Charlie didn't love her. Not like she loved him. He cared about her as a friend, emotions tangled up with guilt and obligation because of their past.

Her chest hurt as if she had taken a vicious fall on an icy sidewalk, knocking the wind out of her.

As much as she wanted to keep driving, Taryn forced herself to park behind his truck and climb out of her SUV, summoning all her strength. She had to face him again, if only to figure out how she was going to navigate this heartache.

Anyway, Charlie wasn't the reason she was here.

The Greenes weren't at the house, she knew. They were currently ensconced in a luxury condo at the resort. Taryn had visited the day before to make sure they were comfortable and had found a glowing, relaxed family. Chloe had told her all about how she and her brothers had gone swimming every day since they took up residence and how Harry Lange had given them all-day passes to the tubing hill at the resort.

"Do we have to go home?" Chloe's younger brother had asked.

Taryn smiled at the memory as she walked toward the porch, where a sign invited volunteers to come in.

When she walked into the kitchen, she found four men working on the new island in the center of the kitchen: Sam, Taryn's father, a guy she didn't know and Charlie.

He wore a long-sleeved Henley work shirt, jeans and a low-slung tool belt. She had to swallow hard and look away so that everyone here couldn't see how bad she had it for Charlie Beaumont.

"Hey, Taryn," her dad greeted her. "If you came to help us, you might want to change out of that pretty sweater."

She shook her head. "I just came to check on things and bring you all a snack. I made brownies for a school potluck tomorrow and have extras."

She was pretty proud of her caramel pecan brownies. Whenever she took them to a school function or party with friends, they received rave reviews and were always the first thing to disappear.

"You're a lifesaver. I'm starving." Sam reached for the plate with a smile. Her dad and the guy she didn't know grabbed one. Charlie, she noted, didn't even look in her direction.

"I can't believe how much work you've already done."

"Thanks to Charlie, here," Sam said. "He's working like a dog. I keep telling him to slow down or he's going to make the rest of us look bad."

At that, Charlie finally looked toward them with an expression she couldn't interpret.

Taryn looked around at all the work remaining. And that was only the kitchen, not the bathroom where Sage had designed a roll-in shower by taking out a linen closet and moving the toilet.

"How are we possibly going to finish the house before Christmas?"

Her dad made a dry sound, low in his throat. "Maybe you and Sage should have thought of that before you came up with the brilliant idea of doing this right now."

"Don't listen to him," Sam said. "You've arranged enough volunteers to help that we can basically keep going 24-7. The only thing stopping us will be complaints from the neighbors about the noise ordinance violations if we end up working through the night."

"That's another reason I'm here," Taryn explained. "I made extra brownies for everyone on the street, to apologize for all the chaos and explain what's going on, in case they didn't know already. I figured I would go drop them off now."

"By yourself?" Her father frowned. "I don't know how I feel about that. Half the houses on this street are vacation rentals, and we don't know anything about the people staying there."

Somehow, she managed to refrain from rolling her eyes. Her father had barely survived having her live three states away in California, too far for him to check up on her constantly.

"I'll be fine," she assured him. "I have pepper spray, if that makes you feel better."

"It would make me feel better if you took someone with you before you start knocking door-to-door."

Her father couldn't seem to stop worrying about her. She understood his fear. If she had almost lost a child, she would probably be overprotective too.

Brodie looked at the other workers in the kitchen, and his gaze landed on one in particular. "Hey, Charlie. You've been breathing sawdust all day. Why don't you take a break and go suck some fresh air into your lungs for a few moments while Tare does a little public relations for our project here."

Charlie looked up with such reluctance in his expression, she was certain he would refuse.

If anyone else had suggested it, he probably would have come up with an excuse, but Charlie liked and respected her father. More than that, he seemed to feel like he owed it to Brodie to do everything necessary to protect her, especially when he still blamed himself for the accident that had nearly killed her.

"Sure," Charlie said after a pause. He laid down the tool he had been using and moved toward her.

Taryn swallowed at the sight of him, gorgeously male. He grabbed a worn denim jacket off a chair in the living room and headed outside.

Laura Beaumont probably wouldn't have recognized her son right now, sawdust in his hair, wearing work clothes, rugged boots and a jacket that had definitely seen better days.

She liked this version of Charlie better than the polished, obnoxious prep school boy Laura had tried to mold him into.

"You don't have to help me," she finally said after they walked out to Lynette's front porch, where a new ramp had already been installed. "My dad worries too much. Nothing will happen to me. This is Hope's Crossing."

"It's his job to worry. And he's right. I've seen a few rough customers driving around the neighborhood during the few days I've been working here. I wouldn't want you to run into any of them on your own."

After several sleepless nights and a day of wrangling students, Taryn was too tired to argue with him. How dumb would that be anyway, when she wanted to spend all the time with him she could before they parted ways?

"Where are the brownies?"

She pointed her key fob to her small SUV and opened the hatch electronically. "I already have them packaged in gift boxes."

"Naturally."

He headed to her vehicle and pulled out a basket filled with small square bakery boxes wrapped in festive ribbons.

"This is a nice idea, but you might not find too many people home this time of day. The guests in the vacation rentals are probably still skiing, and the locals might not be home from work yet."

"I thought of that. I've written little notes we can leave with the boxes, explaining about the project."

"Let's start on this side of the street and then work our way down the other one," Charlie suggested.

They walked to the house next door and knocked. Taryn knew the occupants of this one, an elderly couple who were friends with her grandmother Katherine. They assured her they didn't mind at all about the noise and traffic.

"I'm half deaf and Mary is half blind," Boyd Taylor told her. "We're not bothered by it at all."

"I'm so glad you're doing that to help them. That family are all dears," Mary said. "Even after they had been through such a tragedy, losing their father that way, those children came and helped me weed my vegetables several times this summer and their mother is always calling to ask if we need anything at the store."

"Yes," Boyd said. "Let us know how we can help, won't you?"

After she assured him she would, they took the brownies gratefully and she wished them a good afternoon.

"Good thing you're along to protect me from

the terrifying Taylors," she said in a dry tone to Charlie after they left the house. "Who knows? They might hug me to death."

He shrugged. "Your dad asked. I obeyed."

She wished it were that easy for her, that he would do whatever she asked. She would simply tell Charlie she loved him and wanted happily-ever-after with him, and he would have to obey and do everything in his power to give her what she wanted.

To Taryn's relief, the occupants of nearly all the houses answered their respective doors. Everyone seemed interested in the project, and a couple of snowboarders visiting from Texas in one of the vacation rentals even offered to skip the slopes the next day so they could lend a hand.

By the time they had dropped off goodies to nearly every house on Balsam Lane, the sun had set and Christmas lights had switched on up and down the neighborhood.

"Three left," Charlie said, looking at the basket. "Do you want to go back and check on the places where no one was home?"

"I still don't see any lights on. We can just leave them on the porches, along with the notes. If they have questions, they can always stop by the Greenes' house and ask what's going on."

They retraced their steps, and he waited while she tried one more time. Each house remained dark so she set the treats somewhere protected but visible, hoping neighborhood cats didn't get them first.

"Thank you for helping out, Charlie," she said as they left the final house and headed back. The light snowfall of earlier had slowed to a few stray flakes. "I don't just mean this afternoon. All of it. Working so hard with Sam to get it done before Christmas. It will mean so much to Lynette and her children."

He gave her an inscrutable look. "I was glad for the distraction. It's given me something to do besides rattle around in that big house by myself while I wait for the attorneys to wrap up a thousand details of my father's estate."

"Any progress?"

"Some. The real estate agent spent all day there yesterday, taking pictures. She hopes to list it by the end of the week."

"And then you'll be off again."

Though she tried to speak in a matter-of-fact tone, she feared some of her anguish must have come through in her voice. Charlie stopped and looked down at her.

"I don't belong here, Taryn." He spoke almost gently. "We both know that."

His calm manner had the completely opposite effect on her. She was suddenly furious with him. More angry than she remembered being in a long time.

"Don't tell me what I'm supposed to know,"

231

she said, her voice low and fierce. "I am so sick and tired of you telling me how you don't belong in Hope's Crossing and how much you don't like it here. It's all . . . bull pucky."

He blinked at her. "Bull pucky."

She wanted to swear up a storm at him but working in a school where the students always had their phones out, ready to record, had taught her to hold her tongue when it was necessary.

"Can't you come up with something more original?" she demanded.

"Than bull pucky? That's pretty original."

She frowned at him. "More original than the excuse you are always giving about how you don't belong here in Hope's Crossing and nothing can ever change your mind."

"Doesn't matter whether it's original or not. It's true."

"Hope's Crossing is a wonderful place, full of caring people. Just look at what is happening twenty feet away from you." She pointed at the Greene home.

"I never said there weren't caring people here. But we have different perspectives. You're Taryn Thorne, the town sweetheart. Everyone loves you because they were all invested in helping you heal. I, on the other hand, am Charlie Beaumont. The guy who nearly killed you."

She reached for his hand, desperation giving her a courage she wouldn't otherwise find. "Sure, there might be a few people with long memories who can't seem to let go of the past. Are you seriously going to let them dictate the rest of your life?"

"That's an oversimplification of the situation."

"Is it? Most people treat you like Sam Delgado and my father do. As a friend they like and respect."

He slid his hand away from hers. "On the surface, maybe. But I know what they're thinking."

"That's funny. You never told me you picked up mind reading on your travels."

"I don't need to read minds. I can hear the whispers and see the accusing looks. Why would I want to spend the rest of my life on the receiving end of that?"

"You think people in town can't forgive you for being behind the wheel the night Layla died. As I said, there might be a few. They're the same small-minded people who still gossip about Sage McKnight having a baby out of wedlock and about Claire McKnight's first husband, who left her for his receptionist."

Needing the contact he was trying to avoid, she reached out and grabbed his hand again, cool from the December evening. "The truth is, Charlie, there is only one person in Hope's Crossing who can't forgive you, at least only one who matters. You. You've been running away from that night for years. Aren't you tired yet?"

He made a raw sort of sound, gazing down at her with an intensity that took her breath.

"It was an accident," she said softly. "We were clueless kids who all made dumb choices. Every one of us. You were just unfortunate enough to be the one behind the wheel, but it could as easily have been one of us. Who knows? The consequences might have been even worse."

She pulled her hand away. "You have to decide. Are you going to let that one night dictate the rest of your life? Or are you willing to put it behind you and embrace all that life has to offer you?"

All that I *have to offer you?*

She held her breath, waiting, hoping. He looked as if he wanted to kiss her. She thought he even leaned forward to do it but then he checked the movement and grew rigid, armoring himself with control and discipline.

When he spoke, his voice was as tight as his shoulders. "If we're done here, I need to get back."

The finality in his voice was unavoidable, sharp as a chop saw through her heart.

Pain sliced through her, raw and relentless, and she almost doubled over right there on the sidewalk.

He couldn't have made it more clear. Charlie would never welcome her love. On the night of the accident, he had erected an impenetrable wall between them. He would let her through to be his friend but would push her back if she dared to want more than that.

She felt as if all the dreams and hopes that had carried her for years were spiraling away into the starry sky.

"We're done," she said, her voice low. She clicked open the hatch of her car with the key fob, set the basket inside and then closed it with muscles that seemed to be working in slow motion.

He stood beside the car, his expression closed, and said nothing as she climbed in.

Only when she put the vehicle in gear did he turn to go back into the house.

With tears dripping down her face onto the steering wheel, she drove toward her snug little house a few streets away, where she would have to start trying to figure out the rest of her life.

17
Mason

Nerves crawled through him like hungry spiders as Mason drove through a lightly falling snow toward the Lange house.

He hadn't been able to stop thinking about Sage since the day before, when she had shocked the hell out of him by kissing him out of the blue.

His hands tightened on the steering wheel as those moments flashed in his memory again, her skin warm and soft, her mouth tasting like plump strawberries.

How could he face her again and pretend those moments hadn't happened? He had no idea. If he could have avoided this trip, he would have. What was he supposed to do, though, when Grace had come home after school asking if she could go to Nick's to work on a project for school?

He did what his daughter asked, even if it meant facing the woman he couldn't get out of his head.

"Thanks again for giving me a ride to Nick's house, Dad."

He sent her a sidelong look. "Did you think I was going to make you walk? He lives two miles away from our place."

"I could have asked Grandma to take me. She would have."

Rebecca was always ready to chauffeur Grace where she needed to go, whether Mason wanted her to or not.

"I don't mind taking you," he said. It wasn't wholly a lie. He wouldn't have minded at all, if he were taking her anywhere else but to the home of Sage's parents. Who were in Europe, leaving her in charge.

"Anyway, what's this special project you're so excited about?"

"I can't really talk about it. It's a surprise," she said. She looked away, as if afraid he would glean the truth simply from her expression.

He had a feeling she was making some kind of Christmas present.

"How long will you be?"

"Nick said it might take a few hours. But you don't have to pick me up. He said his sister can give me a ride back home when we're done."

"I'll pick you up. Text me when you're ready to go."

She gave him a worried look. "Are you sure? I know it's not very easy for you to get in the car and everything."

"I'm sure," he said. He immediately regretted his curt tone. It certainly wasn't Gracie's fault her father was a wreck of a man.

"I really don't mind. It's good for me to learn

my way around the streets of Hope's Crossing."

"Okay. I'll text you," she promised as they turned onto the charming street where Sage's parents lived.

"Hey, guess what?" Grace said. "I totally forgot to tell you this earlier. We found out today that real ballet dancers are coming to Hope's Crossing to do a show at the arts center, and guess what it is?"

He had been to a few ballets but wasn't exactly proficient in the various productions available in the world. He quickly said the first one to come to mind. *"Swan Lake?"*

"The Nutcracker!" she exclaimed. "The same one we're doing at our school! It's tomorrow night, and it only costs five dollars if you're a student. Do you think we can go?"

"That would be fun."

"You don't have to take me if you don't want to. Grandma can take me. She said she wants to see it."

"Did she?" he asked woodenly.

"She loves to dance. Sometimes we turn on the radio and dance together. I think she would really like to see the show."

He knew that among her various incarnations, Rebecca had spent time in Vegas. She said she was a showgirl, but his grandparents had basically acted like she had been a stripper. For all he knew, she had been.

"You can ask your grandmother. That's very

thoughtful of her. I can find out tomorrow how to buy tickets for us."

"You want to go?"

About as much as he wanted a colostomy bag. "Sure. It sounds like fun. I love the music of *The Nutcracker*. Especially that 'Dance of the Sugar Plum Fairy.'"

"You can always see it next week when my school does it." She made a face. "Except we're not dancing, only singing. Our show will probably be pretty boring compared to a real ballet."

She sounded glum, as if it had only just occurred to her that putting on a show after only a few weeks' practice would probably not result in a professional-grade performance.

"Are you kidding? I would much rather see fourth-graders singing their hearts out than a bunch of grown-ups dancing. I'll call the arts center about tickets in the morning."

"Okay. Three, right? For you, me and Grandma?"

"Sure thing. Three tickets," he said as he pulled into the driveway of the Lange-McKnight home set among the trees, a gorgeously designed place that seemed made entirely of glass and hewn timber.

He turned off the engine.

"Thanks, Dad," Grace said, reaching for the door.

"Give me a second and I'll come with you to make sure Sage is okay with all of this and to let her know she doesn't have to take you home."

Grace watched him pick up the forearm crutches. "Are you sure? Can't you just text her?"

"I could, but I'm here. It's more polite to talk to her in person."

He swung out of the van, holding on to the specially installed grab bars for support until he had the crutches in place, then he walked with Grace toward the front door.

He had to face Sage sooner or later. He might as well get it over with, while they had the children as a buffer between them. At least he wouldn't pull her into his arms again with three children looking on. At least he didn't *think* he would.

Sage answered the door. She didn't seem her usual polished self. Her curly hair was up in a haphazard messy bun instead of tamed into its usual professional twist. She was wearing a ruffled Christmas-patterned apron and had a slight smudge of flour on one cheek.

He wanted to lick it off and keep going until he had tasted every inch of her.

Her face turned pink when she spotted him. "Mason. And Grace. Hi."

He could look at her all day. She seemed wholly unaware of how very lovely she was, soft and luscious.

"Hi," he said. He should say something more, but all the words in his head seemed to have scattered.

"Come in."

Feeling awkward and uncomfortable, both physically and emotionally, Mason made his way inside.

He hated feeling so ungainly on the crutches. Which was worse? Hobbling his lopsided way inside using the forearm crutches or relying wholly on the wheelchair, which limited his access to places?

After two years, he still wasn't sure.

"Hi, Grace!" Nick bounded down the floating wood staircase, his younger sister right behind him.

"Hi, Grace," she said with her cute lisp.

"Hi, Anna. Hi, Nick."

"I didn't want to just drop Grace off without making arrangements for the time I should pick her back up," he explained, lest Sage think he had followed Grace to the door simply as an excuse to see her again.

Which, okay, might have been part of the reason.

"I was planning to take her back," Sage said. "You don't have to make the trip again."

"It's fine. I'm planning on it. I have errands to run and can swing by when I'm done. Would six give you guys enough time? That's two hours."

"That should be good," Nick said.

Grace inhaled a deep breath. "Your house smells yummy."

For the first time, Mason noticed the scent of something cooking, something rich and comforting, of roasted tomatoes and onions and vegetables.

"What are you cooking?" Grace asked.

"Soup. Minestrone, to be exact."

"I love soup," Grace announced. "It's my favorite thing."

Mason winced as his daughter dropped a not-so-subtle hint.

Sage smiled. "So do I. There's nothing better on a cold day."

"Can Grace stay for dinner?" Anna asked.

"Yeah. Can she?" Nick chimed in.

"Fine by me, as long as it's okay with her father," Sage said.

"Oh please, Dad?"

All four of them looked at Mason with the same looks of entreaty on their faces.

He shifted on the crutches. "You weren't planning on an extra guest for dinner. I wouldn't want Grace to impose."

"She wouldn't. I always end up making far more than necessary. She's more than welcome."

She hesitated for only a moment before she went on. "In fact, if you would like to join us too, there's plenty of soup. I also just mixed up some dough for fresh bread sticks."

Mason figured it would be rude to admit he wasn't sure he should spend any more time with her, especially now that he was so painfully aware of her.

"Please?" Grace asked again. She looked so excited at the possibility of having dinner with her new best friends, and Mason didn't want to disappoint her. It seemed churlish to refuse a direct invitation. But then rudeness seemed to be completely on brand for him right now.

"Sure. That's very kind of you," he managed to say, which earned exclamations of glee from the children.

Sage, he noticed, smiled again, but he was almost positive he saw nerves flash in her expression.

"Why don't I take care of dessert?" Mason suggested. "I'll run in and grab a pie from the Center of Hope Café in town."

"I can never say no to one of Dermot Caine's pies," she said with a laugh that seemed to sing through his veins.

"Great."

"Why don't we say dinner at six thirty? The breadsticks need a few hours to rise, and that will give you plenty of time to go downtown and run your other errands."

"I'll see you in a few hours, then. Be good, Grace."

"I will. Thanks, Dad." She wrapped her arms around his waist in a tight hug, and he balanced on the crutches so he could hug her back.

Sage grabbed the door for him, which meant he had to brush past her on his way out the door. The smell of her, citrusy sweet, tantalized him long after he reached his vehicle and climbed back inside.

By the time six thirty rolled around, Mason was asking himself what the hell he was doing.

After that stunning kiss the day before, he should have taken a solemn vow to stay away from Sage, not make up some flimsy excuse to see her again and then agree to have dinner with her.

What was the point in torturing himself? Sage McKnight reminded him of all the things that were now out of reach.

If he could figure out a way, he would make his apologies, pick up Grace and return to Wolf Ridge.

He couldn't do that to his daughter. To any of them.

As he couldn't back out now, better to suck it up and be polite through dinner. After that, he would do his best to return to a safe distance between them.

Anyway, what did he think was going to happen when they would be sharing a meal with three children?

He parked in the driveway of her parents' house again.

As he made his way toward the house gripping the bag that contained the boxed pie from the café, Mason drew in a deep breath of mountain air.

After his childhood in the flat farmland of Nebraska, he loved living amid the Colorado mountains, solid and comforting.

It was snowing steadily now, but someone appeared to have recently shoveled off the walkway. Sage? He didn't know whether to be touched or embarrassed that she had most likely ascertained how difficult it was for him to maneuver the crutches over ice and snow.

She opened the front door before he could knock. Her nose was a little pink, as if she had just come in from the cold. She had also tamed her hair a little, which gave him a pang. He liked the curls.

He looked around. It seemed suspiciously quiet. "Where are the kids?"

"Anna's room. She's got a table in there, and apparently they needed room for their big project. I'm trying not to pry but I've made a point to knock a few times to check in and they quickly hide whatever they're working on. I've heard a lot of giggling and whispering coming from there."

"Any hints what it might be?"

"It's Christmas. Even if I knew, do you really want me to spoil the surprise?"

"I suppose not."

"Their options are fairly limited. Maybe a picture of some kind? They do have all the markers and crayons out. I don't know. I guess you'll have to wait until Christmas to find out."

He tried to summon up excitement for the upcoming holiday but couldn't find much. Christmas had always been simply another day for him. His grandparents hadn't celebrated it, at least not in the traditional sense of the word. As fundamentalist Christians, they believed Christmas was a pagan holiday, full of idolatry and commercialism, more about Santa Claus than the birth of Jesus.

If anything, their rules about no television were enforced even more strictly during the holidays, as if they feared one little glimpse of Santa Claus would send Mason spiraling to hell.

"Why don't you come into the kitchen?" Sage suggested now. "The breadsticks should be coming out of the oven shortly, and then everything will be ready. I'm setting the table now."

She looked at the bag from the café dangling from his hand, and he could tell she wanted to offer to take it for him. She said nothing, though, which he appreciated.

"Wow. It really does smell good in here."

That mouth he had kissed the day before tilted into a pleased smile. "Thank you for saying so, but I do feel I should add another disclaimer about

247

my cooking. My breadsticks are misshapen, and I probably added too much Parmesan to them."

"I'm sure they'll be delicious. You have to be better than I am. I cook grilled cheese sandwiches and food in the microwave. That's about it."

She glanced at him. "How do you manage?"

"From a wheelchair, you mean? I usually try to stand when I'm cooking, but it's not always easy."

"I wasn't thinking about that at all, if you want the truth. Though I will say that with the adjustable height countertops, your new kitchen is exquisitely designed for people of all abilities who want to cook there."

"It is amazing," he agreed. "But I'm afraid most of the features will go to waste on me."

"That's what I meant. You're a single father with a daughter who needs to eat healthy food. You can only feed children so much fast food and processed frozen meals, apparently, as my mother was quick to remind me before she left town."

He was completely charmed by her. He didn't want to be. But then, he didn't want to have legs that didn't work either. Apparently both were his reality now.

"I cheat," he confided.

"Oh?"

"Rebecca likes to cook and she ends up making something for us a few times a week, which I have to admit I very much appreciate. The rest of the time, I work with a personal chef who stocks my freezer with healthy, ready-to-make food, all with clear instructions. I only have to pop one in the microwave or slow cooker. All the delicious taste with none of the work. Or at least not much of it."

"That's brilliant."

When she smiled at him like that, he felt brilliant. He also wanted to yank her into his arms again and explore that soft, delicious mouth.

Their gazes locked and he saw her swallow, desire flaring in her eyes.

How was he supposed to resist her when she looked at him like that?

All of his lectures to himself about how their earlier embrace was an anomaly they couldn't repeat seemed pointless, especially when the urge to kiss her again surged through him with relentless ferocity, like a flash flood breaking through the banks of his self-control.

Grasping for sanity, for any handhold of control, he reminded himself why this was a bad idea. He had a dozen reasons not to kiss her again.

None of them seemed to matter right now, when she looked warm and soft and lovely.

"Sage."

That was all he said. Only her name. She gazed at him, swallowing hard again. In her gaze, he saw the same confusion and conflict he was fighting.

She wanted him.

He didn't know why or how she possibly could. He only knew he couldn't resist the pull of her another moment.

18

Sage

She held her breath, aware of each pulse of her blood, each beat of her heart as he moved closer.

She wanted to kiss him again, to taste him again and be surrounded by the intoxicating scent of him. This time was different. He was standing up, using the kitchen counter for support behind him, and he towered over her, making her intensely aware of how big he was.

"I have not been able to get that kiss out of my mind," he said, his voice hoarse as if the words had been wrung out of him against his will.

"Same," she admitted softly, even though she knew perfectly well she shouldn't tell him that.

His gaze sharpened. Mason had a way of looking at her as if he could see every thought, every secret dream.

She really hoped not. If he had any idea how much she ached for him, he probably would grab his daughter and rush out the door.

"I would like to kiss you again," he murmured, asking the permission she hadn't thought to when she kissed him the day before.

"Even though we both know it's a mistake?"

He gave a short, rueful laugh. "Maybe *because*

we both know it's a mistake. I can't seem to get you out of my head."

This was the part where she should be the strong one and tell him that all the reasons they shouldn't kiss should carry far more weight than the one reason they should. Because they both wanted it.

She couldn't find the words. She couldn't find *any*. Instead, in tacit permission, she took a step closer and lifted her face to his.

His eyes blazed and he made a low, hungry sound then lowered his mouth to hers.

Yes. Where their first kiss had been a shock to both of them, coming out of nowhere, he kissed her now as if he had been thinking about it, remembering it. As if he had learned her mouth the day before and now wanted to sear the taste of her into his memory.

She could feel heat and strength emanating from him, seductive on a cold winter night. She wanted to lean against him and soak it up.

He pulled her against him, and the feel of his hard chest and strong arms left her aching for more.

His tongue licked along the edge of her mouth and she opened for him, heat pooling inside her as the kiss intensified.

He eased away from her, his blue gaze locked with hers. "You're enough to knock a man clear off his feet, Sage McKnight," he murmured.

Sage swallowed, not knowing until that moment how very desperately she needed the words.

"Good thing you have me to hold on to, then," she murmured. His gaze flared hotter, his arms tightened and he kissed her again, until both of them were breathing hard.

The timer on the oven chimed at the very same moment Sage heard the clatter of feet coming down the stairs. Somehow the sounds together managed to penetrate through the fog of heat and hunger.

The children would burst into the kitchen at any moment. The last thing she wanted was for his daughter and Nick and Anna to stumble through the door and find the two of them wrapped in each other's arms.

But, oh, she hated ending the kiss.

Somehow she found strength to ease away from him barely in the nick of time before all three children rushed into the kitchen.

"Are the breadsticks ready?"

Sage had to clear her throat twice to make any coherent words emerge. "That's the timer for me to take them out," she answered Anna.

"They smell soooo good. I'm starving," she declared. "I could eat every single one."

"So could I," Grace agreed.

Nick, however, gave her and Mason a suspicious look, as if he sensed something crackling in the air.

He was the first one to come through the door. Had he seen more than she wanted him to?

"So is dinner ready?" Anna asked.

"Five minutes," she managed to say. "Why don't you all finish setting the table?"

"Okay," both girls said at the same time, while Nick continued to study them.

What was he thinking, this child she loved with all her heart?

After a few seconds, he seemed to shrug off the moment and moved to help finish setting the table.

"What can I do?" Mason asked.

Oh, I think you've done enough, kissing me until I can't think straight.

"Can you take the filtered water pitcher to the table?"

"I think I can manage that."

To her relief, the children chattered enough through the hearty, comforting meal to make up for her and Mason's distraction.

She always found the conversation of Anna and Nick entertaining. They were smart, curious little humans, with wide and varied interests, from dinosaurs to their favorite video games to books they had checked out of the library.

Adding Grace to the mix turned out to be a delight, as the conversation encompassed everything from their Hogwarts house to a fan theory they had seen on YouTube about the latest Disney animated movie.

She and Mason didn't have to say much at all, which Sage found a relief. She was still feeling shaky and off-balance after that kiss.

"That was all really delicious," Mason said after his second bowl of soup.

"I think it was the best soup I ever had," Grace informed them.

"That is quite a compliment. Thank you," Sage said, smiling at the girl.

She found Mason's daughter sweet and unaffected. Considering all the girl had been through in her young life—losing her mother as well as dealing with her father's serious injuries and long recovery—Grace was remarkably mature for her age, with an expansive vocabulary and a clear compassion for others.

"I'm glad you could have dinner with us," Sage said, which earned her a bright smile from the girl.

"I can't believe I almost forgot to tell you guys," Grace said. "We're going to see *The Nutcracker* tomorrow. The real ballet! My dad said he was able to get three tickets for me, him and for my grandma."

"Hey!" Anna exclaimed. "We're going tomorrow too. I wonder if we'll see you there."

"The Hope's Crossing arts center is not exactly huge, so I imagine there's a good chance we will run into each other," Sage said.

"Yay," Anna said.

"Do you want to know something interesting? The arts center is named for our grandmother."

"Really?" Grace's eyes went wide.

Sage nodded, feeling a little sad to think of her grandmother, Jack's mother and Harry's first wife. Sage had never known Bethany as she had died before Sage was born. Sage only knew she struggled with mental illness all through Jack's childhood.

Her death and the aftereffects had contributed to the final rift between Jack and Harry, which had resulted in Jack leaving Hope's Crossing and staying away for the next twenty years.

"Yes. It's named for my grandmother, our father's mother. The Bethany Lange Arts Center. And our dad designed the whole building. Do you know what acoustics mean?"

"The way sound waves travel," Grace said promptly.

"That's a big part of it, though people in all kinds of areas can research acoustics, from those who study the ocean to engineers to medical researchers. In this case, I was talking about music and sound waves. The acoustics inside our small arts center are supposed to be some of the best in the world. Professional performers come here to practice and record because they love the way it sounds inside there," she said.

"Cool!" Grace exclaimed. "Now I can't wait to see the ballet even more."

"I love to see the dancers," Anna said. "The Sugar Plum Fairy is my favorite."

"I can't wait to see Herr Drosselmeyer," Grace said. "I bet he won't be as good as you, Nick."

Nick seemed both pleased and embarrassed at her praise. "Except I can't dance."

"I'm sure both performances will be great in their own way," Sage said.

"Hey, we should go together," Grace suggested brightly.

Sage instinctively wanted to protest. She would need more than twenty-four hours to process the disturbing truth that she had zero self-control when it came to Mason Tucker.

"Not a bad idea," he said, before she could come up with an excuse. "We're both going to the same place, and carpooling is good for the planet. What do you think?"

She was already spending more time with him than was wise. Their lives were becoming far too entwined.

She was going to leave Hope's Crossing at the end of the holidays with a broken heart. She could sense it lurking just over the horizon.

She should say no. It wouldn't be that hard. She could make some excuse about scheduling and seating. How could she refuse, though, when the children were all gazing at her and Mason with so much expectation in their eyes?

"Sure. Sounds like a great idea. We likely won't

be seated together, though, since we bought our tickets separately."

"That's okay," Grace assured her. "At least we can see each other on the way there."

"We planned to grab dinner somewhere in town close to the arts center before the show. Since I owe you a meal after this delicious soup and of course the lopsided breadsticks, would you all like to join us? It won't be anything fancy. I was thinking Tex-Mex. Maybe Estrella or La Gente."

"Both good choices." Her aunt Alex was good friends with the chefs of both.

"My grandma is going too," Grace informed them again, clearly excited at the prospect.

"That's nice," Sage said, touched all over again at his efforts to include his mother in Grace's life.

"Can we go, Sage?" Nick asked.

Her instincts warned her against spending more time than necessary with Mason to protect her heart as much as possible. At this point, it probably wouldn't do any good, she had to admit.

Maybe Sage could help negotiate some measure of peace between him and Rebecca. He tolerated his mother now, but wouldn't it be better if he could actually forgive her and move forward to build his own relationship with her?

"Dinner would be lovely," she said quickly, before she could change her mind. "Any time I don't have to cook is a win, as far as I'm concerned."

"Great. The show starts at seven thirty. Why don't we have dinner at six? It's early, but before is probably better than after on a school night."

"Definitely." Hungry children probably wouldn't enjoy *The Nutcracker* nearly as much.

Nick, Anna and Grace all looked thrilled at this development. "I can't *wait!*" Grace exclaimed.

"Me neither," Nick said. "May we be excused? We're not quite done with our . . . with what we were working on."

"Grace and her dad probably have to leave."

"Ten more minutes, I promise. That's all."

"Fine with me," Mason said.

"Okay. But clear the table and load the dishwasher first, then you can go," Sage said to the children.

She expected the order to be met with groans, but they only nodded and went to work.

Sage sat back in her chair. "I might even enjoy cooking if I had willing minions to come behind me and clean up," she joked.

Mason smiled and her heart seemed to give a little lurch. She loved seeing him smile, when the stern lines of his face relaxed and the man she suspected was the real Mason emerged briefly.

"Looks like it hasn't stopped snowing," he said, gesturing toward the window.

"I should probably go out and shovel again, at least clear the sidewalk so you don't have to battle ice on your way out."

He reached for the crutches beside him on the floor and rose. "I can help."

Oh, he was a stubborn man. "The whole point of clearing the sidewalk right now is to make sure you don't fall. It kind of defeats the purpose if you insist on going outside with me to help."

He gave her a steady look. "I am not an invalid, Sage. I can still do plenty of things."

Yes, she was aware. Like kissing her until she felt like her bones would dissolve.

That wasn't what he meant, she knew, and she felt a pang of guilt.

"I'm sorry," she said, immediately contrite. "That was wrong of me. It must be so frustrating when people want to make decisions for you about what you can and can't do."

He looked startled, as if he hadn't expected her apology. "I am probably more prickly about it than I should be, as I figure out how to navigate this new world."

"You have to speak up for yourself. I've had to learn through my work that communication is everything when it comes to negotiating the needs of people of differing abilities. I have a bad habit of assuming one thing when the reality is far different. I'm sorry. I'll try not to do that again."

"Thank you," he said, looking touched. "And I will do my best to remember that people in general usually aren't trying to patronize or marginalize me. Most people are trying to figure out the way forward right alongside me."

"If you would like to help me shovel, I would be grateful."

The children were finished in the kitchen. It wasn't perfect, with a few splotches on the countertop and they hadn't started the dishwasher, but they had done an excellent job, for the most part.

"Hey, kids," she called up the stairs.

A moment later, Nick poked his head out of Anna's bedroom. "What?"

"We're heading out to clear the driveway and the walks. Do you guys want to come help?"

"Can we build a snowman after we're done?" Nick asked.

"In the dark?"

"We can see enough. It's a full moon. Did you know the December moon was called the Cold Moon?"

"I did not," Sage answered. "Thanks for the info. I don't know about a snowman. It's getting pretty late. Grace and her dad might need to head back."

Grace had popped her head out of the room as well by now. "Can we, Dad?" she begged.

"It won't take long, especially if we're all working together," Nick pressed.

Mason looked torn but then finally shrugged. "Sure. Why not?"

They all threw on coats, gloves and boots. She found an extra pair of her dad's gloves for Mason, who didn't have any. When they walked outside, the snow had stopped and everything was still, silent.

The inside of the house was charming and festive, with live fir trees growing in baskets in all the bedrooms and greenery on the mantel and the stairways. Her parents didn't have many exterior decorations, though, only a trio of birch trees spangled with snowflake lights.

Up and down the street, she could see Christmas lights twinkling against the dark night.

It only took a few moments to clear the inch or two of snow from the driveway. When they finished, the children immediately put down their shovels and started building a snowman while Sage and Mason cleared around the mailbox.

She could tell it wasn't easy for him to balance on the Lofstrand forearm crutches while he pushed the shovel, but he didn't slow down or give any indication it was a struggle.

At first, she was nervous he would fall but after a few moments she forced herself to relax. He had boots with good treads and he was being careful, she saw.

And if he fell, she was absolutely sure Mason could pull himself back up again.

As soon as the walkway was moderately cleared, the kids started building a snowman while she and Mason worked on the sidewalk in front of the house.

"There's something magical about Hope's Crossing at Christmas time," Sage said. "When I was a kid, I thought it was the most wonderful place in the world."

"You've traveled all over. What do you think now?"

"I love the Bay Area. Don't get me wrong. But Hope's Crossing and the holidays just go together like hot chocolate and marshmallows."

He smiled at her words, and she had to tell herself the flutter in her stomach was only her core muscles complaining about the exertion of shoveling.

"What about you?" she asked. "Why did you decide to settle here? You must like it or you wouldn't have bought a house in Hope's Crossing."

He appeared to consider as he held himself upright with one hand while pushing snow off the steps with the shovel held in the other.

"I do like it. Years ago, I came out to visit Spence Gregory along with some of my teammates. We were doing a fundraiser for the Warrior's Hope foundation he and Charlotte work with."

"Oh yes. Of course. That's a great organization."

Sage knew Charlotte and Spence Gregory had created the program as a way to offer recreational therapy opportunities to veterans who had sustained life-changing injuries. The impetus had been when Dylan Caine, Charlotte's brother, had returned from serving in the Middle East without one hand and one eye. In the nearly a decade since, the program had gained world recognition and had served hundreds of wounded warriors and their families.

"I was just a dumb jock with more money than sense, but I fell in love with the area. It was summer and everything was beautiful and green. I remember thinking it was the most gorgeous place on earth. I loved all of it. The scenery, the downtown area, the people. Especially the people. Wolf Ridge happened to be for sale so I bought it, both as an investment and because I liked it here so much. I thought it would be a good off-season place. It didn't quite turn out that way."

"Why not?"

"Shayla didn't hate it here but she preferred Portland, where her parents live, and the Oregon Coast. We bought a vacation house in the Manzanita area and spent a lot of our free time there so I rented out Wolf Ridge. It went downhill from there, I'm afraid."

The place had been in bad shape when Sage had first taken on the renovation.

"After the crash, I couldn't stop thinking about how at peace I had always felt here," he added quietly. "I felt like Grace and I both needed a new start after everything. Renovating Wolf Ridge seemed . . . right. I can't really explain it. Like this was where we needed to be."

She wished she had known all of that before she started working with him on the house, after Charlotte and Spence recommended her to him. Knowing his reasons for relocating wouldn't have altered any of her designs for the house, but she couldn't help regretting that she hadn't probed harder. She had a feeling, though, that Mason wouldn't have been comfortable sharing anything like that with her when they first started working together.

"How do you feel now, after being here for several weeks?"

"It still feels right. Grace loves school here. She's already been skiing a few times and loved it. She has made good friends. Anna and Nick, especially."

"They do seem to like each other."

"I'm glad we're here. Grace doesn't seem like the same sad, lost shadow of a girl she's been for the past two and a half years."

"What about you?"

"People here have been kind, in general. I'm still finding my way, trying to figure out what I'm going to do with the rest of my life."

Without baseball.

He didn't say the words, but she sensed them

anyway and her heart ached for him. What would she do if she suddenly lost the ability to design, all the skills and tools that enabled her to have a career she loved so much?

"What are some of the options?"

"Still working on it," he admitted. "Nothing seems the right fit for now. I don't have any interest in being a commentator or a coach, which are some of the offers I've fielded over the past year. I don't know. I can't sit around on my butt all day."

She knew that since the crash, he had been working through intensive physical therapy to come as far as he had.

"When it feels right, you'll know. You're lucky enough to have the freedom to take your time."

"I guess."

Nick came over to them before she could probe a little more.

"We need someone tall. Do you think you could help us?" Nick asked Mason.

"Help you do what?"

"We have to put the head on the snowman, and none of us can reach that high."

While she and Mason had been talking, the children had finished, she realized, working only by porchlight and the Cold Moon filtering through the clouds.

"That looks amazing," Sage said. The two large snowballs together were as tall as she was. She had no idea how they had built a snowman that big in a relatively short time.

"It's not done yet," Grace said. "We need the head. Can you help us, Dad?"

"I'll have to see."

He made his way carefully across the snow, Sage holding her breath with each step, hoping he wouldn't fall.

When he reached their creation, Mason sized up the situation. To pick up the large ball they had rolled for the snowman's head, he would have to use both arms, which would leave him without support from the forearm crutches.

He looked back at Sage. "I might need some help keeping me steady."

That he would actually ask for her help felt like a huge leap forward in their friendship, since she knew how hard it must be for him.

"You've got it," Sage said, touched and honored at his trust. "I'll be right here."

Something kindled in his eyes, something warm and almost tender. "Stand behind me while I lift. I expect I'll be fine, but I don't want to fall into the snowman and knock the whole thing over."

She stood close by, ready to offer help if he needed it, while Mason reached down to pick up the snowman's head.

This was how a good relationship should be, she thought. How her parents' was.

Everyone had weaknesses, wobbly parts that

weren't as strong as they would like. Maybe a good relationship meant finding someone willing to step up and help give support when needed. And, maybe more importantly, being willing to ask.

She was *not* in a relationship with Mason Tucker other than the professional one of architect and client.

The assurance she gave herself rang hollow after the heated kisses they had shared and these tender feelings growing to life inside her.

She was falling for him.

The truth of it seemed to settle into her bones, into her heart. Her feelings for him had been growing from the moment she took the commission to design the renovation of Wolf Ridge. She had certainly worked harder on the project and was more excited for its completion than anything else she had achieved in her career.

"There you go," Mason said, grabbing on to his forearm crutches again once the head was firmly set on the trunk. "It looks great."

"It really does," Sage agreed. "Mom and Dad will love it. We can even hang a sign that says Welcome Back on Saturday."

"Thanks, Mr. Tucker."

He smiled at the children. "It's late, Gracie. We need to go. You all have school tomorrow."

She made a face but nodded. "I just have to grab my backpack. It's in the hallway."

"I'll get it for you," Nick offered.

A few moments later, they were loaded into Mason's vehicle. She, Nick and Anna stood on the step watching them back out of the driveway.

"That was fun," Anna said, her last word almost swallowed up in a giant yawn.

"It was, but if we don't go inside soon, my boots might freeze to the porch."

The children giggled, and they went back inside the warm house. Sage followed more slowly, wondering how she possibly would be able to return to normal life after the magic of this holiday season in Hope's Crossing.

19

Mason

This wasn't a date, Mason reminded himself for about the hundredth time as he drove his SUV through the festive streets of Hope's Crossing toward the Lange house.

If he needed a reminder, he only had to look at the passenger seat where Rebecca sat next to him, hands folded on her lap and a look of pure anticipation in her eyes. In the back seat, Grace was practically bouncing out of *her* seat.

Definitely not a date. Simply an outing with his family and Sage's, as he had been telling himself all afternoon.

So why were nerves jumping through him like the first time he had gone to the plate in his first Major League game?

"I've never seen *The Nutcracker* in real life," Rebecca admitted.

"Never?" Grace asked, clearly shocked.

"Not a live performance, anyway. I've watched it on TV before, plenty of times. I imagine seeing an actual ballet will be quite different. We're in for a treat, aren't we?"

In the rearview mirror, he saw Grace's eyes sparkling. She was more excited than he had seen her in a long time.

He thought again that this move had been undeniably good for her and was suddenly grateful for whatever instinct had told him moving to Hope's Crossing was exactly what they both needed.

"I'm so glad we get to go with Nick and Anna and Sage," she said. "I would have been excited anyway, but going with them will make it even better."

"Definitely," Rebecca agreed. "I've found that wonderful moments are always more fun when you can share them with friends."

"Do you know if any of your other friends from school will be going tonight?" Mason asked as he turned the corner onto the Langes' street.

"Only like most of the kids from my class. Miss Suarez asked us this afternoon who would be going and almost everybody raised hands. I think we all want to see the ballet version before we do our show next week."

"Makes sense," he said as he turned into the driveway.

"Oh look!" Grace exclaimed. "There's our snowman. He's even bigger than I remembered! Grandma, we made that guy last night. Me and Nick and Anna. Isn't he the coolest? Dad and Sage helped put on the head."

"Did you?" she asked, clearly curious.

"Yes. We had dinner with them last night," Grace said. "Sage made soup and breadsticks. It was *so* good."

"Dinner two nights in a row?" his mother murmured. "Plus ice skating the other night?"

He frowned, not wanting to get into this with Rebecca right now, with Grace in the back seat. "Grace and Nick are good friends. They're working on a project together. When I dropped her off, Sage invited us to dinner. We decided we should repay the favor tonight. No big deal."

"You don't owe me any explanation," his mother said, though her curious expression certainly invited one.

He decided silence was his best option here and opened his door to get out. This might not be a date, but he still wasn't about to sit in the car and honk for Sage.

"Oh, stay here," Rebecca said. "Grace and I can knock to let them know we're here."

Before he could argue, she and Grace both exited the vehicle and hurried toward the house, leaving him feeling awkward and slow.

Probably better this way, he told himself, though he still didn't like it.

As he waited for them to return, Mason reminded himself of all the reasons why he needed to set aside this attraction to Sage McKnight.

The biggest of all was that he was sitting here in the car with these useless legs while his mother and daughter were collecting their guests.

He shifted and curled his hands on the steering

wheel, mostly to keep from punching something.

He hadn't gone to the door to pick her up, but he could at least open the vehicle doors for everyone. He slid out and made his awkward way around the vehicle until all four doors were open.

Though it was harder for him to climb in and out, he had brought the big Suburban because of the third row of seats. Rather than climb back inside, he leaned against the vehicle, lifting his face to the surrounding mountains.

Unlike the night before, when they had cleared the walks and the children had created their mammoth snow friend, tonight held no trace of a storm. The night was clear, with that Cold Moon and a wild sprawl of stars.

That was one of the things he loved about Hope's Crossing, how the night sky was allowed to shine in all its glory.

He had always loved looking at the stars. When he was a kid, fighting against the cold formality and endless rules of his grandparents' house, he couldn't wait for the Perseid meteor shower every August. Night after night, he would sneak out his bedroom window with a blanket and lay in the back of his grandfather's old pickup truck, watching meteorites streak across the sky.

Those starry nights were one of the few pleasant memories he had of his childhood, until he had started playing baseball in high school and discovered he had natural talent.

December featured another meteor shower, the Geminid. It was probably happening around this time, but Mason wasn't about to lay in the Colorado cold to catch a glimpse of shooting stars.

Maybe when the house was done, he could float in the pool and look through the skylights.

He was suddenly quite certain he would think of Sage when he did it.

And then in a rush, she was there, laughing and bright in a red wool coat and checked black-and-white scarf. She was holding her sister's hand, both of them clearly dressed up. Anna wore a pretty red dress and had a big bow in her hair. Sage, dressed in green, wore her wavy hair in a neat updo. Her dangly crystal earrings glinted brighter than the stars and she looked so beautiful, that delicious mouth painted a soft rose, it was all he could do not to yank her against him and do his best to mess up her lipstick.

"Hi," she said, her voice sounding slightly breathless.

"Evening," he said, his own voice gruff.

"Did you say hi to our snowman?" Anna asked. "His name is Robert."

He fought a smile. "Robert? Why Robert?"

Sage shrugged her shoulders in a *who-knows* sort of gesture. Before he could press the matter, his mother arrived with Nick and Grace.

"Sage, why don't you sit up front?" Rebecca suggested. "I'll sit back here with the children."

"Oh no," she said quickly. "I'm perfectly fine in the back. I don't need the legroom you do, unfortunately."

Mason wanted to tell her she was perfectly proportioned, curvy and luscious and exactly right.

Lord. What was wrong with him?

"Well, I won't argue with you," Rebecca said. "Mainly because I don't want to leave Mason standing out in the cold."

The three children piled into the back bench seat, leaving Sage to sit alone in one of the captain's chairs of the middle row.

He closed the door behind them all and then climbed back inside. His leg didn't want to support any weight, and he was grateful for his upper body strength that allowed him to pull himself in.

"This is a different vehicle than you usually drive, isn't it?"

"It has hand controls also but can hold more people than the van. I figured this would be better for a group."

The Suburban did not have a ramp or a lift for the wheelchair, only additional grab bars, so he only drove it when he planned to use the crutches.

He had made reservations at Estrella, a delicious Tex-Mex restaurant that catered to families, with an extensive children's menu and paper tablecloths where kids could color pictures while waiting for their meals.

He and Grace had eaten here several times, and

it was quickly becoming one of their favorite places in town. Mason had never brought his mother, he realized with a pinch of guilt.

He should have, especially after all the meals she cooked for him and Grace.

Could he ever let go of the pain and resentment from those cold, loveless years spent in his grandparents' home?

When they walked inside the restaurant, breath coming in puffs, they were greeted with warm smiles by the hostess, who Mason knew by now was also the owner.

"Sage!" Luz Garza exclaimed, coming around to greet them. "I didn't know you were back in town. I haven't seen you in forever. How long are you here?"

Sage hugged the older woman. "I've been meaning to come in for lunch to say hi but haven't had time. I'm only here through the holidays."

The thought of her leaving left Mason feeling hollow.

She was becoming entirely too important to him . . . and to his mother and daughter. That became evident as they sat down. They all talked easily about everything from Grace's favorite kind of guacamole to Rebecca's temporary stint living a year in Guanajuato, Mexico, with a friend in her early twenties, something Mason hadn't known about his mother.

The meal was lively and delicious and more enjoyable than any Mason had enjoyed in a long time.

He loved listening to the kids giggle when Rebecca and Sage shared some of the embarrassing culture and language faux pas they had made when traveling in other countries. He even chimed in, sharing how he had once meant to tell the mother of one of his teammates in Spanish that he was embarrassed about something and instead told her he was pregnant.

He would remember this night for a long time, Mason knew.

They had nearly finished eating when another group of diners came into the restaurant. The woman was stylishly elegant, lovely and blonde and hugely pregnant.

The man, on the other hand, looked slightly dangerous, with a scarred face, an eyepatch and a prosthetic hand.

He recognized Dylan Caine, a man Mason had met the first time he came to Hope's Crossing years ago, when he had helped out Spence Gregory's fundraising event for the Warrior's Hope facility.

At the time, Caine had seemed gruff and angry. He was the very definition of a wounded warrior, having lost a hand and eye while fighting overseas. Now, he appeared far different. He held the hand of a cute little blonde girl who looked about kindergarten age while an older boy, who looked close to Nick's and Grace's age, greeted them happily.

"You're all dressed up," Dylan's wife said.

"We're going to see *The Nutcracker*," Anna informed the newcomers gleefully.

"Hey! We are too!" the girl exclaimed, beaming.

Apparently everyone in town would be on hand for the big performance.

"I guess we'll you see there, won't we?" Dylan said with a smile that gentled his somewhat frightening features.

"I'm glad I ran into you," Sage said to the couple. "I stopped at the Greene project today, and Sam was telling me you both came last night and helped out for a few hours. Thank you so much."

"We all helped. Didn't we, kids?"

"It was so fun," the boy said.

"Our Finn is good friends with Lynette's youngest, Jayden," Genevieve said. "It's such a great thing you're doing. What a gorgeous kitchen it will be. I love the way the renovation is going and especially seeing everyone in town step up to help. When are you going to be filming for your channel?"

"My videographer and editor and his wife are coming to town next week. Right now we're planning for Wednesday so we can edit it and have it up by the weekend. I'm keeping my fingers crossed everything will be done by then."

"I think I told you, we've watched every single one of your videos so far. Haven't we, babe?" she said.

Dylan nodded. "We watched some of them more than once. A few nights back, we had a real binge night with popcorn and everything."

"You are a natural, Sage," Genevieve Caine said. "It's no wonder you've got so many subscribers. I just love what you're doing with it."

Mason had never seen Sage blush, but she looked completely overwhelmed at the other woman's words. What was the history between them?

"And thank you for those plans you sent over for our clients at A Warrior's Hope," Dylan said. "It's going to help a lot of guys who could never afford an architect on their own."

"Oh, I hope so. If anybody needs alterations to any of the plans because of site factors or zoning regulations, let me know. I am happy to customize any of them. And of course I would never charge your clients."

Guilt had Mason shifting in his seat. She was doing her best to help people like him, giving freely of her time and skill. All he had to do was let her video his house, and he selfishly refused because of his own stupid ego.

"What about your house?" Genevieve asked Mason, as if reading his mind. "It's been so fun watching the progress from our place. Are you expecting to be in by Christmas?"

"It's basically done. The designer is coming tomorrow, actually, to unload and stage all the furniture."

"I get to sleep in my new bed in two more sleeps!" Grace said, her eyes wide with excitement.

"Tell me you're going to let Sage feature it on the Homes for All channel, right?" Genevieve pressed.

"I'm thinking about it," he said. He didn't look at Sage but heard her sharp intake of breath.

Genevieve beamed at him. "Oh, I hope you do."

Once, this woman would have been his idea of beauty. Tall, elegant, blonde. She reminded him a little of Shayla, who had been lovely inside and out.

Lately, he was beginning to want something else. A woman with soft curves, green eyes that always seemed to be smiling and a mouth he wanted to sink into.

"You won't go wrong with Sage," Genevieve said.

"What?" he asked, startled.

"Her videos," Genevieve explained. "She does such a great job. What did you think I meant?"

He did look at Sage now and saw more color dusting her cheekbones.

"Mason has his reasons for wanting to protect

281

his privacy," Sage said. "I totally understand and respect that."

His reasons all remained valid. He didn't want the world peering into his hard-won sanctuary with pity and avid curiosity.

Everything seemed to have changed over the past few weeks. Okay, maybe longer than that. Since the day he started working with Sage on the plans for his house, he realized now. While he wasn't paying attention, too focused on recovery and reinvention, Sage had become important to him.

What mattered to her mattered to him.

She was using her skills and abilities to help others, while he was still self-involved, too busy feeling sorry for himself.

Could he do it? Open his house to the world?

He didn't know. But something told him the very fact that he was considering it was a huge step.

20
Sage

After the Caines said goodbye and headed out of the restaurant, the children all needed to use the restroom at the same time.

"I'll take them," Rebecca offered.

Only after his mother and the children all bustled away in a flurry of scraping chairs did Sage realize that left her alone with Mason.

Had Rebecca done that on purpose? Sage thought she had seen his mother cast a few significant glances between the two of them. Was she matchmaking? Sage wasn't sure how she felt about that.

She instinctively liked the other woman. She had lived a fascinating life and had great stories and insight about people.

More than that, they shared a unique bond, both of them destined because of their choices to remain on the outside of their sons' lives.

"Is there a way for both of us to get what we want?"

Sage gazed at Mason in confusion. He seemed tense, his jaw set in a hard line and his mouth compressed.

"I don't know what you mean," she finally said.

"You want to feature Wolf Ridge on your channel. I need to protect my privacy, for my sake and Grace's. Could we come up with some kind of a compromise?"

Sage sat up straighter. Was he actually considering letting her film the house? She was afraid to hope. Ideally, she would love to show everyone the home renovation custom-designed around the new mobility needs of baseball All-Star Mason Tucker. His name alone would be a huge draw for viewers, a video guaranteed to go viral.

On the other hand, the gorgeous house and the setting could speak for itself and she truly did understand his need for privacy.

"We could keep you out of it. We wouldn't have to say anything about you being the owner of the house. I can just speak as the architect of the redesign about the choices we made."

"You could make that work?"

"I've done it a few times before when homeowners didn't want to appear on-screen."

Now that she thought of it, she was annoyed with herself for not suggesting anonymity before. She supposed she had been so focused on the star power he would bring to her channel, she forgot Wolf Ridge could speak for itself.

"Those in Hope's Crossing would know it's your house, since everybody in town knows about the renovation and will recognize the house. But no one else would likely connect it with you. We could be careful."

"Could I have final review of the video before you go public?"

That wasn't the way she and Anton normally worked, but at this point she was willing to agree to anything.

"If you want," she said, her heartbeat kicking up. "Does that mean you're reconsidering?"

That muscle in his jaw flexed. "Yes. As long as you can promise to keep me out of it."

She smiled broadly. If they weren't in a crowded restaurant, she would have jumped up and hugged him.

As it was, she couldn't resist reaching across the table and squeezing his arm. "Thank you. Oh, thank you! Anton is a fabulous videographer. He'll make Wolf Ridge look like the most gorgeous house in the country." She smiled again. "Which it is, of course."

"I wouldn't go that far," he said, though she thought she saw a little smile playing around his delectable mouth.

"His partner in life and the production company is a wonderful woman who uses a wheelchair as well, one of my dearest friends, so I know they will be sensitive to your concerns. We'll do a good job, Mason. I promise. What made you change your mind?"

"You have a way of working on a guy," he said gruffly.

What did he mean by that? She didn't have time to figure it out before he went on.

"I guess I reconsidered after really seeing how much you care about your work. Not because you want to show off how smart you are or because you're trying to become an internet influencer or something, but because you seem to genuinely want to help people. I respect that."

Oh. Her heart melted like the delicious fried ice cream they served at Estrella.

"Thank you so much," she said softly. "I can't believe you changed your mind. This is going to be fabulous."

"What is?" Rebecca asked as she and the children returned to the table.

Sage looked toward Mason, wondering if he wanted to keep his decision a secret. To her relief, he spoke. "I've agreed to let Sage film the house for her YouTube channel."

His mother's expression registered her surprise. "You did? That's wonderful!"

"We'll see," he muttered.

She would show him, Sage thought. He wouldn't be sorry. This would be the best video they had ever done on the Homes for All site. Sage couldn't wait to call Anton to share the news.

She was still trying to process the unexpected

turn of events when they arrived at the Bethany Lange Arts Center for the performance.

It always gave her a lump in her throat to pull up to this facility. She would have loved to know her grandmother. Bethany sounded as if she had been wonderful. Creative, kind, sensitive. She was also somewhat of a tragic figure, treated poorly for her mental illness both by medical professionals and by some in town, especially uppity sorts like Laura Beaumont, Gen's mother.

Building this facility had been a labor of love for Jackson, as well as for Sage, who had consulted on the plans during the development phase with her father.

Bethany had loved music and flowers, and the design of the building tried to incorporate both of those things. It filled Sage with deep pride to know the center was constantly in use by the people of Hope's Crossing and that each of them came face-to-face with Bethany—and perhaps their own consciences over the way they had treated her—through the gorgeous picture of her hanging in the lobby, painted by the brilliant local artist Sarah Colville.

Right now, the exterior of the building looked like a winter wonderland, with the bare trees strung with thousands of sparkling white lights, giant blue baubles hanging in the branches.

Mason didn't park in the designated handicapped

parking. She wondered why not, considering there were a few empty spaces, but didn't ask.

As soon as they got out, the children rushed toward the door, followed closely by Rebecca. Sage stayed with Mason and matched her pace to his slower one as he made his way with his Lofstrand crutches.

"So this place was named for your granmother?" he asked.

"Yes. My dad's mom and my grandfather Harry's first wife. She died before I was born. I wish I could have known her. She was beautiful. Well, you'll see when we go inside. There's a portrait in the lobby. In every picture I've seen of her, she has this smile, as if she knows all the secrets of the universe."

He sent her a sidelong look. "So you must take after her?"

She narrowed her gaze. Was he making fun of her? She wasn't beautiful. Women like Genevieve Beaumont were beautiful. Sage was . . . ordinary.

"You said you didn't know her?" he went on before she could respond.

"No. I didn't even know she was my grand-mother until I was nineteen, when I found out the identity of my father."

"You mentioned that before. What happened?"

"It's a very long story, but my father left town after a furious fight with his father. My mother was pregnant with me when he left. Jack was her first love. When she found out she was pregnant, she tried to tell him but he wanted a clean break from his father, which trickled down to everyone in town, and wouldn't take her calls after he left, figuring it was better for both of them that way. He never even knew about me. My mom raised me as a single mother until I was four, when she married Chris Parker after a whirlwind romance when he came through town on tour with his band."

He frowned. "On tour. Chris Parker. *The* Chris Parker, from Pendragon?"

"That's the one."

"Wow. I love their music."

"Everybody does," she said with a smile. Praise for the stepfather she adored always made her proud.

They didn't have a chance to continue the conversation as they entered the lobby of the arts center, dominated by a Christmas tree that had to be twenty feet tall.

"Look!" Grace exclaimed with delight. "All the decorations on the tree are nutcrackers!"

The children all hurried to look, joining other children who were pointing out their favorites.

She was about to urge them all inside to find their seats, even though they still had about twenty minutes to curtain, when she spotted two familiar figures making their way through the crowd toward them.

"Grandma! Grandpop! Hi!"

Her maternal grandmother, Mary Ella McKnight, had shocked everyone in town when she had started seeing Harry Lange, the town's wealthiest resident and Jackson's estranged father, who had a well-deserved reputation as an ogre.

Mary Ella had seen what Sage also had, that Harry's gruff exterior concealed the proverbial gooey marshmallow heart.

That softer side of Harry was evident now as he bent down and scooped both Nick and Anna into his arms. He adored all his and Mary Ella's grandchildren and treated them equally, whether they were related to him by blood or not.

He was far different from the man he had been a decade ago, when everyone considered him a cantankerous, abrasive old man.

Sage introduced Harry to Mason and his mother, remembering that Mary Ella had met them the night of the Fire & Ice Festival.

"Where are you sitting?" Mary Ella asked.

"We didn't buy tickets until this week," Sage said, "so our seats aren't that great."

"You can sit with us," Harry insisted. "All of you. There's plenty of room in our box."

As the principal donor of the arts center, Harry had also purchased exclusive rights to one of the prime viewing areas in the theater, naturally.

"That would be wonderful. Thank you," Rebecca said, before Mason could voice any of the objections Sage could see forming.

The children were thrilled at this turn of events, delighted they would be able to watch the show together. They all sat in the front row of the balcony box, their faces bright with excitement.

Sage wasn't sure how she felt about this new development. She had already spent entirely too much time with Mason.

As the lights went down and the curtain rose, she was intensely aware of him beside her, big and muscular in his jacket and tie.

She tried to focus on the children and their excitement instead of the prickling awareness. They all were entranced from the first moment until the curtain closed for intermission.

"That was so cool!" Nick exclaimed.

"I love their outfits," Anna said.

They chattered about their favorite parts until Mary Ella stood up. "I'm in the mood for some hot chocolate," she declared. "Rebecca, what about you?"

"That would be lovely," Mason's mother said. "Though I think I've had more hot chocolate in the past few weeks than the past ten years."

"Can I have some hot chocolate, Grandma?" Nick asked.

"Of course, my dear. All of you can. Harry, what about you?"

"Only if I can add some Bailey's to it," he muttered.

Mary Ella gave him an indulgent smile. "Isn't

that funny? There's a chance I might have some in my purse, which I may or may not have brought along just for you."

"Ah, aren't I the luckiest man in town?" he said, beaming as he pulled her into his arms for a dramatic kiss, which made the children giggle.

"What about you two?" Mary Ella asked her and Mason.

Sage thought she had sensed his growing discomfort in the darkness as they watched the show. Now she saw she was right. He was in pain. She didn't know how she knew but she did.

She had a feeling he was in no shape to make his way through the crowds toward the lobby and back again.

"I'm good," she said quickly, even though she wouldn't have minded stretching her legs and maybe grabbing a glass of wine. "I think I'll stay here."

She caught the look of relief on his expression before he quickly concealed it. "In that case, I'll stay as well," he said.

"Can we bring you something back?" Rebecca asked.

"A water bottle would be fine," Sage answered. That was the only thing allowed in the theater itself.

"Same here," Mason said.

"Of course," Mary Ella answered with a smile.

When they had all left the box, Sage turned to Mason. "Is there anything I can do for the pain?" she asked gently.

He looked startled. "Who said anything about pain?"

"Lucky guess," she said. "You were shifting around a bit like you were uncomfortable."

"I just need to stand up and stretch a little." He lifted the forearm crutches from the floor beside him and levered himself up. A small groan emerged and she wanted to pull him into her arms, her heart aching for all he had endured.

"Sorry," he muttered. "I did a little too much today."

She couldn't imagine the kind of pain he lived with. It made her heart hurt.

Some of her compassion must have shown on her features because he made another small sound. "Don't feel sorry for me," he ordered her gruffly. "I hate that worse than anything."

"I know. I'm sorry. I just . . . wish you didn't have to be in pain."

"It's better than it used to be," he said. "And I'm alive, aren't I? I'll gladly take the pain if it means I can be here to watch the joy in my daughter's eyes as she watches the Sugar Plum Fairy dance across the stage."

How could any woman not be crazy about a man like this?

She was falling in love with Mason. Every

moment she spent with him only confirmed it.

Her impending heartbreak seemed to lurk at the corner of her vision, fleeting and ephemeral.

She felt a sharp ache in her chest when she thought about returning to her life in San Francisco in a few short weeks. Her world would feel dull and colorless without him and Grace.

She couldn't think like that. Her life was busy and rich and fulfilling. She would simply have to channel all that pain and loss by focusing more on the work she loved and on providing help to people through Homes for All.

"I'm so thrilled you've agreed to let us feature Wolf Ridge on my channel. I can't wait to call Anton. Maybe we can release both videos on Christmas."

"We won't be very festive at our place, though, since we won't have any Christmas decorations this year."

She stared at him, shocked. "Not even a Christmas tree?"

"We have one down at the guesthouse but not at the main house. We're ahead of schedule, remember? Jean-Paul has holiday decorations, but he had to rearrange his calendar when he found out the house would be done early. He doesn't have enough time to stage the rest of the house and put up the holiday decorations. I told him having the house ready to live in earlier was more important to me than a Christmas tree and some lights."

"What about Grace? She needs at least a Christmas tree!"

He looked surprised at her vehemence. Sage couldn't have explained it either, she only knew her favorite memories of childhood were holidays spent with her mother and Chris and Layla, when they were one big happy family. They always came back to Hope's Crossing for Christmas, even when Chris was in the middle of touring with the band.

Their house would be decorated with greenery they collected from the mountains, and home-made decorations she and her sister would make.

"Children need a Christmas tree," she said firmly. "Grace especially needs one this year while she spends her first Christmas in your new home. Something to mark the new life the two of you are creating here in Hope's Crossing."

He looked amused at her vehemence. "Okay. Okay. I'll make sure I put up a Christmas tree and find somewhere to hang her stocking."

She reassessed her plans for the video. "I supposed we can tape footage at your house and hold the release of it until after the holidays."

"You don't like that idea," he said.

"At this point, I'm willing to take whatever I can get. I'm thrilled you're going to let us film at all."

"But?"

She felt silly now that she had to articulate

all the random thoughts in her head. "From the moment I started working on your house, I could picture the perfect Christmas there. Can't you imagine a roaring fire and a blizzard howling outside the windows while candles and Christmas lights twinkle through the house?"

"I can now," he said, his voice taking on a deeper note as he looked down at her.

She felt that flutter of nerves again. She could picture it too, with vivid clarity. She wanted that Christmas with him and with Grace.

Her heart ached to realize the image was all she would ever have.

"If it means that much to you," he said slowly, "I can ask Jean-Paul if he can push his crew a little harder and try to throw up a few holiday decorations while he's staging the rest of the house."

She knew the interior designer well after years of working together and knew he ran a tight, well-orchestrated machine. If he said he wouldn't have time, he wouldn't have time.

"He's supposed to be done Saturday, right? If he's already ordered the Christmas decorations and will be bringing them along with the rest of the furnishings, I could talk to some people. Maybe bring a team of my personal elves on Sunday after he's gone to deck the halls of Wolf Ridge. Do you trust me?"

Something flashed in his expression again,

something she couldn't quite interpret. "I don't think you really need to ask that, do you? I gave you free rein with my house renovation."

She coughed. "Is that what you call it? As I recall, you insisted on having a hand in every single stage of the process."

"Have I been so demanding?"

She had wanted to tear her hair out a few times during the process but now that they were nearly done, she understood why he had cared about every detail. "It's been refreshing to work with a client who knows what he wants."

"Even the things he knows he can't have," he murmured, his gaze dancing toward her mouth and then away again.

He wanted to kiss her again.

She caught her breath, aching for him to touch her, even as she knew this wasn't the place or time for it.

"Mason," she murmured.

She wasn't sure what she would have said because an instant later, the others returned to the box in a noisy rush and the moment was gone.

21

Mason

Throughout the rest of the performance, Mason tried to focus on the dancers onstage, but his attention was mostly on the woman beside him.

He was drawn to her in a thousand small ways. How kind she was to his daughter; the light in her eyes when she talked about her passion for architecture; her clear love for her family and community.

Sage was a difficult woman to resist.

He had to try harder. She would leave in only a few weeks, off to return to her life away from Hope's Crossing, while he should be focused on building a new life here with his daughter.

Sage was attracted to him. He couldn't dispute that. He could see it in the flare of her eyes and the slight way her mouth parted and the way her gaze would sometimes flicker to his mouth and then she would get this adorable rosy tint to her cheeks.

He wasn't sure why she would be interested in a broken-down wreck of a man who had probably progressed as far as he was going to in his recovery.

Mason knew he would remember, long into the future, sitting in this darkened theater and watching dancers move across the stage with grace and beauty while his body hummed with yearning for someone he couldn't have.

He seemed to be the only one who wasn't sorry to see the evening end after the ballet was over. They made their way through the milling crowd—not his favorite exercise—and eventually loaded into the big SUV again. The children chattered endlessly, dissecting the show and the music and the dancing.

He took Sage and her family home first, much to the chagrin of the children, who apparently didn't want to be separated even for a few hours' sleep.

"Bye," Grace said. "I'll see you tomorrow at school. We can work on the thing at recess."

"I don't have recess with you, though," Anna said with a pout.

"Maybe you can come to our house over the weekend and we can finish our project and then go swimming," Grace suggested.

"It's probably not a good weekend for guests," Mason said. "We're going to have people coming in and out while the furniture is moved in."

"Grace is welcome to hang out here during all the fun," Sage suggested. "My parents will be home tomorrow night, but I'm sure they won't mind."

So much for keeping his distance from her. "That might work. I'll be in touch."

"Okay. Come on, kids. Tell Grace's dad thanks for dinner and the chauffeur service."

"Thanks, Mr. Tucker," Anna said.

"Yeah. Thanks." Nick flashed him a smile that suddenly reminded him of Sage's.

Feeling like a minibus driver, he took Rebecca to her apartment next. His mother hugged Grace, and he could tell she wanted to hug him too.

"Thank you for letting me tag along," she said quietly.

"You're welcome." After a beat, he added, "It was nice to have you there."

They were simple words that didn't hurt at all to say, but from the way his mother's face lit up, one might have thought he had just hit a grand slam in the World Series.

"Did you have a good night?" he asked Grace after they returned to the guesthouse, to be greeted by the ever-enthusiastic Elsa.

"I loved, loved, *loved* it!" She flung her arms above her head and spun around in a pirouette. Their dog danced right along with her. "Can I take ballet lessons?"

He smiled. "Sure. I'll ask around and see if we can find a class for you in town."

"I think my friend Shannon at school takes lessons somewhere. I'll ask her where she goes at school tomorrow."

"Good idea."

He was grateful again that Grace seemed to

301

be settling in well in Hope's Crossing. She had a wide circle of friends, though Nick and Anna were her besties.

"The hot chocolate was so good, and Nick's grandma and grandpa are super nice. His grandpa acts all grumpy, but he bought all the hot chocolate and he held Anna's hand when she was afraid of the Mouse King."

Mason mentally contrasted that with his own grandparents, who never let him forget what a burden he was to them in their old age.

He pushed away the bad memories. He had managed to move past that to create a better life for him and for Grace. That was all that mattered.

"Are you liking it better in Hope's Crossing now?" he asked. "I know you didn't really want to move away from our house in Oregon."

"I didn't really care about the house," she assured him. "I was just afraid . . ."

Her voice trailed off.

"Afraid of what?" he pressed.

"I guess I was afraid that when we moved out of our other house, we would forget Mom," she said, her voice low.

His chest felt tight, achy, and he pulled Grace into a hug. "We won't ever forget your mom. She'll always be in our hearts. Whenever you want to remember her, you only have to look in the mirror, sweetheart. Her eyes will look right back at you."

She wrapped her arms around his waist and hugged him for a long moment. "Do you think she would have liked *The Nutcracker*?"

"She would have loved it. She was always taking me to operas and ballets and things like that, hoping to make me into more than just a dumb jock."

"You're not a dumb jock," Grace said with a giggle that quickly faded. "Sometimes I feel guilty when I'm laughing and having fun with my friends, thinking I should be sad and missing her more."

His heart ached again. "She wouldn't have wanted that for you, honey. She loved hearing you laugh more than anything in the world. She wouldn't want us to be sad forever."

At his words, a knot of emotions he hadn't realized was tangled inside him seemed to uncoil itself. Shayla would have wanted him to let go, just as he wouldn't have wanted her to close her heart away if something happened to him.

"Sage is nice, isn't she?" Grace said suddenly.

He gave her a startled look and could feel himself flush. He had to hope his nine-year-old daughter didn't notice. "Yes. She's very nice."

"You like her, don't you?"

Exactly what had he revealed to Grace about his growing feelings? "Yes. She's done a fantastic job of helping to make Wolf Ridge a better house for us."

"And she's pretty, don't you think?"

Beautiful. Not flashy but soft, lovely. Like birds soaring through mist on the water on a summer morning or the peace of a quiet forest at dusk.

"She's been a good friend to us," he said, his voice sounding rough to his own ears. "We're lucky we have been able to have her help us with the house."

"I like her a lot," Grace announced, then gave him a sidelong look. "If you wanted to date her or something, it would be okay with me."

Mason was momentarily speechless, both because he had to wonder where this was coming from and because the truth seemed to settle over him like that mist. He *did* want to date her. And more. Much more.

"What made you think I might want to . . . date her?" he asked carefully.

She shrugged. "Nick said he thinks you two like each other."

He didn't know what to say. How did he, a guy, navigate a conversation about his love life with his nine-year-old daughter?

"Um, we do like each other. Sage has become a . . . a friend to me. Just like Nick is a friend to you."

She appeared to digest that. "Okay. But if you *did* want to be more than friends, if you wanted to kiss her and stuff, it's okay with me. I wouldn't mind having a stepmom, as long as we don't

304

forget Mom. She wouldn't have wanted you to be sad forever either."

Whoa. He was okay with the part about kissing Sage. More than okay. But *stepmom* was way ahead of the game.

"I appreciate that but I'm not sad, honey. I have you and Elsa and the new house. That's more than enough for now."

She didn't look convinced. Something told Mason this was an argument he wouldn't win, so he pulled the classic no-fail parent card.

"Right now, it's time for bed. Way past time, actually, and you have school in the morning."

She sighed but gave him one more hug and headed for her room, leaving him to think about all the things he wanted but couldn't have.

22
Sage

"I am so sorry about this." Her mother's features on the FaceTime call were lined with distress. "This storm is a nasty one. They're calling it the storm of the century. Your dad has called every airline, and nobody is flying out of France until at least tomorrow. Possibly Monday. It's horrible timing. I know you have a million things going on right now. I honestly thought we would be home tonight."

Sage shook her head. "Don't worry for a second, Mom. It's no big deal. The kids have been great, and we've been having a lot of fun together. They miss you, but I'm sure they'll understand that this is a weather emergency out of your control."

Maura sighed. "I know you're right, but it's so hard to be away from them. I have to tell you how wonderful it's been to know you're there with Nick and Anna. I don't know how I would have been able to leave them otherwise."

Because they were speaking on a video call, Sage managed not to roll her eyes at that blatant exaggeration. Maura had a large family in Hope's Crossing—her mother, her five siblings and their families, as well as a large network of friends.

Any of them would have been happy to take care of Nick and Anna while Maura and Jack had a well-deserved holiday together to celebrate a big moment in his career.

She also knew her mother was fiercely independent, probably from her days as a single mother, both before and after her marriage to Chris. She still had a tough time relying on anyone.

"It's been a joy, Mom. I have never been able to spend this much uninterrupted time with them, and it's been really great to see firsthand what good humans they're turning into."

Her mother's smile was soft and filled with love. "They're wonderful children. They truly are. I can't imagine my life without them."

If Sage ever questioned her decision to ask her parents if they would consider adopting Nick, she only had to see how much Maura and Jack adored him and the other daughter they had created together.

She would always be deeply grateful that her parents had opened their hearts to Nick, even if some part of her still ached with emptiness.

She didn't think about that often. The decision had been made nearly a decade ago, and she wouldn't regret it.

"Don't worry about a thing. You'll get here when you get here, and we will all be fine until that happens. Just try to enjoy your extended vacation with Dad."

She could hear a male voice in the background and Maura looked at something Sage couldn't see, then returned to look at her through the phone camera.

"Your dad wants to know how Wolf Ridge is coming."

"Finished," she said triumphantly. "Jean-Paul showed up yesterday with the moving vans full of furnishings and started moving things in. By the time you get back, you can ask Mason to give you a tour."

She paused for effect. "Or you can always watch the video I'm doing for my YouTube channel."

"What?" Maura exclaimed. "I thought Mason refused to let you feature his house."

"He changed his mind. What can I say? I'm pretty irresistible."

Her mom laughed, and she could hear her father's deeper laughter in the background. "Yes, you are," Maura said. "Or at least an unstoppable force. I'm so happy he agreed. You will do a fabulous job of showing all the changes you have helped design for that house. It really has been a labor of love for you, hasn't it?"

Her mother didn't know the half of it—and Sage hoped Maura never guessed the depth of her feelings for Mason.

Since the evening of *The Nutcracker*, Sage had come to realize that her feelings for Mason were far more than mere attraction or admiration.

She was in love with him and probably had been since she started working on the project with him. She could look back over the past nine months to see the signs.

She had been more excited and invested in the redesign of Wolf Ridge than any other project of her career. She thought it was because of the beauty of the house and the surroundings and the innovative adaptations Mason wanted. Now she realized it was because of him.

"I'm thrilled with the way it turned out," she said with a smile that felt strained.

"I'm so proud of you, honey. I know your dad is too. You've worked so hard to follow your dreams."

She was extraordinarily fortunate. Her parents had supported her every step of the way, and she would never be able to repay them for that.

"What will you do while you're stranded in Paris?" she asked.

"Probably not leave the hotel. The wind is blowing so hard, I'm afraid we'll both get blown into the Seine if we tried to venture out. But we've had a marvelous time before the weather started. We hit about a hundred museums, none as beautiful as the one your father designed in Rouen, of course, and even made a day trip down to the Loire Valley to see the châteaus."

"I'm so glad you've had fun."

Her mother looked happier and more relaxed than Sage had seen her in a while. As much as Maura loved the bookstore, her family and her life here in Hope's Crossing, no doubt she and Jack had needed this time on their own.

She loved seeing how much her parents loved each other, even while it reinforced how alone Sage was.

"I had better go," Maura said. "I'm afraid we're going to lose internet again. It's been in and out all day. Give the children our love."

"Okay. Au revoir."

The children came down for breakfast shortly after Sage hung up with her mother. She pulled them close. "I have bad news. There's a big storm in France where Mom and Dad are and their flight has been canceled. I know you were excited about them coming home tonight, but it looks like it won't be until tomorrow or Monday."

Nick accepted the news with equanimity but Anna looked nervous. "But you'll still be here, right?"

She hugged her sister. "Of course. I'm not going anywhere."

For now. She would be leaving after Christmas to return to her busy life, but she would take with her great memories of this time with Nick and Anna. She hoped they could say the same.

"Is it still okay if Grace comes over to work on our Christmas present today?" Nick asked.

She had completely forgotten their discussion a few nights earlier at the ballet. While she would have loved to be at Wolf Ridge while the designer and his team staged the house, she knew she would only get in the way. She was no expert on interior design.

"Absolutely," she said now to Nick. "What time?"

"Ten. Is that still okay?"

She had a moment's panic to see that was only twenty minutes away and she hadn't showered yet.

She took the fastest shower on record and was putting the final touches on her makeup when she heard the doorbell. Tempting as it was to let the kids answer, she knew it would be rude. Mason might wonder if she was avoiding him.

By the time she made it to the door, the kids had let Mason and Grace into the house. He was using his Lofstrand crutches again, she saw. Grace was already chattering with Anna and Nick.

"Good morning." She managed a smile, though her ridiculous nerves fluttered at the sight of him.

"Hi. Wow, it's blessedly quiet here."

This time her smile was more genuine. "I take it things are a little bit crazy right now at Wolf Ridge. I'm surprised you're not holed up at the guesthouse."

"Jean-Paul would find me there. He wants me

close by, apparently. As if I care which color towel he hangs in which bathroom."

"You're welcome to hide out here." *I'll be your refuge,* she wanted to say, but managed to bite back the words.

"Tempting." His smile crinkled the lines around his eyes. Was it her imagination or did he seem more lighthearted the past few times she had seen him? Maybe that meant he was settling into his new life here in Hope's Crossing.

"Jean-Paul will probably never forgive me if I blow him off today. Who knows, I might end up with pink towels in all the bathrooms."

"What's wrong with pink?" Grace asked him.

"Nothing. Absolutely nothing," he assured her.

"Can we go to Anna's room?" Nick asked.

Sage nodded.

"Bye, Dad," Grace said. She hugged him, careful not to unbalance him on the crutches.

"Have fun, sweetheart," he said, his eyes warm as he returned the hug. Oh, he was a hard man to resist, especially whenever she watched him interact with his daughter. It was obvious Grace was his world.

"She can stay here all day, if you'd like," Sage said after the children hurried off, chattering and giggling. "Our schedule is easy, only wrapping presents and running a few errands."

"That would actually be great. My mom ran to Denver for some last-minute shopping, and I'll be busy all day with the designers. Grace can entertain herself in one of the rooms that's done at the house, but I'll feel better to know she's happy here. Thank you."

"You're welcome. I can take her home when we're done with our errands."

"Are you sure? What time are your parents coming back?"

"They're not. Apparently there's a big storm grounding all the flights out of Paris, so they're stuck for a few extra days."

"Hard luck, there," he said, his voice so dry she had to smile.

"I'm thrilled to have a few extra days with Anna and Nick."

He gave her a searching look and she flushed, wondering what he could read in her expression. Could he tell how bittersweet this week had been, spending so much time with her son?

"We'll have a great time. I'll bring her back this afternoon."

"Thank you. Jean-Paul says they have to be done by five so he can drive back to Denver. Apparently he has a flight home to Quebec City early in the morning. When you bring her back, I'll give you the grand tour."

"I can't wait. It's always wonderful to see how the furnishings work with my designs. Jean-Paul is brilliant at melding his ideas with the architecture, don't you think?"

"Sure. If you say so. I'm no expert, but I do like what I've seen so far. It feels like a house made for living. That's all I know."

"Oh, I'm so glad." She smiled and he gazed down at her, something hot and fierce in his expression that stole her breath.

He wanted to kiss her again. And she wanted to let him. She wanted to taste his mouth again, feel the silky slide of his lips against hers, the strength of his upper body wrapped around her.

She had to check herself from leaning forward in invitation. Bad idea. She couldn't kiss him again. She would already be leaving Hope's Crossing with a shattered heart. She didn't need to make things worse.

These teasing, tantalizing kisses were only making her fall harder for him.

She shifted her gaze, tucking her yearning away as best she could. "I'll bring her back around four thirty or five," she said in clear dismissal.

"Thanks. I appreciate it," he said after a pause. When she looked back at him, she thought she saw a fleeting hint of hurt in his gaze, but it was gone too quickly for her to be certain.

23

Mason

He did his best to stay with Elsa in his office at Wolf Ridge—one of the first rooms to be finished—while the small army of movers and assistants on the design team did their thing.

His office was near the front door, and he could hear them coming in and out all day and arguments in English and French about where things should go.

He wasn't sure why he had to be part of this. If he had his way, Mason would have jumped into his SUV and taken a drive as far as he could get from Wolf Ridge, but Jean-Paul insisted that he stick close so he could be consulted about the most minor of details.

He had zero interest in most of it, but after about the third or fourth consultation, he recognized the man only needed a little validation for his hard work. It reminded Mason somewhat of working with rookie pitchers, who were always so eager for him to notice them.

Around two, after walking the dog as best he could down the driveway and back, it occurred to him that he should have arranged for food to be delivered to the crew. He was looking up a couple of options when the doorbell rang and a moment later the door opened.

"It's my house," he heard Grace said. "We don't have to ring the doorbell."

A moment later, she called out, "Dad? Where are you?"

He could grab the forearm crutches but since he was already in the wheelchair and since his entire body ached from the walk earlier, he opted to wheel out of his office. "I'm here. I wasn't expecting to see you for a few hours."

"Hi, Dad." She beamed at him and threw her arms around his neck. She loved when he was in the wheelchair, she always said, because it meant she could reach to hug him. One small bonus, he supposed.

Sage followed Grace, with Nick and Anna close behind. She wore that cute red coat and checkered scarf again and looked so delicious, he wanted to pull her onto his lap and wheel straight to his newly decorated bedroom with her.

She was also carrying what looked like six pizza boxes. Nick and Anna and Grace all carried bags of paper products and drinks, he realized.

"Wow," she said, looking up at the massive foyer. "Everything looks amazing! Better than I dreamed."

He felt a surge of pride, which was fairly ridiculous since he'd had little to do with it except shell out copious amounts of money and offer his opinion on which pillows to put where.

The man responsible for the interior design of the home came down the stairs at that moment, and his features lit up when he saw her. "My darling Sage!" he exclaimed in his French-Canadian accent. "I was hoping to see you here today."

They had worked together often, Mason remembered. She had recommended the Dupont interior design firm. He understood why now. She had been right. The designer's vision matched Sage's architectural elements perfectly, a unique blend of rustic and industrial that also matched Mason's own tastes.

She was the heart of his home.

He found the realization sobering. Sage McKnight would always be inextricably linked to Wolf Ridge, from the skylights to the beams to the universal design features for accessibility.

How would he be able to get over this woman when her presence seemed soaked into every wall, every window?

"We brought food," she announced.

"You didn't have to do that," Mason said. "I was just about to order something."

"You're an angel," Jean-Paul said.

"I know how hard it can be to stage a house, so I thought you could use it." She smiled. "And the truth is, I couldn't wait another minute to see how things were going here."

"Come. We will eat in the kitchen then I will

show you the house," the designer said, before speaking into his headset. "Everyone, take a break. We have food."

They all trooped into the kitchen, and Sage set the pizza boxes on the island. In moments, the room was filled with the entire crew of movers and designers.

She knew Jean-Paul's assistants and greeted them warmly, then set the kids up with pizza at the table.

Mason loved watching her. She had a way of putting everyone at ease. She chatted with the team, asking the moving crew where they were from, looking at pictures on the phone of one of the assistants showing the woman's daughter, asking Jean-Paul about his wife, who apparently was passionate about horses and dressage.

She made everyone comfortable, even Mason.

"How's everything going?" she asked. "Are you sure you'll be done today?"

"Yes, yes," Jean-Paul insisted. "We are almost there. Two more guest bedrooms, and then we will be done with everything for now."

"Can I go show Anna and Nick my new room?" Grace asked.

Mason looked at Jean-Paul, who nodded.

"Yes, my dear," the interior designer said. "That room is finished, except for all the little things you will bring to make it your own. Books and toys and the like. I know you will love it."

"Can we use the elevator?" she asked.

"Sure. But remember, it's not a toy," Mason said. "If it stops working, you'll have to carry me up and down the stairs."

She giggled and the children jumped up from the table. He caught Sage giving him an odd look, as if she wouldn't have expected him to joke with his daughter about his disabilities.

Pizza forgotten, the children headed toward the elevator.

"We must return to our work if we want to make it back to Denver tonight." Jean-Paul clapped his hands, and the movers and assistants stuffed a few more bites into their mouths then followed him from the kitchen.

"I suppose you want to look around," Mason said.

She grinned. "Good luck stopping me."

He could always follow through on his compulsion of earlier, to pull her onto his lap and kiss her until neither of them remembered where they were. That might stop her.

"We can start down here and work our way up," he said.

She followed him into the great room, with its soaring ceilings and massive fireplace.

"Oh, this is so cozy, with all the separate seating areas. I hope you're going to put a Christmas tree right there in the corner and a wreath above the fireplace."

"I'll leave that to you and your elves tomorrow."

"Done." She grinned at him. "You'll be choking on holiday spirit by the time we're done."

"Can't wait," he said dryly, though he was surprised to realize his words held some truth.

"Do you mind if I take a few notes of things I want to point out when Anton and I tape here next week?"

"Suit yourself."

She pulled out her phone and dictated notes as they walked through the rest of the rooms.

"Oh. I love this!" she exclaimed when they reached the home theater. "I was worried the space would seem cavernous but the combination of comfy couches and recliners is perfect."

Two of those recliners were lift chairs and were positioned to make it easier for him to transfer either to his crutches or his chair.

The home theater was large enough for at least twenty people. He wasn't sure he knew that many people in Hope's Crossing.

Maybe he should fly in some of his friends from the team for a weekend before spring training started up.

The thought shocked him, mostly because he had spent the years since the crash building walls between him and his old life as a professional athlete. Spence Gregory had been fine to hang out with here in Hope's Crossing. He was retired and had built an entirely different life, rich and rewarding, with his family and friends.

Mason's close friends who were still in the game were a different story. He had assumed seeing them would be too painful, reminding him of all he had lost. What did they have in common now when they couldn't talk about baseball?

While he hadn't cut ties completely and didn't ghost them or anything, still mostly answering texts and calls, Mason didn't go out of his way to reach out to any of them.

He should change that. He missed the hell out of them.

How pathetic, that he had cut off people he loved simply because they reminded him of the man he used to be, a game he loved and a time he could no longer recapture.

They were still friends. He still cared about them and their families.

He could change that. His life was different but it wasn't over. This house was proof of that, his way of planning for the future.

He could still support his team, still maintain friendships.

He would start small, Mason decided. Maybe three or four guys who had been his closest friends on the team. They each had wives he liked and respected and children around Grace's age that she had been friends with too.

She would like having company, this link to their old life.

He also didn't have to shut out baseball completely from his life.

That truth seemed to resonate deep in his soul. He had been a fan of the game long before he ever played, and he could recapture that. Maybe he and Grace could even take a trip to Portland over the summer when school was out, during a stretch when they could catch several home games.

"Are you okay?" Sage asked. "You've been staring at the screen for about five minutes straight."

"Sorry. My mind was wandering. I was thinking about inviting some of my old friends out to visit after the new year."

"What a good idea!" she exclaimed.

Sage was responsible for this monumental shift in his thinking. Sage and this house. She was bringing him back to life, ready or not.

She wouldn't be here when his friends came. She would be leaving after Christmas. He tightened his hands on the rims of his wheelchair at the reminder, missing her already.

He was subdued as they finished the tour. When they reached Grace's room, with its built-in bookshelves and window seat, they found Anna and Grace swinging in the hammock chair hung from the ceiling while Nick talked down to them from the loft reading nook.

"This is the coolest room," Anna said. "Can you do my room just like this, Sage?"

She smiled. "You'll have to talk to Mom and Dad about making any changes to their house. They might have something to say about that. But this is a pretty cool room."

"I love it! I can't wait to sleep here tonight. Hey, can we go swimming?"

"We have errands," Sage said. "We were only supposed to be here for a moment to drop off the food, but we got distracted looking at your awesome house."

After a few more moments, she ushered the children away and Mason couldn't help thinking the house was emptier without them, as if Sage took some kind of light with her.

24
Taryn

Taryn did her best during the week following her scene with Charlie to throw herself into the holidays.

In addition to helping out where she could at the Greene project, she went to two concerts at the middle school, found a last-minute ticket to *The Nutcracker* at the town arts center, finished her shopping and organized a cookie swap among the faculty.

By the weekend, she knew her frenzied efforts weren't working. She went to bed exhausted each night but didn't sleep well, waking up after tortured dreams of all she couldn't have.

As a last-ditch effort, she had offered to spend Saturday with her siblings while Evie and Brodie finished their own shopping.

They were making a mess of the kitchen and singing along loudly to Christmas music when their parents returned.

"Looks like a party in here," Taryn's dad said with a grin.

"Don't worry. We'll clean it up, won't we, kids?"

Sasha, thirteen, beamed. "Not me. Anthony can clean it up."

"Hey. No fair," Anthony complained. "It's your turn to wash the dishes. I did them last night."

At ten, Anthony had caught up with the rest of his class after he had been adopted by Evie and Brodie three years earlier. His low vision caused some learning challenges, but he more than made up for them in hard work and determination.

"We'll all work together," Taryn said.

"I can help," offered Zoey, the child Brodie and Evie had together, who was in first grade this year and extremely proud of her missing front teeth.

Her father and Evie had created a beautiful family. Sage could admit now that she had been a little nervous when they told her the year she left for college that they were planning to open their home as foster parents to Sasha, a young girl with Down syndrome who had been neglected by her drug-addicted young parents and had been nonverbal at the time, with significant developmental delays.

Within two years, Sasha had been talking up a storm and charming everyone in town with her bright smile and tender heart.

The social worker who had helped them foster and then adopt Sasha later told them about Anthony, whose loving grandmother had raised him from birth until she recently had a stroke. Evie and Brodie hadn't hesitated to bring him into their family, which by now also included Zoey, who had been a precocious toddler at the time.

Taryn loved all of them dearly and especially loved seeing how happy their brood made Evie and Brodie. They were another reason she had taken the job at Hope's Crossing Middle School, so she could have more of an active role in their lives.

"Thanks for letting me steal them for the day," Taryn told Evie after the children had all helped her clean up the kitchen and then put on their coats to go help Brodie deliver the cookies to neighbors. "We had a great time. They were exactly what I needed to help put me in the holiday spirit."

Evie gave her a searching look. "Okay. Out with it. What's going on with you?"

Taryn shifted. "What do you mean?"

"You aren't yourself. I thought I was imagining things, but your dad commented on it while we were shopping too. Something's wrong. Is there anything we can do to help?"

She looked away. "I've just been a little blue this year. I'm sure it will pass."

"Is it something to do with Charlie?"

She stared at her stepmother, even more lovely than she had been a decade ago when Brodie had hired her to help with Taryn's physical and occupational therapy during the darkest time of their lives.

Evie had become much more than her therapist.

Even before Brodie had fallen in love with her, Taryn had come to care for the woman dearly.

Unfortunately, Evie knew her better than just about anybody, even her grandmother, Katherine, who had helped Brodie raise Taryn after her mother died when she was three.

"Why would you . . . think it has anything to do with Charlie?"

"Sasha was asking about him the other day. You know how she adores him."

She did. It always warmed her heart to see Charlie interact with her siblings. He was so good with them all.

"When she mentioned him, I realized we've hardly seen him since he's been back in Hope's Crossing. Usually whenever the two of you happen to be in town at the same time, you're inseparable."

A lump rose in her throat at Evie's words. They used to have so much fun together. In the summers, they would hike in the mountains and go boating on the reservoir. In winter, they would go out on snowshoes or hit the slopes or sometimes they would just hang out here, watching movies and pigging out on popcorn.

And laughing.

Always laughing.

Tears burned, and she did her best to blink them back before Evie could see.

"Nothing's going on. He's just been busy," she

mumbled. "He's dealing with his father's estate and trying to get the Beaumont house ready to sell. If that's not enough, I also roped him into helping out with the Greene project."

As Taryn hoped, Evie let herself be distracted, if only momentarily. "I am so happy you and Sage put your heads together to help Lynette Greene," she said. "She's a lovely woman who has been through far too much. When will you be done?"

"Only a few more days. They're close."

"How wonderful of everyone to come together like this."

"Definitely."

The project was a bright light piercing the gloom that seemed to surround her this week.

As she feared, Evie returned to the original subject. "How's Charlie doing since his father's death?"

"Okay, I guess. He doesn't say much about it. You know they weren't close."

William Beaumont had been a difficult man. Ambitious, driven, politically savvy. But also self-absorbed and demanding to his family.

With a distant father who ignored him and a mother who had smothered and indulged him, it seemed a miracle Charlie had turned out to be a decent human after all. Taryn attributed that to the influence of people like her dad and Sam Delgado in his life, as well as Charlie's own strength of character.

"I'll be honest," Evie said. "I guess I always kind of suspected the two of you would end up together."

"You . . . you did?"

Evie gave a gentle smile. "He was always so protective of you, from the first day he came to help me with your rehab. I mean, he's clearly been in love with you since you were teenagers."

Taryn stared at her stepmother, feeling her face heat. "Why would you say that?"

"It was obvious to everyone. Why do you think his mother was so eager to send him away from here for college? So she could keep him away from you. She was happier than anyone when you decided to go to school on the coast, several states away from where Charlie had gone to school in Texas."

She didn't know what to say, what to feel. She had always suspected he had feelings for her but hadn't realized others in town had seen the same things she did.

Apparently they were all wrong. Charlie wouldn't keep pushing her away, if he truly loved her.

"He's not," she said, her voice sounding strained. "If he cares about me at all, why does he keep shutting me out?"

Evie looked closer at her. "You're in love with him too. I suspected but was never quite certain."

Taryn closed her eyes, feeling those tears welling precariously close to the surface. "Yes," she whispered. "He knows how I feel about him. I've told him clearly enough. He doesn't care."

Her stepmother took her hand and gave it a comforting squeeze. "Charlie carries a heavy load of guilt and pain because of how badly you were injured in the accident. He has seen firsthand how hard everything has been for you and how hard you've had to work to get to where you are today. I suppose he feels like he can't ever make up for what happened to you."

Those tears broke free of all her efforts to restrain them and trickled down her cheeks. She had never felt so hopeless. "I only want him to give us a chance. How can I convince him to let me in?"

She wiped at her cheeks, feeling as if the future she wanted so desperately was slipping through her fingers and she had no idea how to grab hold of it.

"Oh, honey." Evie wiped at Taryn's tears and hugged her close, reminding her of all the times her stepmother had pushed and prodded her and supported her during her recovery, when she had been a frightened girl trapped in a body that didn't work the way she wanted. She had been afraid she was broken forever back then. Now she feared her heart would never survive losing Charlie.

"I'm so sorry," Evie murmured. "I wish I had a good answer for you. Charlie doesn't see what the rest of us do, that he's no longer the same person he was that night."

"None of us are." She had been a fifteen-year-old brat, rebellious, angry, feeling trapped by her father's rules and expectations. She had no idea where she might have ended up, if not for the accident.

She could never consider it a positive event in her life, but she did know that nearly dying and then having to claw her way back to health had given her a strength and resilience she wasn't sure she would have found inside herself otherwise.

"You're right. I'm certainly not. Neither is your father. But Charlie is trapped by his guilt. He can't see that he's no longer that spoiled, thoughtless boy, indulged by his mother and constantly seeking his father's approval. He still sees himself as the screwup whose terrible mistake of driving under the influence killed Layla and seriously injured others, especially you."

"He's so much more than that," she said, the tears flowing faster now.

"Yes. He has become a good, honorable man who deserves to be happy."

"Who deserves to be happy with *me*," Taryn said. "How can I convince him? Why won't he see himself like everyone else does? Nothing I say makes any difference."

"I don't think you can convince him. This isn't

about you. It's about him, honey," Evie said, her voice sad. "Charlie has to forgive himself, which is sometimes the hardest thing any of us have to do."

Taryn couldn't help the small whimper that escaped her. She rested her head on her stepmother's shoulder and wept, until she heard the door open from the garage.

She straightened and wiped her eyes with a tissue Evie quickly handed her as her siblings came in, followed by Brodie.

Her father frowned and gave Evie a questioning look. Her stepmother shook her head, and Taryn knew Evie would fill him in later.

Sasha, ever sensitive, came to stand in front of Taryn, clearly in tune to her distress.

"What's wrong?" her sister asked with a frown. "Why are you crying, Tare? Did you hurt yourself?"

Taryn hugged this precious girl on the cusp of womanhood, who loved so generously and without judgment. "I did. But I'll be okay. I promise."

The last was meant for Evie and her father, who she knew would worry about her even more now.

She would be okay, she told herself. She simply had to convince Charlie he would only truly be happy if he gave them a chance.

If not, she would have to figure out how to live without him.

25
Sage

"This house is gorgeous, Sage. Absolutely stunning."

She smiled at her aunt Claire, married to her mother's brother Riley.

"It was gorgeous before but what you all have done has made it stunning," she said to the women gathered in the great room of Wolf Ridge, most of them related to her in one way or another.

Most of the women here were either related to her or such close friends that it felt as if they were family. She loved being part of a large, loving family, always ready to lend a hand, whether to one of their own or someone else in town.

"Thank you all so much for taking time during your busy holidays to help me out with this."

"Are you kidding?" Sage's grandmother Mary Ella beamed. "This has been so much fun."

"Yes," Claire's mother, Ruth, said. She actually had a smile on her usually sour face. "Really fun."

"Any excuse I can find to hang out with friends and decorate a gorgeous house is a win, as far as I'm concerned," Katherine Thorne Caine said.

"I've been dying to see what changes you've made to the house," Charlotte Caine Gregory said. "I visited here with Spence shortly after Mason bought it. I had no idea how you were going to make it work for him now. I can't believe the difference."

Sage had to admit, it was better than she had dreamed.

The more she saw of Jean-Paul's furnishings for the house, the more she loved how well his interior design meshed with her vision for Wolf Ridge.

The Christmas decorations he had included for the house were perfect, subtle and warm, intended to bring the outside in.

The centerpiece of the holiday decor was the fifteen-foot tree in the great room with its white lights and rustic ornaments. As she had suggested to Mason, a huge wreath hung from the river rock fireplace, ornamented with ribbon and pine cones.

She loved this room, with its cozy conversation nooks. Sage could imagine Mason and Grace spending evenings here, with the girl doing homework while her father read nearby.

Throughout the rest of the house, candles and greenery complemented the other furnishings to make the house feel cozy and festive without going over the top.

"Thank you for your help. You've all been so kind to reach out and help us, especially considering we're virtually strangers to most of you," Rebecca Tucker said to the group. Sage wanted to think Mason's mother had made friends with several of the women during the past few hours as they had worked together.

"You might have started out as strangers to some of us, but you'll find after you've been here for a while, people don't stay strangers long in Hope's Crossing," her aunt Alex said with a smile.

"Where is the man of the house?" Mary Ella asked. "I was hoping we might have the chance to say hello to him and his cute daughter."

"Mason wanted to stay out of our hair so he and Spence took Grace and our kids, along with Nick and Anna, ice skating in town," Charlotte said.

Ruth frowned. "Ice skating? How can Mason go ice skating? He's in a wheelchair."

Behind her, Claire rolled her eyes and mouthed an apology for her mother to the group in general. Ruth was not always the most tactful of people, though Sage liked to think her heart was usually in the right place. She had mellowed over the years she had served as Maura's right hand at the bookstore for the past decade.

"He was probably going to cheer from the sidelines," Sage said quietly, astonished at how protective she felt for Mason.

She wanted him to be able to do anything. No limits. More than that, she wanted people in town to accept him as he was, whatever he did, and not pity him or treat him as if he had some fatal disease simply because his mobility needs were different from theirs.

"Grace was doing her best to convince him to let her cheat by holding on to his chair for balance while she pushed him around the ice," Rebecca said with a smile.

"I hope he lets her. It would be fun for both of them," Sage said softly, wishing she could be there to help persuade him.

"Well, the point is, you've done a wonderful job with the house. I can tell you've really put your heart and soul into this project."

Sage smiled at her grandmother, who studied her closely in return.

What did Mary Ella see? Could she tell how Sage's emotions had become wrapped up not only with Wolf Ridge but with Mason and Grace? She expected so, especially when her grandmother's expression shifted to one of concern.

"Is there anything left for us to do?" Claire asked.

Sage looked around. Anton would have a great time filming all the beautiful details. "I can't think of anything. Thank you so much for your help."

"I can't wait to see your YouTube video," Charlotte said. "It's going to be your best one yet."

"I hope so."

They all spent a moment gathering up discarded ribbon ends and broken ornaments and then they were pulling on hats and coats to leave when the front door opened.

An instant later, Grace raced in, followed by Nick and Anna, then Mason in his wheelchair.

Spence must have traveled separately, she guessed.

Grace stood in the middle of the great room, her features rosy from being outside and her eyes glittering with the suppressed excitement and happiness of most children during the season.

"Oh. It's beautiful! That Christmas tree is *huge*. I love it so much. I can't believe we really get to live here."

Katherine and Mary Ella both gave Grace the same indulgent smile, clearly charmed by her enthusiasm.

"Wow. It does look great," Mason said. He smiled at the group of women, though Sage could tell he felt uncomfortable around them all. "Thank you for going to so much trouble for us."

"It was really no trouble," Katherine assured him. "We're always looking for any excuse to get together."

"Anyway, it's tons more fun to decorate someone else's house," Charlotte said with a warm smile that reminded Sage the other woman and her husband were among Mason's closest friends. "We don't have to put your Christmas decorations away afterward, only our own."

"We're more than happy to help you take them down, though, if you need us," Claire assured him.

"I'm sure we'll be fine," he answered. "I've hired a housekeeper who will start after the new year. That will be one of her first jobs."

"And I can help," Rebecca said.

"This house is stunning," Mary Ella said. "Even without the Christmas decorations, it would have been perfect for Sage to show on her channel. We all can't wait to see the video."

"I hope you'll let her interview you," Alex said. "My favorite clips are the ones where she talks to the homeowners and they go in-depth about the things they love most about their house."

Mason looked clearly alarmed and she quickly stepped in. "It will still be great without that," she assured him.

"We'd best be off," Katherine said.

"I forgot to ask. Any word on the travelers?" Alex queried.

"Mom called this morning and said the airport in Paris is still socked in, but they're hoping to get a flight home tomorrow."

"I hope they've had a wonderful time," Mary Ella said. "It's been so lovely of you to stay with the children. I know how much a trip away together meant to your parents."

"It's been a blast. Hasn't it, kids?"

Nick and Anna nodded. "Super fun," Anna said.

"Can we go see the rest of the decorations?" Grace asked her dad when everyone had left, including Rebecca who said she was scheduled to FaceTime with a friend in another state.

"Sure."

"Not too long, though. We have to go soon," Sage said.

The children rushed off. Sage, abruptly left alone with Mason, suddenly felt awkward. Needing something to do, she fiddled with some of the greenery on one of the side tables.

"Our friends and family can be a little much sometimes. Thanks for putting up with us."

"Most of them are related to you?"

"About half of those who were here. Two of my aunts were here, Alex and Claire, as well as Claire's mom, Ruth. You know my grandmother Mary Ella. The rest are related to Charlotte. Katherine is married to Charlotte's dad, Dermot. Second marriage for both. One of her sisters-in-law was here, Lucy. She runs a B and B in town. And you remember Genevieve, right? Dylan's wife? We met them at dinner the other day. Gen wanted to be here but her kids had a piano recital."

"I'm never going to remember everyone's name."

"You'll figure it out eventually. They'll all make sure you settle in." She smiled, even as she felt a pang that she wouldn't be here as he came to know the people of Hope's Crossing.

"You're lucky to have them," he said, his voice gruff. "Everybody needs a group of people to count on when life hits them hard."

Did Mason count on anyone besides himself? He seemed so self-contained, an independent island in a sea of turmoil. He couldn't even fully accept his own mother's help.

She again wished she could help the two of them. Every time she saw Rebecca with Mason, the woman's desperate longing to have a better relationship with her son nearly broke Sage's heart.

"You mentioned hiring a housekeeper. Will she live on-site?"

"No. She's coming from the next town over. She'll be here two or three days a week. We're still working through a schedule."

This was none of her business. But perhaps she could help bridge the gap between him and his mother. Then he wouldn't be so alone.

"Have you thought about letting your mom move into Wolf Ridge?" she finally ventured.

He stared at her. "Why would I do that?"

"I don't know. Maybe because you have eight bedrooms in this house and are only using two. Maybe because she's your mother. Maybe because she loves you and wants to be part of your life."

"She had her chance," he said abruptly,

wheeling away from her and into the kitchen. She followed, heart pounding.

No, this wasn't her business. But it wasn't healthy for Mason to hold such anger and resentment toward his mother.

"She was seventeen years old and had to make a difficult choice. I'm sure she did what she thought was best for you."

With blunt, jerky movements, he grabbed a glass and filled it from the touchless water dispenser on the refrigerator then swallowed hard before responding.

"I needed her when I was a kid and she wasn't there. I certainly don't need her now that I'm a fully grown man."

Oh, he did. He talked about how lucky Sage was to have a network of friends and family in her life and how everyone needed a support system. Did he think those relationships all came automatically?

"Fine. You might not. But Grace does. She loves her grandmother. More than that, she needs her."

"I'm not stopping them from having a relationship. Rebecca lives two miles away. She can be here in five minutes. Ten in bad weather. I've never once told her she couldn't be part of Grace's life."

Maybe not in so many words but he put roadblocks up. Sage could see them, even if Mason couldn't.

"What about the guesthouse? Why couldn't Rebecca move in there, once the renovations are complete? That way she would be close by for Grace but far enough away that you don't have to live in the same house with her."

"You may have designed my house, but that doesn't give you any right to design my whole damn life," he snapped.

She gave him a steady look, unfazed by his anger. "I'm not trying to design your life. I was only pointing out how your stubborn determination to prove you don't need anybody is hurting two people who care about you."

And me.

She wanted him to need her too.

"Why do you care where my mother lives? You'll be in San Francisco, making your mark in architecture."

"You were the one talking about my support system and saying everybody needs one. It's obvious to me your mom wants to be one of those people you count on, but you keep her very carefully at arm's length. I don't understand why, when she's trying so hard. What more does she have to do to prove herself to you?"

He glowered at her, frustration stamped on his features. "Why does letting Rebecca into my life have to mean having her underfoot every single damn minute? What we're doing now works. I don't need to go changing everything just because my bossy architect wants to try saving the world."

She threw up her hands, both literally and figuratively. "Fine. Forget I said anything. It was just an idea. I thought it might be good for all of you but obviously the Mighty Tuck doesn't need any help from anyone. He's completely—"

Whatever else she meant to say was cut off in the next second when out of nowhere, Mason reached out, grabbed her and hauled her onto his lap. His heated gaze met her shocked one for only an instant and then he was kissing her with a ferocity that stunned her almost as much.

She didn't want to respond to him in the middle of an argument. Who did that kind of thing? But his mouth was warm and delicious and he was so sweetly grumpy that she made a low sound and kissed him back with the same ferocity, falling in love with him all over again.

She also loved that this position, with her sitting on his lap, put their faces at exactly the same level. She grasped his shirtfront, kissing him with all the emotion that had been growing inside her for all these months.

The heat and strength of him seeped through her skin and Sage wanted to stay right here forever, locked in this delicious battle they both seemed to be winning.

He was the first to pull away, shifting to catch his breath, his eyes stormy and aroused.

"What am I going to do with you?" he muttered.

"What do you want to do?"

He gave her a steady look. "I'm not sure you want to know the answer to that."

Oh, she did. She wanted to know exactly what ran through his head when he kissed her. This gorgeous man was attracted to her. She couldn't miss it, especially when she was sitting on his lap.

She wasn't sure why, she only knew it felt like the most precious Christmas gift anyone had ever given her.

"Just kiss me again," she said, her voice husky.

He gave a short, raw-sounding laugh and did exactly as she asked.

26
Mason

He didn't want to move from this moment, with the blood surging through him and his heart pounding and her mouth tangled with his.

She kissed him as if she were trying to memorize every angle of his mouth, every curve of his lips.

He meant what he had said to her. What was he going to do with her? He couldn't bear the idea of her leaving after Christmas. But she had a life and career away from Hope's Crossing, and he still had no idea what he could possibly offer a woman as vibrant and alive as Sage.

They couldn't go hiking in the glorious mountains around Hope's Crossing. They couldn't go skiing. He could never whirl her around a dance floor.

Sage wouldn't care about those things.

He knew it with a sudden surety. When she loved a man, Sage McKnight would love him with her entire heart, regardless of any physical limitations.

He wanted to be that man.

What the hell was he doing? He should have kept their relationship professional. Instead, he had let her into his life and his heart, and now he realized Sage had become infinitely precious to him.

He spent every day reminding himself of all the reasons he and Sage could never have a relationship, then the moment she came within reach, he forgot all his good intentions and ended up kissing her again.

Never again. This had to be the last time. He closed his eyes, imprinting the taste and smell and feel of her into his memory.

He might have stayed there all afternoon, lost in the sensory overload of Sage, if a distant voice hadn't intruded from outside the kitchen somewhere.

"Hey, Dad, can we go swimming now?"

Grace's voice pierced the haze of desire he was caught up in, and Mason froze to the realization that Sage was lying across his lap and he was about two seconds away from lifting her sweater and exploring all those soft, delicious curves.

The two of them were in serious danger of being caught in a compromising position by three children, and Mason couldn't seem to make his brain work fast enough to extricate them.

Fortunately, Sage seemed to grasp the impending disaster as clearly as he did. Seconds before the children hurried into the kitchen, she slid off his lap, looking so tousled and rumpled and gorgeous, it was all he could do not to pull her back.

The children stopped and stared at them. "What

were you guys just doing?" Nick asked, his voice suspicious.

"Um, talking," Sage managed to say.

"Why was Sage on your lap?" Anna asked. "Did she fall?"

So apparently she hadn't left his lap in time to keep from being discovered. Neither of them seemed to know how to answer that.

"You were kissing," Grace accused. She looked stunned for a second before she laughed and punched Nick on the shoulder. "I knew it. You like each other. You were right, Nick!"

Mason shifted. "We don't like each other," he growled, then cursed under his breath when he saw Sage flinch as if he had punched her.

He winced. "Sorry. That came out wrong. We do like each other. Sage is a very good architect who created a beautiful house for us to live in. She has also become a . . . a friend I value."

The truth of his own words seemed to resonate deep inside. Somehow during the process of remodeling Wolf Ridge, Sage had become vitally important to him. He didn't have that many close friends in his life. Sure, plenty of people had wanted to stay close, but he had shut them all out after the crash.

Sage wouldn't let herself be shut out. She pushed and pushed until he had no choice but to let her in.

He had let her in too far.

She had become a woman he respected, admired and . . . was starting to care about deeply.

"Yes. We are friends but that's all," Sage said, her voice a little wooden.

He narrowed his gaze. Did she want to be more than friends?

She cleared her throat. "We need to go, kids, or we won't have time to change before the Christmas concert at the church. We promised Aunt Angie we would go hear her solo."

"So we can't swim?" Anna asked in a dejected voice.

"Maybe another time," she said quickly.

"You can come back again," Mason said, his voice ragged. "The swimming pool is not going anywhere."

Sage was, though. She would be leaving after the holidays to return to her busy, fulfilling life.

What would he do without her? She was thawing the parts of him he thought permanently frozen after Shayla's death. He didn't want it. He wanted to stay in his state of suspended animation, focused only on Grace and on trying to regain as much function as he could.

He didn't want to feel again.

After the crash, doctors had kept him so drugged up that he hadn't felt the pain of more than a dozen broken bones at first. His spine, both legs and ankles, several ribs.

It had been so tempting to stay in that warm

haze, where all his emotions were muted, the jagged edges of all he had lost smoothed by narcotics.

Eventually he had started weaning himself off the drugs, against the doctors' advice. The pain had been excruciating but at least it was better than living in that numb state, where he couldn't even grieve Shayla properly.

He had a feeling that losing Sage would be like that pain. Raw. Intense. Endless.

Would he have preferred that he had never let her inside? That she had never kissed him that day a few weeks earlier and opened the floodgates to all these feelings that had been building inside him for longer than he cared to acknowledge?

Mason didn't know the answer to that, he only had a feeling this ache in his heart wouldn't heal nearly as easily as a dozen broken bones.

27
Sage

By the Tuesday before Christmas, two days after that intense, emotional kiss in Mason's kitchen, Sage knew her heart would not recover from this season in Hope's Crossing.

As she dressed in her favorite red sweater and jeans for the elementary school performance of *The Nutcracker*, Sage looked in the mirror of the room she stayed in whenever she came home. Could everyone else see the shadows of impending heartbreak in her gaze?

She was so frustrated with herself for letting this happen.

When she came home for the holidays, she had expected a nice break from the hectic pace of her life, a chance to catch up with her family and friends, with the bonus of being on hand when the work wrapped up at Wolf Ridge. She expected she would return to San Francisco renewed and refreshed and ready to jump back into the fray when the new year rolled around.

Instead, she had once more fallen for a man who was completely unavailable.

How had it come to this? Sure, she could understand it when she had been a foolish girl of nineteen, imagining herself in love with

Genevieve Beaumont's fiancé. Her twenty-nine-year-old self could look back with sympathy at that young woman who had been lost and vulnerable after Layla died, aching with an overwhelming need to have something, anything, to hold on to, even a man who belonged to someone else.

She couldn't delude herself about Mason. She had known he wasn't emotionally available from the moment she started working on his house.

She should have been smarter. She should have protected her heart better. Instead, she had let herself fall in love with him, even knowing it would end in heartache.

A knock sounded on the door of the guest room. "Are you ready?" her mom called. "We're about to leave."

She suddenly didn't want to go. She wanted to stay here, to climb onto that comfortable bed and pull the covers over her head.

Mason would be at the school, and she wasn't sure she was ready to see him. Or that she would ever be ready.

She would have to face him eventually. Anton and Rachelle would arrive in Hope's Crossing that evening. The next day they were to video the renovations at Lynette Greene's house then Thursday, two days from now, they were scheduled to tape at Wolf Ridge.

Sage would have to put on a casual air as she

walked through the house she had designed exclusively for him and try to pretend she didn't love him.

"Sage?" her mom called again.

"Yes. I'm nearly ready. I'll meet you downstairs in a moment."

She had to go. She couldn't miss seeing Nick's performance as Herr Drosselmeyer and Grace as Clara.

She should have known her turmoil wouldn't escape her eagle-eyed mother. She and Maura talked about inconsequential things until they were nearly to the elementary school, when her mother sent her a sidelong look.

"Is everything okay? You've seemed a little down since we made it home yesterday. I hope the kids weren't too much for you."

The urge to confide in her nearly overwhelmed Sage. She usually told Maura everything. The two had always been close, probably in part because they were only eighteen years apart, Maura more like an older sister than a parent, and also because they shared the pain of losing Layla.

She wouldn't. Not yet. This pain felt too raw right now to share with anyone.

She forced a smile. "I'm fine," she lied. "And no, the kids weren't too much for me. We had a great time together, like I told you."

"I'm so glad."

"As much fun as we had, I'm very happy you're home again. I was worried you would miss Christmas."

"I would have chartered a plane myself to get home by Christmas if I had to," Maura said fiercely. Despite the ache in her heart, Sage had to smile, not doubting for a second that her mother meant the words.

"I'm glad you made it back for Nick's performance today."

"Right? I would have hated to miss it."

"And I hope the trip was worth it, even the part where you had to endure a blizzard."

"It was all so wonderful," her mother replied with a dreamy sort of look as she parked in the elementary school parking lot. "The new museum is stunning. I would love to take all of you to France to see it."

"That would be great."

"You know, even after a decade, I sometimes still have to pinch myself to make sure I'm not dreaming, that I'm actually living the happy-ever-after I always imagined with your dad when I was a girl."

Sage forced another smile, feeling as if her face would crack apart.

Jack was already there, saving them a couple of seats in the crowded elementary school gymnasium. Every grade would be performing a few numbers for the holiday event, though the fourth grade production of *The Nutcracker* would be the highlight.

Only after Sage sat down did she see Mason sitting a few rows ahead of them, his crutches on the floor at his feet. Rebecca sat beside him. As Sage watched, Mason said something to his mother, who smiled brightly. Sage could only hope the fact that they were there together and seemed to be talking was a good sign.

She did her best to focus on the play instead of the man in front of her. The production was adorable, a shortened version of the classic story they had seen only the week before, with enthusiastic songs instead of graceful dancing.

Afterward, while the parents and other guests enjoyed light refreshments, she carefully avoided talking to Mason, focusing instead on chatting with her parents and other friends she knew in town.

Still, she was aware of him. He stayed in his seat but she saw others approach him and chat for a few moments.

The year-round residents of Hope's Crossing were generally kind. Still, Sage was aware of a protective streak she knew he wouldn't appreciate. A few of the old-timers, like Claire's mom, Ruth, for instance, weren't always the most tactful.

He could take care of himself. In a few weeks, she wouldn't be here to watch out for him.

Mason and Grace would be fine. Sage did not

doubt that people here would welcome them into their midst. They would have a good life in Hope's Crossing, in a beautiful house that perfectly met their needs. She needed to focus on that and not on the ache in her heart, knowing that she couldn't be part of that future.

She was sipping a cup of water from the refreshments table when Rebecca approached her.

"Wasn't that a wonderful show?" Rebecca asked with a cheerful smile. "In my humble opinion, it was even better than the professional version last week."

"Grace was fantastic. She made a perfect Clara."

"And Nick totally owned Herr Drosselmeyer."

"They're great kids, aren't they?" Sage said.

"Truly great. Nick and Anna have been wonderful friends to Grace. I'm grateful. She doesn't always make friends easily." Rebecca made a face. "Neither do I, actually, which makes me especially grateful to you and your family for being so welcoming to me and introducing me around. Everyone has been so kind."

"Oh, I'm glad."

"And I'm sorry I didn't have more opportunity to speak with you the other day when we were decking the halls of Wolf Ridge. It always seemed as if we were working in different parts of the house."

"It was a hectic afternoon, wasn't it? But I love the results."

"Yes. It's a beautiful home." She paused. "I've been wanting to tell you how shocked I was to hear Mason agreed to let you film his house. He's such a private person, I never thought he would do it in a million years. How on earth did you convince him to agree?"

Did Rebecca think she had some kind of magic power over Mason? The idea was laughable.

"I am not sure, to be honest. He's not doing it for me. I know that much. The ad revenue I make from the channel goes to help renovate houses for others with mobility challenges. I think that was what finally decided him."

Rebecca raised an eyebrow. "Don't sell yourself short. If that was all he cared about, it would have been easy for him to simply hand you a check. No. He agreed for you."

Sage shifted, not knowing how to respond. His mother obviously didn't know him as well as she thought, if Rebecca could believe that.

"I don't think so. But whatever the reason, Wolf Ridge deserves to be seen by a wider audience, if only to show that universal design elements can bring style and grace to a house."

"You did that."

"And Jean-Paul," Sage said. "Don't forget him and his team."

Rebecca smiled a little. "How could I? He's quite a character. I loved seeing what he did to the spaces. I found the whole process fascinating.

Do you know, I once dreamed of being an interior designer. I even took a few classes at a community college once, years ago, when I was living and working in Vegas."

She made a face. "But then I got married and my husband thought it was a waste of time. He didn't want me to work so I could be free to travel with him. He was a wealthy developer with enough money in the bank that I didn't have to work, so I kind of gave up on that dream."

Missed opportunities always made Sage feel a little sad, as well as deeply grateful that her parents had continually pushed her to achieve her own dreams.

"It's never too late," Sage said. "If interior design is something you love, you should pursue it. Why not?"

"Oh, I wouldn't know where to start," Rebecca said, looking stunned at the idea.

"What about by working with one of the interior designers here in town? We have some good ones. I know a few people. I could make some calls, if you want."

Rebecca's eyes went wide. "Really? Why would you do that for me?"

"Why not?" Sage asked simply.

To her surprise, Rebecca gave her a quick hug. Only through fast reflexes did Sage avoid spilling her water cup all over both of them.

"You know, it was sheer luck that my son ended

up buying a house years ago in Hope's Crossing and decided to renovate it and move here after he was injured. Since I've been living here, though, I can't help thinking this is exactly where Mason and Grace need to be."

Sage had to agree.

"And while I don't believe in a God who manipulates every circumstance in our lives like some grand puppeteer," Rebecca went on, "I do believe sometimes we are led to the places and the people who will impact our lives in ways we can't even imagine."

Rebecca gave her a steady look. "You're one of those people, Sage McKnight. You're making a difference to all of us. Mason, Grace and me."

Sage blinked, deeply touched. "Oh. That's a lovely thing to say."

"And true. I have loved seeing Mason start to smile again."

She wanted to tell Rebecca she had nothing to do with that, but her mother came over to say hello to Mason's mother and the moment was gone.

28

Mason

What were Sage and Rebecca talking about so intently that had both of them looking so serious?

Mason wasn't sure he wanted to know. Rebecca was becoming entwined with every part of his life, like it or not.

He shifted, trying to find a more comfortable position on the hard folding chairs. Now that the performance was over, he wanted to take off but his mother had asked for a ride since her car was in the shop for new brakes. He couldn't hobble out and leave her here. Nor did he particularly want to go over and interrupt the women's conversation.

Grace had already come over for a hug and then had run back to her friends, who were eating all the cookies at the refreshment table.

He was ready to get up and head for the door, hoping his mother took the hint that he was ready to leave, when Dylan Caine slid into the seat beside him.

"I hear you're all moved in."

"Yeah. We've slept at the house a grand total of three nights. I almost know my way to the bathroom now. I've only been lost a time or two."

Dylan smiled. "Great to have you in the neighborhood."

They chatted about general things for a few moments before Dylan broached the subject Mason had a feeling was the reason he had approached him.

"I'm glad I bumped into you. I've been meaning to talk to you about something."

"Oh?"

"You may know I'm on the board of directors of A Warrior's Hope with Spence Gregory and my sister Charlotte."

"I remember."

"I hope you don't think I'm overstepping, but I wanted to make sure you know we don't only help veterans through A Warrior's Hope. That's the main mission and focus of our work, but we are always happy to loan out adaptive outdoor equipment to local people in the community who might need it. If you ever want to take your daughter skiing, we can set you up."

Mason shifted. "Good to know."

"We've got monoskis, tri-ski bikes. All kinds of winter gear. And in the summer, we have accessible mountain e-bikes, kayaks, even a catamaran you can use to go out on the Silver Strike Reservoir. You're welcome to borrow anything we have and try it out so you can decide what works best for you."

Mason had been so focused on making Wolf

366

Ridge work for him and Grace that he hadn't given a lot of thought to what he would do with his time once they moved in.

They lived in the beautiful Rocky Mountains, and he should be taking full advantage of his surroundings.

"Thanks. I might do that."

Dylan hesitated for a moment before he spoke. "Again. I don't want to overstep, but if you ever need to talk, I'm here. I can't completely relate to what you've been through. We each have our own journey. But I do understand a little about how damn hard it can be to reconfigure your whole life."

"I'm sure you do."

He held up his empty sleeve. "When I came home, I thought my life was over. I climbed into a bottle for more than a year and didn't want to climb back out."

Why was Dylan telling him this? Mason shifted again, wondering if the other man sensed how Mason sometimes felt like a volcano of seething, boiling, frustrated emotions, on the brink of eruption?

"What changed?"

"I did, I guess. I lost a lot of friends. Good men and women with families and futures, snuffed out in a minute, either by the enemy or by themselves when the pain grew too unbearable. At some point, I sort of woke up and realized that would be my fate if I didn't change something."

Dylan looked over at his beautiful pregnant wife, currently talking to one of the teachers, and his harsh features seemed to soften. "I realized my life would never be what I had once planned, but that didn't mean it was over. I still had things to do. I'm not saying it's always been easy, but I can tell you that the years since have been some of the happiest of my life. It sounds cliché, but it's true."

"I'm glad things have worked out for you."

Before Mason could say more, the principal of the elementary school went to the microphone to announce all students were excused to go home with their parents or they could ride the bus if they preferred, and a moment later, Dylan left to rejoin his family.

He was still thinking about his interaction with Dylan as he drove with his mother and Grace back toward the apartment Rebecca rented.

"Thanks for coming to my play, Grandma," Grace said.

"You're welcome, sweetheart. You were wonderful. I'm so glad I could see it. I haven't been feeling all that festive, but that program filled me with all kinds of Christmas spirit. I might have to even put up a little tree in my apartment now."

"I can help you, if you want," Grace offered. "Maybe I can come over tomorrow after school."

Rebecca gave Mason a sidelong look, as if she were bracing herself for his rejection. "Thanks, honey. We'll have to see. Your dad might have plans."

"I don't," Mason said gruffly. "I can bring her after school."

His mother looked delighted. "I don't mind picking her up."

"Grandma, why do you need a Christmas tree anyway?" Grace asked. "We have a giant one. You can share ours. You helped decorated it."

"That's *your* tree. I was thinking of one for my own place."

Grace continued to frown. "You should stay with us for Christmas. We have like a hundred extra bedrooms, don't we, Dad?"

"That might be a slight exaggeration. But we do have a few." He wasn't about to offer one to Rebecca, though.

She apparently had come to the same conclusion. For a moment, hope had sparked in her eyes but it quickly faded.

"Oh no. I'll be fine at my own place. You and your dad have your own traditions on Christmas."

"Christmas would be way more fun with you there. Wouldn't it, Dad?"

Mason didn't know how to answer. He wanted to instinctively protest. He had never told Grace the reason his relationship with Rebecca was stilted. She had never asked, though he knew she sensed the wide chasm between him and his mother.

He thought of what Sage had said the other day, about his mother already being part of his support network but he was too stubborn to acknowledge it.

For the past two and a half years, Rebecca had stepped up to be a wonderful grandmother to Grace when they had both needed it.

He would have been lost without her help.

He suddenly felt ungrateful and childish that he had continued erecting barriers she was constantly trying to hurdle, without much success.

Would he have preferred a different childhood than the one he had? Hell yeah. Every child deserved to grow up in a home filled with warmth and love, not strict rules and harsh discipline.

Rebecca had been a child herself when she had him. Seventeen. Hadn't he been an idiot himself when he was seventeen? He certainly wouldn't want to be judged forever by some of the stupid decisions he had made at that age.

How hypocritical and unfair of him, then, to continue blaming Rebecca for the choices she had made. He had to let go of the pain at some point, didn't he?

Christmas was a time of renewal and hope. He and Grace were making a new start here in Hope's Crossing. It was long past time he tried to make a new start with Rebecca. Sage had been absolutely right.

"Nobody should be alone on Christmas. We would be happy to have you join us for Christmas Eve and Christmas Day. You're welcome to stay at Wolf Ridge."

His words sounded gruff, stilted, but he could see they were enough for Rebecca. Her eyes filled with tears.

"Oh. I would love that. Truly love that. Thank you."

"Yay!" Grace said. "It will be so fun, Grandma. We can go swimming and make cookies and read Christmas stories. I can't wait! You can sleep in the room next to mine, if you want. It's really nice, with a big bed and it even has its own fireplace."

"That will be great. I can't wait either."

Her eyes were bright, and she looked suddenly happier than he had ever seen her.

He should stop there. That was enough, wasn't it? He had made an effort.

But he couldn't help remembering that conversation with Sage, how she had been such a passionate advocate for Rebecca.

Not only Rebecca, he realized now. For Grace and for him. She thought it would benefit all of them to have his mother closer.

She was right, as hard as that was to admit.

He spoke quickly, without giving himself a chance to change his mind. "Now that the main house is finished, Sam Delgado will be working on fixing up the guesthouse after the new year. You don't have to answer right now but . . . I was thinking maybe you could move in there. If you wanted to, anyway. No sense paying the crazy rent for your apartment when we have so much room."

Her eyes widened with stunned disbelief, as if he had stripped off his clothes and started dancing to the car radio. "Are you serious? You . . . you would let me move into your guesthouse?"

The shock in her voice made him feel about as low as a snake. This conversation should have happened a year ago. If he hadn't been so stubbornly determined to hold on to old pain, he would have brought this up a long time ago. "It makes sense. That way you could be closer to Grace. She needs you."

His mother had seemed happy before. Now she looked positively radiant. A tear trickled down her cheek, but he somehow knew she was crying tears of joy.

"Oh, Mason. I would love that," she breathed.

"It will take a few months. Maybe more," he warned. "Sam is basically gutting it and starting over."

"That's fine. Totally fine. I can wait."

He took a breath and plunged forward. "Meanwhile, if you want to move in to Wolf Ridge, we can find room. Grace is right. We have plenty of extra bedrooms."

"I have a lease until the end of January but after that I . . . I might consider it. If you'll still let me. Thank you."

She reached across the car and kissed his cheek and Mason had the oddest feeling, as if he had been wearing a heavy backpack full of rocks without realizing it until it had suddenly been lifted from his shoulders.

A few weeks earlier, he never would have taken such a monumental step forward in his relationship with his mother.

Why now? Rebecca had been trying to build a relationship with him for two years and he had shut her down again and again.

What was different about this moment?

He knew the answer. Sage McKnight.

She had worked her way into his life, his thoughts. And into his heart, whether he wanted her there or not.

29
Taryn

"Are you ready for this?"

Taryn nodded to Sage, wishing she could summon a little more enthusiasm at this culmination of the whirlwind Greene home renovation.

She did her best, mustering a smile so fake, it made her mouth hurt. "I'm ready," she said. "This has been so much fun. Thank you for letting me play a small part in the latest Homes for All project."

Sage laughed. "A small part. Right. Is that what you call it? You only organized the whole thing, coordinated the volunteers, reached out to every neighbor and even fed the crew a few times, from what I understand."

"I was happy to do it."

She decided not to share with Sage that focusing on this project had been the single bright spot in what was turning out to be a miserable holiday season.

"It's been a team effort," she assured Sage.

"That's true." Sage smiled at Sam and Charlie, who waited on the lawn with several other volunteers.

Taryn did her best to avoid Charlie's gaze, not sure she trusted herself around him, with her emotions feeling so close to the surface right now.

"My sources tell me Lynette and her children will be here in about five minutes," Sage said to the assembled crew. Taryn noticed her videographer, Anton James, was presumably filming.

"Before they arrive," Sage went on, "I wanted to take a moment to thank you all for making this happen. I know some of you have sacrificed time with your families during this busy holiday season. Thank you for your willingness to help. You make me proud to say I'm from Hope's Crossing."

A moment later, a van pulled up in front of the house, emblazoned on the side with the emblem for the Silver Strike resort, where Lynette and her children had been staying during the renovation.

Taryn held her breath as the woman climbed out slowly and transferred to a waiting scooter. She waved to everyone gathered in the lightly falling snow and then wheeled up the new ramp to the cheers of the onlookers and excited exclamations of her children.

She waited on the porch for Sage and Anton to precede her into the house so they could film her reaction. Taryn followed close behind.

"Oh!" Lynette exclaimed as she made her way to the gleaming kitchen, with its marble island for rolling out cookie dough, the double oven provided by an appliance store in town and the lowered shelves for a stand mixer that she would be able to reach easily from a wheelchair or a scooter.

Lynette burst into tears. "It's beautiful. Better than I dreamed!"

"This can't be our house!" Chloe exclaimed, walking past her mother. "It doesn't feel real."

"Isn't it beautiful?" Sage said happily. "I predict many delicious cookies will come out of this kitchen in the coming months."

"You can count on it," Lynette said, her features glowing. "I can't believe you did all this in only a few weeks!"

Was that really all it had been? It felt like a lifetime ago that she and Sage had bumped into Chloe and her mother that evening at the café in town and then had driven here to talk to Lynette about Homes for All.

So much had happened. The dance. The kiss. Her heart shattering into tiny pieces.

"We had an excellent crew," Taryn said, gesturing to Sam and Charlie.

"Thank you. Thank you all. This is amazing. I love the tile backsplash. And the farmhouse sink is gorgeous."

"This is so cool!" her older boy exclaimed. "Check it out. The sink works just by waving your hand."

He proceeded to demonstrate, and of course his younger brother had to try too.

"There's also a hot water spigot by the cooktop so you don't have to carry a heavy pan when you're making pasta, as well as a small sink to drain the water or to wash vegetables," Sam pointed out.

"It's perfect. Absolutely perfect. How can I ever thank all of you?" Lynette asked through tears.

"By enjoying your house and making tons of cookies for the rest of us to savor," Sage said softly.

"Count on it," Lynette said, smiling through her tears. "All of you are going to be so sick of my cookies."

"Never," Sam assured her.

Charlie, Taryn noted, remained quiet, watching the family's excitement with an expression she couldn't read.

"I'm so happy you like it," Sage said.

"I can't wait to see the rest. First, can I say something?"

"Of course."

Lynette slowly rose, gripping the edge of the counter for support. She turned to face the assembled volunteers.

"We will never forget what you all have done for us, taking time out of your busy holiday schedules to help me and my children. My grandmother always told me Hope's Crossing was a special place, overflowing with kindness.

Unfortunately, I have mostly known sadness and grief and fear here after losing my husband."

She gave a tremulous smile, wiping away tears. "You have all reminded me that I'm not alone on this journey. My children and I are part of something more, a community of people who take care of each other. Who reach out to those who need help, even when they are afraid to admit it. Thank you all. From the bottom of my heart. You have reminded me that the sun always shines again, even after the hardest storms of life."

The crowd applauded her. Several wiped away tears. Even Charlie seemed touched by her words.

While Sage showed Lynette some of the other features of the kitchen, filmed by Anton, Chloe approached Taryn.

"Thank you, Ms. Thorne. It's gorgeous. I can't wait to show my friends."

"You're very welcome. I was thrilled to be part of it."

"This will make things so much easier for my mom."

"That's the idea."

Chloe's expression grew thoughtful. "You know, it's not as weird as I thought it would be to let people help us."

Taryn had to smile. She gave the girl a hug. Though technically she wasn't supposed to hug her students, sometimes rules were meant to be broken in certain situations.

"I know what you mean. When I was fifteen, the people of Hope's Crossing helped me too."

"Did you get a new kitchen?"

"No. My help was a little different. I was injured in a bad accident that also killed my best friend."

"Oh man. That's rough." The sympathy in Chloe's expression made a lump rise in Taryn's throat. Those who struggled most with grief and loss in their own lives often showed the most empathy for others.

"You were okay, though?"

"Not at first. I was in a coma for a while and then had to relearn everything. Walking, talking. How to eat. How to hold a book. I was in pretty rough shape."

"Wow. I'm sorry."

"My friends and family always had faith in me. They pushed me. No matter how I whined and complained, they wouldn't let me give up, even on the days when I didn't want to wake up in the morning because everything hurt so much."

"That must have been so hard."

It had been. She wanted to think that was the worst thing that had ever happened to her, but she would rather cope with that physical pain than the emotional trauma of losing Charlie forever.

"Nobody wants to have hard things happen to them. But I wouldn't have become the person I am without going through that time. It made me stronger, more kind, more compassionate."

"I get that."

"Do I wish my friend hadn't died? Of course. Every single day. So does her sister." She pointed toward Sage.

"Really? Your friend was Ms. McKnight's sister?"

"Yes. Layla was bright and funny and kind. Sort of like you."

Chloe looked touched at her words. "Thanks."

"More than anything, I wish my friend could be here celebrating the holidays with us. She would have been the first one to volunteer for a project like this."

"I wish my dad were here," Chloe said softly. "The first Christmas without him is hard."

"I know how much you must miss him. I'm sorry." She hugged the girl again.

"He would be really happy about this, though. Anything that made my mom happy made him happy."

Taryn felt tears rise up in her throat again, wishing she could be loved like that. Against her will, her gaze lifted to Charlie's.

He was watching her from across the room with an expression on his features that was so fierce and full of aching emotion, it took her breath away.

The crowd of volunteers inside the house

seemed to fade away, leaving only the two of them.

I love you.

She almost mouthed the words. Instead, she only thought them, wishing she knew how to convey everything in her heart with only a look.

His jaw clenched, his expression suddenly tortured, and then he shoved a beanie on his head and pushed his way through the crowd and out the door, into the cold.

She stood frozen for a moment, not sure what to do. Every instinct screamed at her to stay where she was. Charlie had made his feelings clear. Why continue banging her head against the wall, when she had no hope of changing the outcome? He would continue pushing her away, and she would end up even more heartbroken.

Or maybe not.

She could always pray for a miracle.

She had to try, didn't she? Her heart was already broken. If he pushed her away again, what would change? Her heart couldn't break apart again.

"Will you excuse me for a moment?" she said impulsively to Chloe.

"Um. Sure," the girl said, looking confused. Taryn hardly heard her, already pushing her own way through the crowd toward the front door.

He was walking down the street, probably heading to his pickup that she could see parked in front of the nearby park.

She hurried after him as snow started to fall, big, fluffy flakes that clung to her hair, her eyelashes.

"Charlie," she finally called. "Stop. I can't walk as fast as you can."

He froze, still facing away from her, then slowly turned. "Taryn. What are you doing? You shouldn't be out here in the snow. You might slip and hurt yourself."

She continued moving inexorably toward him. "I might. But I know how to get back up again."

"Why are you out here? The celebration is inside."

Now that she was here, she didn't know what to say. What more could she say that she hadn't already tried?

She couldn't think of any words that might persuade him to give them a chance. Nothing she said seemed to work, maybe because words weren't the answer.

When she reached his side, she did the only thing she could think of. She stood on her toes, heart pounding, wrapped her arms around his neck and brushed her mouth against his.

With her touch and her kiss, she tried to convey all the love and tenderness she felt for him, as well as the pain of the past week without him.

He stood immobile, as if etched from the same granite as the mountains around them. After a moment, he made a low, raw kind of groan and then grabbed her against him, kissing her with hunger and need and a yearning that more than matched her own.

He kissed her for a long time while snow fluttered around them and lights began to flicker on as dusk started to give way to night.

"I love you, Charlie," she murmured. "Please don't push me away."

He jerked away, his expression stunned. "No, you don't."

She made a face. "Don't pretend you didn't know."

When he continued to stare at her, she shook her head. "You didn't know. Seriously? How can you not know? Everyone else in town seems to."

"What are you talking about?"

"Charlie Beaumont. I've been in love with you as long as I can remember. Since I was at least twelve or thirteen. At least I thought it was love back then. I knew for sure after the accident, when you came every single day of my rehab, no matter how angry my dad was at you or how poorly I treated you."

She would never forget his patience and compassion during that time. He pushed her, challenged her, coaxed her back to health when she feared she would be trapped forever with a body and mind that didn't work the way she wanted.

He came every day. No matter what. And in

the years since, he had been a constant source of strength to her.

"You love me too," she said. "Please don't deny it. Can we at least have honesty between us?"

He stepped away, taking his body heat with him, and she immediately shivered.

He gazed at her, and this time she saw what he usually tried to conceal. Anguish. She had been wrong. Her heart could break more than once. It seemed to crack apart all over again at the look in his eyes.

"What does it matter if I love you?"

"It matters," she whispered. "It matters so much."

"Why? I'm not planning to do anything about it. You deserve better, Taryn. We both know you do."

She swore, something she rarely did. "I never thought I would say this but you are a coward, Charlie Beaumont."

She could see he instinctively wanted to argue, but then he shoved his hands into his pockets and turned away.

"When it comes to you, maybe I am," he muttered.

"No *maybe* about it. I just told you I love you. The correct response to that is to sweep me into your arms, kiss me again until I can't breathe and swear your undying love. Instead, you make some lame excuse about how I deserve better."

"Because you do."

She swore again. "I'm so sick of you saying things like that. You are the most decent, most compassionate person I know. You just spent a week helping to give a new kitchen to a family you didn't even know that has seen more than their share of pain, simply because I asked you to and because it was the right thing to do."

He frowned. "So what? That doesn't change anything."

"What would change things? What can I or anyone else say or do to hold a mirror in front of your face so you can see the good man the rest of us do?"

She wasn't getting through to him. She could see by the angle of his jaw and the tense set of his shoulders.

"Have you made mistakes in your life? Yes. Who hasn't? I certainly have, which you know all about, in glaring detail."

She felt shaky, her stomach twisted into knots and her heart pounding. This felt like the biggest gamble of her life, but she had to try. Their future together depended on it.

She stepped forward and slid her fingers to his face, strong and beautiful despite those haunted eyes.

"You have a choice, Charlie. We both do. We can continue to let the past control us. One horrible night we can't change. Or we can take the lessons we learned from it—lessons about courage and resilience and second chances—and embrace a future together."

He closed his eyes, and she could feel her fear growing again that her words still wouldn't be enough.

"What if I screw this up?" he finally said, his voice ragged. "What if I . . . hurt you again?"

This was the crux of the matter. He carried the weight of the pain he had caused her and was afraid to let it down.

"You won't," she murmured with a certainty that seemed more solid than anything else in her world. "I have trusted you with my heart since I was fifteen years old. The only way you can hurt me is if you walk away."

He gazed at her for a long moment, and she could almost see the internal battle he waged with himself.

Let love win, she wanted to tell him. *Love should always, always win over fear.*

At last, just when she thought he would push her away for one final time, he said her name on a sigh. Hope surged through her, bright and joyful, and then he kissed her with a stunning, heart-wrenching tenderness.

She was crying, she realized, tears of joy and relief and love. She didn't care. She didn't want to move from this spot. She wanted to stand here forever on Balsam Lane, kissing the man she loved.

Eventually a car came down the street and the headlights slicing toward them seemed to jolt Charlie back to awareness. He drew away, and it was as if those few magical moments had changed him. There was a softness to the hard edges of his features, and she thought he looked as if he had finally let go of a burden he had carried far too long.

"I can't believe I made you stand out in the cold so long," he murmured. "We could at least go make out in my truck or something."

"I'm not sure I've ever been more warm," she said truthfully.

"You won't say that when your feet have to be treated for frostbite."

"It would totally be worth it. But I should point out I do have a house that's only a few streets away."

He smiled down at her, their hands joined, then he completely charmed her by lifting her cold fingers to his mouth. "I love you, Taryn. I love you so much, sometimes I can't breathe around it."

She would never get tired of hearing that. "I wish I could tell you how much I have needed you to say those words."

He met her gaze, and the emotion in his eyes took her breath away. "All I have ever wanted since that terrible night was to somehow find the same kind of courage inside myself that you showed every minute of your recovery. You taught me that true courage means showing up, no matter how hard. I won't forget that lesson, Taryn. I promise."

She had no choice but to kiss him again, until finally the cold did start to sneak through the layers of her coat.

"You know some people are going to wonder what the town sweetheart is doing with someone like me. Charlie Beaumont, the troublemaker who spent time in the system for causing the death of a friend."

"Do you really think I care about those tiny-minded people who can't see what an amazing man you have become, in spite of one horrible night?"

She shrugged. "Anyway, I never wanted to be the town's sweetheart. I only wanted to be yours."

"You have been. You are. Always."

He kissed her again then held her hand as if he couldn't bear to let her go as they finally hurried out of the cold and into the warmth of the future.

They still had things to work out, Taryn knew as he helped her into his truck and turned on the heat. He lived hundreds of miles away in Utah and for now he had a job he loved that required him to travel.

She wasn't sure whether Charlie could ever be happy in Hope's Crossing. His memories here were filled with pain and regret. She didn't want to leave the town she loved, but she would in an instant if that was the price she had to pay to be with him.

She wasn't going to worry about those details right now. Somehow she knew they would face every challenge, handle every decision together.

For now, as Charlie drove toward her house past the magical holiday lights of her neighbors and friends, Taryn couldn't seem to stop smiling.

Christmas was about miracles. Hope, peace, joy. She felt like she had just been handed every single Christmas wish she had ever wanted, and the reality was so much better than she ever could have imagined.

30
Sage

Two days before Christmas, Sage stood in her favorite holiday sweater inside the foyer of Wolf Ridge while Anton checked the lighting and sound settings on his equipment.

She couldn't remember ever being so nervous before a shoot. So much was riding on her making this video a success. Mason hadn't wanted her to feature his house at all. That he had acquiesced felt like a minor miracle and she owed it to him to give her very best, even when her heart ached at being here again.

Even as she prepared to start taping, she was also grimly aware that this very well might be her last time at the house. After she was done here today, she would have no real excuse to come to Wolf Ridge again. Yes, she was still technically contracted to work on the renovations to the guesthouse, but that was a minor project compared to all they had done here. Sam could handle most of the work without any input from the architect.

She tried not to think about it. Whenever she did, Sage had to fight down tears.

"Oh, Sage!" Rachelle exclaimed, eyes wide as she returned to the small sitting room off the kitchen they were using as base for all their equipment. "You were exactly right. This house is a *dream*."

Rachelle had accompanied Anton for the day ostensibly to be his assistant, but Sage knew that was really an excuse for Rachelle to see the house Sage hadn't stopped talking about for months.

"Talk about aspirational," her friend said, shaking her head. "How can I get me one of these?"

"First of all, you should have married a baseball star instead of a lowly videographer," Anton said.

"Is it too late? Asking for a friend."

He made a face at her teasing, and Sage had to smile. Anton and Rachelle had one of the best relationships she had ever seen. They were both completely committed to each other.

"Where *is* the sexy baseball player in question?" Rachelle asked.

That lump in Sage's throat seemed to grow. "I'm not sure. He knew we were coming today and what time we would be here. If I had to guess, I would say he's probably down at the guesthouse, doing his best to stay as far away as possible from the house today, in case we accidentally on purpose catch a glimpse of him on camera."

"Kind of like Hope's Crossing's version of Bigfoot," Rachelle said brightly.

"Something like that."

"I would never do that," Anton said. "Man

wants to keep his privacy, I totally respect that."

Sage wasn't sure they would even see Mason that day during the taping. While they had texted to confirm the details for today, she hadn't seen him since two days earlier at the production of *The Nutcracker.*

She missed him.

That was a feeling she needed to get used to. She had one week left in Hope's Crossing then would probably be out of his life forever.

"You sure we're not trespassing?" Rachelle asked. "We have permission to be here, right? Tell me we do. Because I don't really feel like being locked up for Christmas in some Podunk Colorado jail."

She had to smile. Her uncle Riley was the police chief in Hope's Crossing, and she knew for a fact that the jail facilities were state of the art.

"I'm sure. Mason gave us full access to the entire property."

"Looks like we're all good on my end," Anton said after adjusting a few more settings on his light system. "Where do you want to start?"

"The foyer would be a good place, I guess."

"Go for it."

She attached her microphone while Anton set the lights up, adjusted his camera on the tripod then pointed to her. "Rolling," he said, the signal he always used to let her know she could start.

Sage stood up tall and smiled into the camera.

"Hello. My name is Sage McKnight with Homes for All, and today I have an amazing house to show you."

For the next two hours, she and Anton made their way through the main living spaces of the house. He moved the lighting and the equipment as they walked from room to room, with Sage expounding at length about all the things she loved about Wolf Ridge—the architectural style features as well as the universal design elements that would make life easier for someone in a wheelchair.

Anton suggested that instead of talking about how some of those features worked in theory, they should feature Rachelle in her chair actually using them. It was the perfect touch, but it meant the taping took longer than she had expected.

During the process of guiding Anton, and subsequently their future viewers, through Wolf Ridge, Sage fell in love all over again with this house. It was open, warm, inviting. Exactly what she had hoped when she started working on plans for the remodel all those months ago.

Mason and Grace would have a wonderful future here. She was certain of it. If imagining their future here without her made her want to cry all over again, that was her own fault for becoming too emotionally involved with her client.

They had finished the ground-floor pool and

workout area and the main living space and were about to head upstairs to the bedrooms when she heard the front door open. A moment later, Mason rolled in using his chair. He looked startled to see them still there.

"Sorry to interrupt. I left a few papers I need in my office."

"You're not interrupting at all," Rachelle said, smiling brightly. "We were just about to head upstairs. I'm Rachelle James, Mr. Tucker. This is my husband, Anton."

If he was at all surprised to see another wheel-chair user in his house, he didn't show it. "Hello. Nice to meet you both."

"Rachelle has been demonstrating some of the universal design features of the house," Sage explained. "It seemed to make more sense to show how they benefit someone with mobility challenges, rather than simply talking about them."

"Good idea."

"Your house is absolutely beautiful," Rachelle said. "Lucky for you, I'm madly in love with my husband or I might think about putting the moves on you, just so I could live here."

Sage gave him a wary look, not sure how Mason would handle Rachelle's lighthearted flirtation.

"I would say Anton is the lucky one," he said with a smile.

"Oh I never let him forget that, believe me, honey."

To Sage's astonishment, Mason chatted easily with both Rachelle and Anton. She would have expected him to grab his papers as soon as he could and escape.

"Has Sage shown you downstairs yet? The workout area and the pool?"

"Yes. I wanted to dive right in," Rachelle said.

"It's hard for me to say what I love best about Wolf Ridge, but that area is definitely up there. I love how the retractable roof can open and bring the outside in. It feels very therapeutic, physically and emotionally. Healing, even. In the water, I feel more like myself than anywhere else. Sage's unique vision for that space has created a true haven."

The rest of them fell silent. Rachelle looked on the brink of tears. Anton was the first one to speak in his deep, calming voice. "That's beautiful, man. Now, how can we convince you to go on camera and say that?"

Mason's jaw hardened. "You can't."

"You have to," Rachelle pressed. "Everybody is rooting for you. We all grieved with you when your wife died and when you were injured so badly. I know I speak for the whole world when I say that everyone would love to know how you're doing."

Mason's temporary congeniality disappeared

in a blink, and he once more went back to the grumpy bear Sage was used to. Even though it had been Rachelle and Anton who had spoken, he glared at Sage as if she had orchestrated their effort.

"I said no and I meant it. If you can't respect my wishes, I'll call this whole damn thing off."

He wheeled away toward his office, leaving an awkward silence behind him.

"Wow, he really values his privacy, doesn't he?" Rachelle said.

"I get the feeling he was hounded by paparazzi right after the helicopter crash," she answered. "From what I've read, they even posed as medical staff to break into his hospital room so they could get pictures of him. That has left him jaded about publicity, especially where he never wanted me to feature Wolf Ridge in the first place."

"Too bad he's so reclusive," Rachelle said. "With his celebrity, he could really offer hope and encouragement to others who are dealing with sudden spinal cord injuries, complete or incomplete."

Mason first needed to feel that hope and encouragement himself before he could help anyone else. Sage's heart ached for him. "Can you give me a minute?" she asked Anton. "I should probably talk to him."

As she walked to his office, she debated what to say. She found him at his desk, gazing into a drawer as if he had forgotten why he came.

"You didn't have to be rude," she finally said, then regretted it instantly when he lifted eyes that blazed with anger.

"I told you how I felt about being on camera. Under no circumstances do I want to be part of your video. Not my words, not my image, not my name. I should never have agreed to let you and your crew inside the house. I wouldn't have, if you hadn't guilted me into it."

She felt as if he shoved the desk into her gut. When had she ever pressured him about the taping? Yes, she had asked more than once but she had accepted his answer and moved on to a different project, the Greene renovation.

The hurt expanded in waves, followed quickly by anger.

"What are you so afraid of? That you're no longer big, tough Mason Tucker, the Mighty Tuck? You're so terrified to show any sign of weakness that you've fooled yourself into thinking you can be happy here, hiding away from the world, pushing away anybody who . . . who cares about you."

He narrowed his gaze. "Like who? My mother? For your information, I offered to let her move into the guesthouse when the renovation is done. Are you happy now? That's another thing you guilted me into doing."

Not your mother. Me, you idiot.

She dug her fingernails into her palms to keep from shouting the words at him. "That's a start."

"More than I wanted to do."

"I'm sure that will make Grace and Rebecca very happy."

A muscle worked in his jaw. "Look, you're a great architect. I appreciate everything you've done. But I hired you to redesign my house, not to try to reorder my whole damn life. I don't know how many times I have to tell this to you and your friends, but I'm not appearing on-screen. End of story. Now finish your taping and then leave, so I can get on with my life."

For a moment, she could only gaze at him as pain and hurt coiled inside her. She felt shaky from it, almost queasy.

She drew a breath into lungs that burned. "Right," she finally said. "Yes. Clear enough."

She turned around and walked away, gently pressing the automatic pocket door to shut him away by himself, just like he wanted.

Somehow she made it through the upstairs bedrooms. To protect Grace's privacy and at Mason's request, they avoided her bedroom, even though it was one of Sage's favorites.

The last room on the filming schedule was Mason's bedroom.

It smelled like him, of pine soap and leather and Mason, and for a moment, she stood inside and simply breathed it in. She didn't want to be here but couldn't figure out a way to avoid it.

Sage knew she had to show all of the accommodations in the room, from the rotating shelves in the closet to the low-profile sliding doors out to the private deck.

After waiting while Anton filmed close-ups of some of those elements, Sage stood near the bed, framed by a huge painting that looked like an original, of a wooded hillside leading to a narrow strip of beach.

"Okay. Rolling," Anton said a few moments later.

Sage compartmentalized her pain and drew in a breath before smiling into the camera.

"I created this space so that M . . . so that the owner can have a retreat from the world, somewhere calm and restful where he can be himself and relax without any expectations. This isn't a therapy room or simply a utilitarian place to sleep. I wanted this to be a refuge, a space where he never has to adapt himself to the environment but where the environment is designed for *him,* where everything is easy to reach and to use. He . . . he should be very happy here."

She tried to smile but couldn't make her mouth work suddenly.

"Oh, honey," Rachelle said. "Cut, Anton."

He lowered his camera and Rachelle rolled closer to her.

"I'm okay," Sage said.

"Are you?"

"Not really. Can I take a short break?" she asked Anton.

"Sure. I've still got plenty of B-roll to film out in the hall and entry. Take your time."

As soon as he took off with his equipment, Sage stood in the room that smelled so much like Mason. She couldn't stay here. Not with her emotions in so much turmoil. Quickly she turned and headed out to a landing near the elevator, where Jean-Paul had artfully arranged side tables and chairs to create a cozy conversation nook. Sage slowly lowered herself into one of the chairs, and Rachelle rolled up in front of her.

"So. How long have you been in love with the Sexy Grump?" Rachelle asked.

If she hadn't been feeling so miserable, she would have laughed at the appropriate nickname.

Sage could see no reason to deny her friend's assumption. Rachelle knew her too well.

"It feels like forever," she admitted.

Rachelle gave her a long look before her features melted into an expression of sympathy. "This house is a love letter to him, isn't it?"

The simple words seemed to reach in and shake her, making her want to close her eyes and sob.

"I suppose you're right. I hadn't thought about it in those terms, but yes. It's the only thing he's willing to take from me."

"So what are you going to do about it?"

She frowned. "What can I do? He has made it clear he thinks I'm nothing but an interfering busybody trying to run his life. Apparently I'm the last thing he wants."

"Funny, but the man didn't look at you like you were the last thing he wanted. I would say exactly the opposite, honey."

Sage closed her eyes, remembering those heady moments in the kitchen when he had kissed her as if she were his salvation.

She wasn't. He had made that clear.

Now finish your taping and then leave, so I can get on with my life.

He couldn't wait to push her out of his life. She was his architect. That was it. Sure, they had shared a few heated kisses, but they obviously meant nothing to him.

She had done her job, and now he wanted her to leave him alone in the love letter she had written for him out of wood and glass and stone.

She drew in a sharp breath and wiped away a tear that trickled down.

She had made this mistake before, of giving her heart to someone who wasn't available. This felt different. Worse. Even when she had been pregnant and afraid and the ass Sawyer Danforth stopped taking her calls, she had never felt as if her insides had been scraped raw.

She was a professional, though. She had to dry

her tears, repair her makeup and finish the job—
no matter how much she wanted to hide away
in some dark corner of this beautiful house and
weep for what she couldn't have.

31

Mason

He had been a jerk, and Mason knew he would have to apologize.

Sage had done nothing to deserve his anger. Quite the opposite. Since they met, she had been generous and kind and giving.

He hated being in the wrong, especially when he wasn't exactly certain what had compelled him to lash out that way.

Sage hadn't been trying to get him to show up on camera. Her friends had been the ones to cajole him, but Sage had become the target of his ire.

Maybe it was better this way. A clean break between them would be less painful. All the way around.

Less painful for whom? Not him, certainly. When she left, he would feel like she was taking a healthy chunk of his heart with her.

She would be doing nothing of the sort. Sure, he cared about her, but he had survived a damn helicopter crash. He could survive losing Sage.

Couldn't he?

Upset at himself and not sure what to do, he focused on finding the papers he had come for in the first place. When he had them in hand, he rolled out of the office and headed toward the massive front door.

He pushed the button to open it and was welcoming the blast of cold December air when he sensed someone approaching him from behind.

"Mr. Tucker."

Turning warily at his name, he found Sage's friend approaching in her wheelchair, which looked to be similar to his but a little less sporty.

He pushed the button again to close the door and turned to face her.

"Rachelle, right?"

"That's right." She gave him a long, steady look that made him squirm.

"What you did out there? Not cool."

His first instinct was to tell her to mind her own damn business. The words died before he could speak them. He could not disagree. He had been rude in front of Sage's team and then had compounded everything by lashing out worse in private.

"I know," he muttered. "I shouldn't have overreacted."

She didn't seem convinced of his sincerity as she wheeled closer to him, gaze narrowed. "Sage McKnight is one of the sweetest people I know. She throws her heart and soul into every single thing she does. But in the years I have known her, I have never seen her as passionate and committed to something as she has been to renovating your home. She has worked tirelessly to make sure this house is perfect for you."

Mason's hands tightened on the rims of his wheels. *Way to pile on the guilt,* he thought.

In an abrupt change of subject, the woman tilted her head and studied him and his chair.

"What's your injury? Incomplete SCI, right?"

"Yes. Incomplete spinal cord injury at T6." The sixth thoracic vertebrae.

As far as spinal cord injuries went, he knew he was luckier than some. With an incomplete SCI, the spinal cord hadn't been completely severed, which meant he still had some neural pathways between his brain and the rest of his body.

"You can still walk, Sage says."

He didn't want to talk about his medical history to this nosy woman that he had only met a short time ago. But she was good friends with Sage, and he also didn't want to be outright rude to her.

"Yes. Not well, but I try." He paused. "What about you?"

"I was sixteen years old when I broke my neck while cliff diving on a family vacation to Mexico. Mine is a complete SCI at the C6."

"That's tough."

"We all have our own path. I've been where you are. Angry, bitter. Raging at the world."

Was that what he was? He let out a breath but couldn't deny it. He struck out from pain and loss, something he hated about himself.

"I hurt the people who cared most for me. My parents. My brother. It took me a long time to make it up to them."

She studied him more intently, and he wondered what Rachelle could see out of those intense brown eyes. "Don't make the mistakes I did. Like I said, Sage is one of the best people I know. I love her like a sister. And I can tell you that any man lucky enough to be loved by her should get down on his knees and thank his Heavenly Father—or his lucky stars or whatever he believes in. If you can walk, you can kneel, can't you?"

Mason blinked, not sure how to answer. He hadn't done much praying lately, on his knees or otherwise. His grandparents' fanaticism had done a good job of completely pushing out most belief in a benevolent higher power. Losing his wife and unborn baby had done the rest.

Grace once told him she thought Shayla must have been his guardian angel, keeping him alive so he could take care of *her*. Their daughter. He wasn't sure how he felt about that.

He was so busy thinking about theology that it took him a moment for the rest of Rachelle's words to sink through his subconscious.

Any man lucky enough to be loved by her.

What did she mean by that? Sage didn't love him. She couldn't.

"Why are you telling me this?" he managed to ask.

"Figure it out, champ," she said with an arch look, then turned and rolled away from him quickly, leaving him staring after her.

Could it be possible? Could Sage . . . have feelings for him?

Mason stared blankly around, and his gaze took in the warm, inviting entry of the house. The massive front door, the metal beams and buckles, the glass streaming in with light and warmth despite the cold outside.

She had poured her heart into this project, working tirelessly to make sure he had everything he could ever want or need. Even things he had never thought of himself.

Yes, she was an excellent architect and probably did the same thing for all her clients. But the care she had taken with his house seemed different.

It *was* different.

Could she love him?

His heart pounded and he closed his eyes. He wanted her to. Sage had brought light and warmth to his life just like she had brought it into his house. She had made him smile, laugh, *feel* again.

Whether she loved him or not, he loved her.

He suddenly remembered what Dylan Caine had told him the other day.

I realized my life would never be what I had once planned, but that didn't mean it was over.

Mason's wasn't either. He still had things to do.

And people to love, particularly one very determined, very passionate architect.

He didn't deserve her. He still didn't know why she could ever care about him, but he remembered how generously and sweetly she had kissed him and he was suddenly quite certain Rachelle was right.

By some miracle, Christmas or otherwise, Sage McKnight had feelings for him. He closed his eyes again, wholly overwhelmed at the idea.

He wanted to find her right then, to get on his knees if he could—which, okay, he probably couldn't, but he could try. He wanted to ask her if there was any chance they could figure out how to make things work between them, any chance she could see beyond his current disaster of a physical body to the man he still was inside.

He was at heart a man who loved her and wanted to do everything in his power to make her happy.

He had hurt her, he suddenly remembered. She had paled at his harsh words as if he had slapped her.

Regret burned through him. How could he fix it?

As he looked around at the house she had worked to bring back to life, Mason could only think of one thing.

Yeah, it was the absolute last thing he wanted to do. But for Sage, for the joy and love she had brought back into his life, he somehow knew it was the right move.

Pushing down his trepidation, he rolled through the house in search of her camera guy.

32
Sage

Somehow, Sage managed to repair her makeup. Props for the genius who invented waterproof mascara.

She would have been done quite some time earlier if she hadn't spent so much time staring in the mirror without really doing anything as she tried to regain her composure.

By the time she emerged from a guest bathroom on the second floor, nobody else was around. She assumed Anton must still be shooting close-ups of the house and its various features that he would edit together with her commentary.

While she wanted to escape, to take her heartache and go, Sage knew she had to stick around in case Anton might need her to reshoot something.

She took the back staircase that ended near the kitchen. From here, she could hear her videographer but couldn't see him. He was speaking with someone, though she couldn't hear the words. A moment later, she was shocked to hear him say "Rolling." That was usually the signal he gave her to let her know he had started recording.

A moment later, she heard a male voice speaking. Puzzled, she made her way to the doorway into the great room, where she found the lights set up and Anton standing behind his video camera and tripod, which were aimed toward the stone fireplace.

To her utter shock, Mason was sitting in his wheelchair, in full view of the camera. He looked big and gorgeous. And he was wearing a microphone.

Rachelle, she saw, was parked in her chair a few feet away from her, wearing a sound headset. Sage shifted, eyes wide, to look at her friend.

What's going on? she mouthed.

Rachelle picked up an extra headset and held it out for Sage, who snatched it and shoved it on her head.

Mason's voice came through, clear and commanding, with no trace of anxiety or uncertainty.

"Most of the world knows what happened to me two and a half years ago. After the crash that killed my wife and the baby she carried, along with a very good helicopter pilot and friend, I didn't know why I survived. I'll be honest. For a long time, I wished I hadn't. How could I surrender to those demons, though, when I still had a daughter who needed her dad? Because of her, I hung on and worked hard to come back. It's been a tough journey, I won't sugarcoat it. I still haven't made it along that path as far as I would like, but I'm further along than I was at the beginning."

He gazed into the camera without flinching.

"Nine months ago, Wolf Ridge was a house that

414

didn't work for anyone, really. Wheelchair or not. But a good architect sees beyond the brokenness to what can be. All the hidden possibilities the rest of us can't see for the clutter and noise. A good architect can take a dark and closed-in house like Wolf Ridge and turn it into something beautiful, a place of joy and peace and comfort. A refuge from the pain and heartache in the world."

She made a tiny sound, so small she hoped no one could hear. Mason did, though. He shifted his gaze and she knew the moment he saw her. Something sparked in his gaze, something glittery and bright and wonderful.

When he spoke again, his voice rasped with emotion. "I consider myself the luckiest of men to have found Sage McKnight, who is as passionate about her work as she is brilliant."

Oh rats. There went her makeup again. Sage could feel a tear drip down but she decided she didn't care. Mason was speaking on camera, the very last thing he wanted to do. For her. This was his way to apologize for his harsh words, and Sage couldn't have loved him any more in that moment.

"This house represents more to me than walls, a foundation, a roof. It represents hope, potential, the promise of a much brighter future. When we started this project nine months ago, I didn't have the first idea what I needed. Now I know precisely what that is."

This time when his gaze met hers, he didn't look away. The intensity of his expression stole her breath. In his eyes, she saw apology, she saw regret. And she saw love.

Sage wasn't aware of moving. One moment she stood beside Rachelle, the next she was running toward Mason. She didn't slow down, simply launched herself at him. He caught her with a rough laugh.

She threw her arms around his neck and kissed him fiercely with all the love that had been building inside her for months. She didn't care that they had an audience, though she would make Anton delete that part of the footage. This was a moment for them alone.

Only this part, though. The rest was perfect.

He met her kiss with the same unflinching emotion, until she felt more tears roll down her cheeks and into their joined mouths. Mason finally broke away and looked over her shoulder at Anton. Sage turned to see her friend had put his camera down.

"Grab your new coat, babe," he said to Rachelle. "I've got what I need here. I think we should go outside and grab a few more exterior shots."

"Yes. Yes, that's exactly what we need to do," she said with a grin toward Sage and Mason.

A moment later, they were alone and she didn't wait for the door to close behind them before she kissed the man she loved again.

"I should probably tell you that I'm in love with you, if you haven't figured that out by now," she said breathlessly.

His arms tightened around her, and the tenderness of his kiss told her everything she needed to know about his feelings.

"I meant what I said to Anton," he said, his voice rough. "When you were rebuilding my house, infusing new life and new hope into it, you were rebuilding me too."

"Oh," she said softly, moved beyond words.

"When Shayla died, I thought this part of my life was over. I never expected to fall in love again. But then a certain feisty architect pushed her way into my life and, well, here we are."

"Here we are," she repeated, her heart overflowing with emotion.

"I think I fell for you long before I ever kissed you. Probably the first time you refused to add something I wanted into the plans and instead offered me an even better solution."

"I think I fell for you the first time you accepted the change I suggested," she said softly.

"How could I not? I believe I've said on record what a brilliant architect you are."

If there was anything more seductive than a man who thought she was brilliant, Sage couldn't imagine what it might be.

She wanted to stay here forever, lost in his arms. Anton and Rachelle would be coming back soon, unfortunately. Her friends could only stay out in the cold so long.

She slid off his lap. "Thank you, for what you said on camera. I have never been so touched."

He gripped her hand as if he didn't want to let her go. "You know this won't be easy, right? I might never be able to walk any better than I can right now."

"I don't care about that. I hope you know me well enough by now to see that."

"I do." He let out a breath. "I also want you to know I would never stand in the way of your career. You're doing important work, Sage. Work that makes a real difference in people's lives."

"We'll figure something out. I don't have to travel as much as I have been. I can focus on jobs closer to home. I still may need to travel when Anton and I are taping something for the YouTube channel, but I can try to minimize those trips. Maybe you and Grace can come with me sometimes."

"That could work, but you've forgotten one thing."

"What's that?"

He kissed her forehead. "You've created the perfect house for me. So perfect that now I never want to leave."

He could not have paid her a greater compliment.

She kissed him again until she heard the door

open quietly as Anton and Rachelle came back inside.

As she looked out the window, she saw it was snowing lightly, plump flakes that fluttered past her view. With the huge Christmas tree in the corner and the wreath on the mantel, the great room looked like something out of a dream.

Not a dream. This was real and right.

She had come home for the holidays to spend time with her family and enjoy being back in Hope's Crossing.

She never imagined this season would change her life forever, that she would find a love she never expected and a man who was better than any dream she could have imagined.

Epilogue

Two years later

"Wow. You sure we're going to have enough popcorn?"

Sage made a face at Mason as he scanned the massive island in the Wolf Ridge kitchen, currently covered in red-and-white-striped popcorn bags.

"I only made ten batches," she said, defending herself. "We have twenty people coming over, counting my family and Rebecca. That should be about right. Knowing how much the kids eat popcorn, I think we're going to be lucky to have a kernel or two left over for ourselves."

"I better grab one now, then," he said.

"Help yourself," she said in a distracted voice. "Actually, maybe I better make another few batches."

She was adding more popcorn kernels to her microwave popper when she felt his arms wrap around her. "On second thought, it's not popcorn I'm craving," he murmured, kissing the back of her neck until she shivered.

After six months of marriage, she never grew tired of his touch.

"Mmm," he said, his mouth sliding across hers. "Who needs popcorn? You taste even better. What time is everyone coming again?"

"Fifteen minutes. Not enough time for what you're thinking."

"Too bad," he said, sliding away again. He was moving better every day. After an experimental surgery a few months prior to their wedding, Mason had regained a little more sensation in his left leg. The increased function allowed him to use only one cane for stability instead of the two Lofstrand crutches. He still used the wheelchair at times when he was tired, both around the house and in public in his role as coach of the high school baseball team.

Mason had settled into life in Hope's Crossing as if he had lived here forever. In addition to coaching the baseball team, which he had discovered he loved, he was now one of the main fundraisers for both A Warrior's Hope and Homes for All. He had an almost uncanny knack for persuading people to part with their money for the sake of a worthy cause.

To her relief, he had also taken over much of the business end of her foundation, allowing Sage to focus on what she did best, designing houses.

"How are you holding up?" he asked.

She gave a rueful laugh. "Terrified, if you want the truth. What if it's terrible?"

"It won't be," he said calmly. "With you and

James Productions involved, how could it be terrible? You know what you're doing."

She released a breath. "Anton does. But what if *I'm* terrible?"

"Trust me. Rachelle would have been the first to tell you."

He leaned back against the kitchen counter and wrapped both arms around her. She had not realized how much she needed his support to calm her nerves until this very moment.

"Stop worrying," he ordered her. "It's going to be fantastic. Homes for All has millions of subscribers, each of them clamoring to watch your streaming debut."

The last two years had been the happiest of her life, despite the challenges, professionally and personally, of moving from San Francisco to Hope's Crossing. She now worked out of her father's office here, only taking a few handpicked projects while devoting more time to the work of the Homes for All foundation and the YouTube channel, both which had grown exponentially.

The video featuring Wolf Ridge and Mason had indeed gone viral, especially when news trickled out that he was now dating the architect who had designed his home renovation. The same one he had spoken such glowing words about in the video.

No matter how many times she had seen it, watching that clip always made her cry.

If not for that video, she wouldn't be standing here right now, getting ready for one of the biggest evenings of her career, the debut of her home renovation show on Netflix.

She and Anton had filmed ten episodes, each one focused on providing a renovated home for someone with mobility challenges.

She was thrilled to be part of it and even more thrilled that the show allowed her more opportunity to make a difference in people's lives.

None of it would have been possible without this man she loved with all her heart.

"Thank you," she said to Mason now.

"For?"

"A million things. Mostly for having faith in me."

She kissed him, wishing she had never had the wild idea of inviting her loved ones over for a viewing party.

She heard a sound and slid away just as Grace came into the kitchen.

Apparently she didn't move quickly enough. Grace looked at the two of them with an exasperated expression. "Can't you two find anywhere better to kiss than the kitchen?" she said, rolling her eyes.

"Nope," Mason said, giving Sage a noisy smack on the lips, which made his eleven-year-old daughter roll her eyes again.

She might make faces but Sage knew it was all for show. Grace loved seeing her father happy, and she and Sage had a warm, loving relationship that Sage considered one of the true joys of her life.

"What time will Nick and Anna be here?" Grace asked.

Sage looked at the clock in the kitchen.

"Not long, unless they get caught in weather. Looks like it's snowing again."

"Yeah. I forgot to tell you Grandma texted me about a half hour ago and said she might be a few minutes late. She just left the house she's working on in Breckenridge and said she has to drive slow because of the weather."

"Better safe than sorry," Mason said.

"That's what I told her."

Rebecca had taken a job with one of the interior designers in town, as a receptionist at first but gradually as an assistant. She adored the work and seemed to be thriving.

While Sage wouldn't have said everything was perfect between Mason and his mother, their relationship was worlds better than it used to be.

"How's the book coming?" Mason asked his daughter.

Grace sighed. "Writing is hard. All my ideas are dumb."

"I'm sure it's not as bad as that," Sage said.

"It is. I wish we didn't have to finish it."

Mason shrugged. "You don't have to finish it. But then you three will have to find something else to give everyone on your Christmas list."

"I know. Don't remind me."

The gift the three of them had worked so hard to make during that magical holiday when Sage had come home and fallen in love had turned out to be a charming and sweet Christmas story, written and illustrated by the three of them.

They had printed out several copies for family and friends, to overwhelmingly positive response. The next year, Mason had paid to have that first book, as well as the sequel they had written last year, bound and printed with their original illustrations.

He had promised to do the same for the third book in the series as soon as they finished it, which apparently was slow going. They had been working on it for a month.

"You'll get it. You've got to finish by next week if we want to have it back from the printer's before the holidays. Maybe you need to have Nick and Anna over tomorrow to pound it out," Mason said.

"Can we go swimming too?"

"That can probably be arranged."

The doorbell rang again and Grace jumped up. "I'll get it. That's probably them."

A moment later, Grace led the way, followed by Taryn and Charlie Beaumont. Charlie was carrying a large plate covered in plastic wrap.

Taryn looked around the empty kitchen. "I

was afraid we were going to be late," she said.

"Nope. You're the first ones here, which means you get your pick of the treats and the chairs."

"Perfect." Charlie set down the plate and picked up a bag of popcorn.

"Ooh. Are those your caramel pecan brownies? You know how much I love those," Sage said.

"I made them in honor of your big day. Can you tell I cut them in the shape of houses?"

"Thank you!" She couldn't really see a house shape, but she wasn't about to tell Taryn that.

"She's been so excited for this all day," Charlie said. "I wanted to binge the whole series at midnight when it dropped, but Taryn hid the remote from me."

"Can you blame me? My best friend is a celebrity!"

While Sage and Taryn had been friends for many years—since Layla died, really—over the past few years of Sage spending more time in Hope's Crossing, their bond had solidified.

She loved seeing Taryn so happy with Charlie. Nobody had really been surprised when they started dating after the same Christmas when Sage and Mason had found each other.

They had married in a beautiful autumn ceremony later that year on a mountaintop over-looking town, which somehow seemed symbolic of the difficult path they had climbed together since that night when Layla died.

As they exchanged vows, Sage wasn't the only one who had wept at the love and joy on their faces.

Charlie had opened his own carpentry business in Hope's Crossing and was constantly busy, though he still occasionally helped Sage out with projects for Homes for All.

The doorbell rang again, and for the next half hour, a steady stream of family and friends crowded into the house.

Mason greeted them all with a warmth she never would have expected to see two years earlier, when he had been withdrawn and remote, lashing out at anybody who wanted to help him.

Her Sexy Grump.

She still teased him by calling him that sometimes, which usually earned her a glower and then a long, delicious kiss, as if he intended to prove her wrong.

When everyone arrived, grabbing popcorn and heading into their comfortable home theater, Sage moved to the front near the screen and cleared her throat.

She looked out at everyone who had loved and supported her through the years, especially Mason who was her rock and her biggest cheerleader.

How empty her life had been before he and Grace had entered. She felt immeasurably blessed.

He smiled now and nodded his head in support

and encouragement. Sage drew in a deep breath, gazing out at everyone she loved. Her parents. Nick. Anna. Her grandmother and Harry Lange and all her aunts and uncles.

And Mason, who knew every one of her faults and somehow loved her, anyway.

She was part of Hope's Crossing, and these people were part of her. A rich, intricate tapestry.

"Thank you all for coming. I . . . I don't know what to say, other than thank you. This is an exciting night for me, which wouldn't have happened without every single one of you."

When she sat down, Mason reached for her hand and squeezed her fingers. As the cheerful opening credits rolled, Sage could feel her anxiety dissipate.

Even if the show flopped, which she was suddenly certain was impossible, she had everything she could ever need, right here in this room, in the house she had designed, built on a foundation of love.

Center Point Large Print
600 Brooks Road / PO Box 1
Thorndike, ME 04986-0001 USA

(207) 568-3717

US & Canada:
1 800 929-9108
www.centerpointlargeprint.com